An Unexpected Husband

Against her better judgment, Lady Gillian Marley needs to find herself a husband—and quickly. To claim her uncle's unexpected bequest she must marry by her next birthday, which leaves only two months to find a malleable mate. Topping her list of eligible candidates is the Earl of Shelbrooke, but one look at the very handsome but enigmatic nobleman and Gillian knows that cajoling him into a marriage of convenience will be hardly convenient at all.

A Marriage of Inconvenience

Far from immune to Gillian's entrancing charms, the last thing Richard Shelton is about to bind himself into is a chaste marriage. Though the inheritance is more than tempting, Richard knows the lady herself is the real prize and isn't about to allow Gillian to deny the burning fervor that sparks between them. Now he has only two months to convince her to be his wife in full . . . before his mysterious secret is revealed and their lives explode irrevocably into scandal.

VICTORIA ALEXANDER

The HUSBAND LIST

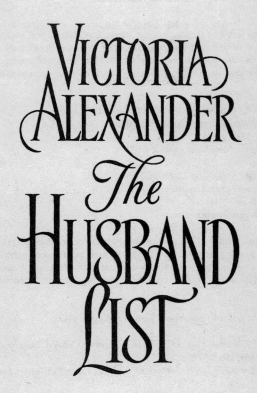

An Avon Romantic Treasure

AVON BOOKS

An Imprint of HarperCollinsPublishers

This is a work of fiction. Names, characters, places, and incidents are products of the author's imagination or are used fictitiously and are not to be construed as real. Any resemblance to actual events, locales, organizations, or persons, living or dead, is entirely coincidental.

AVON BOOKS
An Imprint of HarperCollins*Publishers*
10 East 53rd Street
New York, New York 10022-5299

Copyright © 2000 by Cheryl Griffin
Inside cover photo by the author
ISBN: 0-380-80631-2
www.avonromance.com

First Avon Books paperback printing: August 2000

Avon Trademark Reg. U.S. Pat. Off. and in Other Countries, Marca Registrada, Hecho en U.S.A.
HarperCollins® is a trademark of HarperCollins Publishers Inc.

Printed in the U.S.A.

10 9 8 7 6 5

This book is for
Cindy Rutledge, Louise Foster,
Melissa McCoy and Diane Kirkle.
Dear friends who lead me to the edge of the cliff
and, more often than not, push me over.
And then help me to fly.

A List of Potential Husbands
(as compiled by Lords Weston and Cummings with notations by Lady Gillian Marley)

Viscount Reynolds
    a gambler unrepentant and worse, unsuccessful

The Marquess of Dunstable
    pleasant enough but with nine children more in need of a governess than a wife

Lord Tynedale
    remarkably well spoken for a man with few teeth

Baron Raitt
    charming gentleman, although advanced age has left its mark

Lord Clevis
    excellent dancer in spite of vast proportions that shake the foundations of any house with his first steps upon the floor

Lord Runley
    elegant in appearance but with the intelligence of a small mutton chop

Lord Harkin
    short, bald and altogether unaware of his distinct resemblance to a hairless rabbit

The Earl of Shelbrooke
    entirely too handsome but apparently quite reformed

Chapter 1

Spring 1818 . . .

Where on earth was the blasted man?

Lady Gillian Marley resisted the urge to stalk to her front door, throw it open, and scour the streets of London for him herself.

What if he wasn't coming at all?

The thought tightened the muscles in her shoulders, but she refused to let her well-practiced smile so much as twitch. Instead, she surveyed the room with the air of serene confidence worn only by a hostess who has accomplished the difficult task of melding a diverse group of people into a cohesive gathering.

There were perhaps twenty in attendance at her salon tonight. In one corner, several members of Parliament argued amicably about some obscure issue. Another grouping dissected the latest work of a rising poet, while the merits of a new exhibit of paintings held the attention of yet another cluster of guests.

Gillian's skill as a hostess in such a setting was unrivaled, her reputation for gatherings of this nature unequaled. The picture she presented to the world was, as always, cool and controlled and competent.

Not a single guest here would suspect every nerve in her body was stretched as taut as a piano wire. Not even the most astute observer would imagine the upheaval in her stomach. And absolutely no one would ever dream it took every ounce of self-discipline she possessed not to scream aloud in sheer frustration.

Where was Shelbrooke?

Gillian glanced at the doorway once again, just as she had every few minutes since her guests had begun arriving. He should have been here half an hour ago. Oh, certainly it was not unusual for attendees to arrive late. But tonight the only guest whose presence she wished for, the only guest who mattered, was the only guest who had not yet seen fit to cross her threshold.

Surely, he had not changed his mind? He'd responded to her invitation with a terse note of acceptance, and it would be unforgivable of him to renege now. How could the man be so impolite? Had he no sense of proper behavior? She was not about to align herself with anyone as rude as to accept an invitation then fail to appear without so much as a message of apology. It would certainly serve him right.

Still, her rejection would not have the desired effect on Shelbrooke, since the man had no idea of her intentions.

Gillian forced the subject, and the accompanying flurry of nerves, to the back of her mind and turned her attention to her guests. She dutifully meandered from group to group, offering an observation here, a comment there. Any other evening, she would have taken part enthusiastically in one discussion or another, but tonight she simply couldn't concentrate. She paused at a small knot of guests gathered before a new painting her brother Thomas had sent her and listened halfheartedly.

". . . surely, Sir Edmond, you're not suggesting art has no merit unless it includes figures?"

Sir Edmond, a collector noted for his extravagance but not necessarily his taste, adopted a smug expression. "Come now, Mr. Addison, without depictions of the human form, this is nothing more than a pretty picture. There is a reason why great art typically portrays some significant moment in history."

"And is there something wrong simply with a pretty picture?" A wry voice sounded behind her, and she turned sharply.

Richard Shelton, the Earl of Shelbrooke, stood with his hands clasped behind his back, studying the painting with an air of thoughtful consideration. Her heart skipped a beat.

So this was the man who'd filled her thoughts in

recent days. She hadn't stood this close to him in years. He was a good six inches taller than she, his dark brows pulled together in concentration. His hair was a deep, rich walnut, with an unruly curl and just a shade too long, as if he'd forgotten to keep it trimmed or simply didn't care. Wasn't he able to afford a valet?

Sir Edmond's eyes narrowed as if he couldn't believe this unknown newcomer's temerity to question his opinion. "Without an aspect of humanity, a painting has no emotion. No soul as it were."

"Nonsense," Mr. Addison, a critic of some note, snorted in disdain. "How can you look at a scene like this and say it has no soul? Why, you can almost smell the fresh scent of the grasses and feel the winds blowing the clouds across that sky."

"One could say the painting expresses not the soul of man but the soul of God," Lord Shelbrooke said mildly.

"The soul of God." Sir Edmond's face reddened with outrage. "What blasphem—"

"What perception . . ." Mr. Addison laughed. "I don't believe we've met."

"I have just now arrived." He turned to her and took her hand. "Please forgive me, Lady Gillian, I was unavoidably detained." He raised her hand to his lips, his gaze never leaving hers.

His eyes, too, were brown, deep and endless and intense, and for the briefest moment she wondered if he could see her soul in her eyes as he'd seen the soul in the painting. The touch of his lips on her hand was unexpectedly warm and intimate even here in the midst of the crowded room, and an odd shiver ran up her spine. She resisted the desire to jerk her hand away and forced a cool note to her voice. "Were you late, my lord? I hadn't noticed."

"Then I shall save my apology for a more notice-able offense." He released her hand and straight-ened. A twinkle lurked in his eyes, but he did not smile.

She raised a brow. "And do you plan on more noticeable offenses?"

"I plan little beyond the moment, my lady." He nodded and turned to introduce himself to Mr. Ad-dison and the others.

At once, the debate over the value of the work before them resumed, and she was left with an an-noying sense of dismissal. Why, she had been right in the first place: the man was definitely rude. Al-though, she had to admit, his immediate immersion in the discussion saved her from conversing with him alone. And at the moment, she had no idea what to say and not the faintest notion where to begin.

She murmured an appropriate comment and withdrew, preferring to observe him from a safe distance. The mere touch of his hand had had a startling effect on her. It was absurd, of course. They shared no more than a passing acquaintance and even that was nothing more than a vaguely remembered dance during her first and only season years ago. Surely, she could attribute her reaction to her own state of nerves brought on by her plans.

What would he think of her proposal and all that

went with it? Her stomach churned at the thought.

For the next hour or so she watched him join in one discussion then another. He was as intelligent as she'd been led to believe. His comments were well spoken and to the point. Shelbrooke acquitted himself in a knowledgeable manner whether the conversation centered on literature or politics or art. She couldn't help but be impressed. Still, even when his contribution was amusing and those around him laughed, he was restrained. She had the strangest impression he was more concerned with observing the reactions of others than permitting his own emotions to be noted.

"I must say, Lady Gillian." Lady Forester joined her beside a table laid with refreshments. "What an intriguing man Lord Shelbrooke is."

"Do you think so?" Gillian murmured and sipped at her third fortifying glass of wine.

"I do indeed. He is so wonderfully mysterious."

"Mysterious?"

"Why, yes." Lady Forester fluttered her fan. "While he is not reticent to express an opinion, nothing he says reveals anything whatsoever of himself."

Gillian studied his tall figure. "What is there to reveal? There are few true secrets in London. The circumstances of his life are common knowledge. His father squandered the family fortune and Shelbrooke has spent the years since his death trying to restore what was lost."

"I suppose it could be the sorry state of his financial affairs that explains his reserve. Still, men as attractive as the earl do not usually go out of their way to avoid attention. Why, the man never even smiles. I have often noticed him at social occasions, but he seems to linger on the fringes of any gathering, never quite joining in, as if he was there only to observe and not participate." Lady Forester slanted her a curious look. "However, I've never seen him at one of your salons before. Why did you invite him?"

Gillian raised a shoulder in a casual shrug. "I simply like a varied group of guests, and someone suggested he might be an interesting addition."

"Well, I do always meet the most fascinating gentlemen here." Lady Forester's gaze lingered on the earl. "Shelbrooke used to be quite a rogue, if I remember correctly, before the death of his father. Now, *there* was a true scoundrel." A speculative smile played on her lips. "What a shame his son is not in need of a patron. You don't suppose he has any artistic or literary tendencies that need nurturing, do you?"

Gillian laughed. "I think not."

"Pity." Lady Forester sighed. Only a year or so older than Gillian, Lady Forester fancied herself a great patroness of the arts and had contributed substantially to the careers of several struggling artists and writers. In return, they had contributed to her more amorous, although according to gossip, no less creative, pursuits. Gillian was at once grateful Shelbrooke was in no need of her type of patronage.

Shelbrooke's gaze caught hers from across the

room and he lifted his glass slightly in acknowledgment, as if he knew the direction her thoughts had taken. A hot flush swept up her face and she nodded politely, pointedly turning her gaze away.

Lady Forester considered Gillian carefully. "You've been a widow far too long, my dear. It's been my experience that men who are reluctant to talk about themselves do so because they have something to hide. Secrets, if you will. Oh, it's usually nothing of significance to anyone other than the man himself. Still, secrets are always dangerous, and always," she smiled wickedly, "more than a little exciting."

"We all have our secrets, Lady Forester. I doubt his are any more dangerous, or exciting, than . . . mine."

Gillian smiled and excused herself, then quickly crossed the room and stepped into the foyer. She headed down the hallway leading to the servants' stairs and a pair of matching doors. The right served as a delivery entrance. She pulled open the left and stepped outside onto a tiny terrace surrounded by a small but well-tended garden, the entire area kept private by a tall brick wall.

The evening air washed over her and she rested her back against the doorjamb, closing her eyes and lifting her chin to the cool, refreshing breeze. For a long moment she stood and enjoyed the delightful sensation, trying her best to ignore the reasons behind her heated cheeks.

Botheration, she hadn't blushed in years. Obviously, it was the circumstances and not the man that brought this rush of fire to her face. Still, there was something in the way he had looked at her. . . . She wasn't entirely certain if it was thrilling or terrifying. Or both.

"It is exceedingly warm inside."

Her breath caught, and she snapped her eyes open.

Shelbrooke's arms were folded over his chest, and he lounged against the opposite side of the doorframe. "I too felt the need for a momentary respite."

"Did you?" she said curtly.

He raised a brow. "If you'd prefer to be alone—"

"No." Her voice softened. "Not at all. Do forgive me. That was insufferably rude. I'm not usually this sharp with my guests. Particularly guests who are new to my home." She smiled and willed her heart to slow to a normal rhythm. "I trust you are enjoying yourself?"

"The evening is as entertaining as I had been led to believe. Your reputation for salons of this sort is well deserved."

"Thank you." She waved in an offhand manner. "I simply prefer evenings where the discussion is of a more stimulating nature than the usual gossip found at typical social gatherings."

"Why?"

"As I said, I prefer . . ." She hesitated. It was not too soon to be honest with him, and honesty was as important to the success of a relationship as respect. Gillian drew a deep breath. "I see a great deal of waste in the society we live in. Lives wasted by war and indolence. Minds wasted by far too much concern paid to the cut of one's coat as opposed to the state of one's world."

"Really? Yet it seems to me I rarely attend a ball or soiree where you are not present."

"You are observant." She laughed. "But there I am no more than another guest. I see nothing wrong with frivolous entertainments, I simply do not wish to devote my life to them. Instead I fill these evenings with artists and critics, writers and scholars, poets and politicians. Men who think of matters beyond the complexity of a well-tied cravat."

"And what of your female guests?" Was that a note of amusement in his voice?

"I find women no less intelligent than men and just as capable of perceptive observations when free to express them." She drew her brows together. "Do you disagree?"

"Not at all. Intelligent women willing to speak their minds have long been the bane of my existence," he said dryly.

Was he talking about his sisters? He had four, if her information was correct. Or was there another woman in his life?

Silence stretched between them, and she couldn't think of anything to say that did not sound inane or insipid. She had no wish to sound foolish in front of him. There was far too much at stake.

The light from the hall cast half his face in shadows and sharpened the line of his profile, straight and strong and determined. *And dangerous?* He studied her, his gaze unwavering, his expression considering.

"Why did you invite me tonight?" he asked abruptly.

"Why?" The question caught her by surprise. She forced a teasing note to her voice. "You do ask a lot of questions, my lord."

"Only when I have no idea as to the answers." An intensity underlaid his words. All at once she was aware of how little space separated them and how very alone they were here. Was he aware of it as well?

"Lady Gillian?"

She drew a deep, steadying breath. "I have a . . . a business proposition for you."

"A business proposition?" he said slowly. "About painting?"

"Painting? Why on earth would you think that?"

He shrugged. "A passing thought, given much of the discussion here tonight, nothing more. Please, go on."

"My proposal is of a more personal nature."

"Indeed?" He straightened, and the movement brought his body to within a bare few inches of her own. Her heart thudded. His voice was low and colored with a meaning she did not care to examine. "I must admit, I am intrigued. Precisely how personal?"

"Extremely personal." An immediate need to place distance between them gripped her, and she stepped across the threshold and into the house. "But this is not the moment to discuss it. I have already left my guests unattended for far too long. If you would be so kind as to remain later, after the others have left."

"As you wish." His voice was noncommittal. "Later, then."

She nodded and turned to walk briskly down the hall. She could feel his gaze following her. Observing her. Thoughtful and curious. From his angle he couldn't possibly notice a slight tremble in her hands or the flush that once again heated her face or the butterflies cavorting in her stomach.

Anticipation mingled with dread and washed through her. She at once wanted to avoid their meeting, yet knew the remaining hour or so until then would last a lifetime.

Appropriate enough, since it was indeed the remainder of a lifetime in the balance.

"Do you really like it?" Richard said over his shoulder.

He had heard Lady Gillian enter the room behind him after bidding good night to the last of her guests. Guests who had seemed to linger for an eternity. Throughout the interminably long evening he'd been hard-pressed to hide his growing impatience. What did the woman want from him?

"Yes, I do." She stepped to his side, tilted her head, and studied the painting. The tension he'd noticed in her during their brief encounter earlier had vanished, and she now seemed relaxed and at ease. "Quite a lot."

"You say your brother sent this to you?"

"Yes. It was something of a surprise. Thomas and I have never been particularly close. Older brothers being groomed to inherit the title and responsibilities of a duke do not have a great deal of time for younger sisters. Yet we are fond of one another." She considered him the same way she had just regarded the painting. "I believe you know him, don't you?"

"We were in school together," he said as if it was of no significance. In fact, at this moment, he wasn't entirely certain if he wished to thrash the future Duke of Roxborough or embrace him. He forced a casual note to his voice. "Do you know the artist?"

"Not personally, although I have been hearing a great deal about him lately. Apparently, he is as accomplished with the ladies as he is with a brush. He's French, you know."

"Is he?"

"Have you heard of him? His name is Etienne-Louis Toussaint."

"Rather a mouthful," he murmured.

"Rather. I should like to invite him here, but he is apparently quite reclusive." A slight smile quirked the corners of her lips. "In spite of his rakish reputation, I have yet to encounter anyone who has actually met the man in person."

"Not even Lady Forester?"

"Not even Lady Forester." Gillian laughed, a delightful sound that echoed through his blood. "Why, my lord, you're actually smiling."

"Am I?" He widened his eyes in mock surprise. "How could that have happened? I must have lost my head for a moment. I shall have to take care it does not happen again."

"I've never noticed you smile before."

He raised a brow. "I was not aware you had noticed me at all."

A charming flush colored her cheeks, but she ignored his comment, staring at him with amused suspicion. "Lady Forester thinks you're quite mysterious. She suspects you have some deep, dark secret."

"Then I shall do my best not to disappoint her. Besides, I much prefer the illusion of a mysterious keeper of deep, dark secrets than the all too boring truth of my circumstances in life." He turned back to the painting. "Now, the artist who created this obviously has secrets. No doubt all of them deep and dark."

"No doubt." She examined the work with the critical air of one who knows good art from bad, and he observed her out of the corner of his eye. "There is a great deal of passion here. Unbridled. A passion born from a love of life. It's extremely compelling. Almost irresistible. I suspect he has quite a future ahead of him."

"Do you?"

She nodded thoughtfully. She was barely half a head shorter than he, her figure a bit more voluptuous than he'd thought, but then he hadn't been this close to her in years. Not since before her marriage, and then she was a mere girl fresh from the schoolroom.

The woman now beside him was lovely in the

fair-haired, creamy-skinned tradition of classic English beauty, with an intelligence that only enhanced her appearance. This was a woman to fulfill the fantasies of any man. Even a man with deep, dark secrets.

"I liked what you said about it. About the soul of God."

He raised a shoulder in an offhand manner. "I don't know a great deal about art."

"Yet you are extremely perceptive."

"Not at all. For example, I don't have so much as an inkling of what your business proposition entails."

At once her casual air vanished. She raised her chin and stared into his eyes. He sensed a determination in her even as she appeared to gather her courage.

She drew a deep breath, the blurted out her request. "I need a husband. I must wed within the next two months." Her voice was resolute, her gaze steady. "I think you will fill the position nicely."

Shock held him still and stole his voice. For a long moment he could do nothing but stare in disbelief. "You wish to marry me? *Me?*"

"Yes, I do," she said, her voice a shade less adamant than before. Again, she seemed to summon strength.

"My lord, would you do me the honor of becoming my husband?"

Chapter 2

"**Y**our husband?"

Without warning, the absurdity of her request struck him, and he laughed long and hard.

"This is not funny," she said indignantly. "I expected any number of possible reactions to my request, my lord, but laughter was not among them."

"Richard." He sniffed and wiped a tear from his eye.

"Richard?"

"It's my name. You should call the man you intend to marry by his given name." The very idea of this eminently desirable woman proposing to him . . . he struggled to contain himself against a fresh wave of mirth.

"I wish you would stop that. I am quite serious. And I must say, this is all rather disquieting. First a smile and now a laugh? From a man who has never been observed to do either?"

"I neither laugh nor smile, at least not in public, because I do not wish to become the target of any number of women who are more than willing to disregard the state of my finances in exchange for my title. In addition, I'm not completely unattractive, and I learned long ago that that alone is enough to attract the unwanted attentions of marriage-minded females." He chuckled and shook his head. "You, however, are obviously made of sterner stuff. I find your courage quite intriguing—"

"Well, I don't—"

"As well as your blunt nature. None of that coy, flirtatious banter for you. No, it's straight to the point. I can do no less." He stepped toward her, unable to stifle a grin. "What was it that attracted you, Gillian?"

"Lady Gillian." Her eyes widened, and she stepped backwards.

"Gillian," he said firmly. "Formality will not do with my betrothed."

"I am not yet—"

"But you wish to be." Again he moved closer. "Was it my brooding, aloof manner?"

"You don't seem particularly aloof now," she said cautiously and once more backed away.

"I'm not and never have been. Lady Forester was right—I do have deep, dark secrets." He narrowed the space between them. She tried to step back, but a sofa blocked her retreat. "My demeanor in public is one of them."

"That isn't why—"

"Then what is it, Gillian?" He stood close enough

to touch her, her body within a hairsbreadth of his own. His voice softened. "Why me?"

She stared up at him, a stunned look in her eyes, blue and bright as no sky an artist could ever capture on canvas. At once he knew, regardless of her reasons, he was not at all adverse to having her as his wife. Or anything else. "I . . ."

It was more a sigh than a word. For a long moment his gaze held hers. Without warning, he wanted to pull her into his arms, press his lips to hers. Electricity arched between them and . . . what? Desire?

"No!" She pushed past him and fled to the other side of the room. "There will be none of that!"

"None of what?" He exhaled a long breath.

"You know perfectly well *what*." She aimed an accusing finger at him. *"That!"*

"I didn't do a thing."

"But you wanted to!"

"Did I? Are you certain?"

She paused and considered him, then nodded. "Yes."

"Apparently, you too are quite observant." He folded his arms over his chest. "It will be bloody difficult to have a marriage with none of that."

"It will not be that kind of marriage." She mirrored his stance with her own and glared.

"What precisely do you mean by *that kind of marriage?*"

"You know perfectly well what I mean. We will each continue to live our separate lives," she said loftily. "It will be a marriage in name only."

He snorted in disbelief. "Not with me it won't."

"But *you* are the only suitable candidate on the list."

"What list?"

"The list of possible husbands." An uneasy expression crossed her face as if she suddenly comprehended the unflattering nature of her admission.

"You have a list? A list?"

"You come very highly recommended," she said weakly.

"Bloody hell." He strode across the room to the table still bearing refreshments, poured a glass of wine, and downed it in one swallow. All sense of amusement had vanished. By God, the woman was serious. Worse, she apparently aimed to select a new husband the same way she'd pick a dressmaker or milliner.

"I have brandy if you'd prefer something more substantial," she said helpfully.

He ignored her. "And what propelled me to the top of this list? I assume I am at the top?"

"Of course you're at the top."

"Why?" He eyed her cautiously.

"Well . . ." She glanced around the room as if to find the answer lurking in the shadows. "Everything I know about you indicates you're an honorable man with a strong character and sense of responsibility and honor and . . ."

"And what?"

She smiled apologetically, and her gaze met his. "And you need money."

"Go on."

"I am the beneficiary of a substantial inheritance. But to receive it, I must be married by my thirtieth birthday."

"In two months' time?"

She nodded.

Suspicion narrowed his eyes. "How substantial?"

"Very." She stepped to him, took his empty glass from his hand, and moved to a cabinet, opening a door and selecting a decanter of brandy. "It's from a distant relative in America. It includes ships—"

"How many ships?"

"Eight, I think, more or less." She pulled the stopper from the decanter and filled the glass. "Plus there's a great deal of land, in America of course." She replaced the stopper. "And there is a fair amount of cash." She turned and held the glass out to him.

"How much cash?"

"Six hundred thousand pounds." She took a quick sip of the brandy, as if she needed its bracing effect.

"Six hundred thousand . . ." He stepped to her, plucked the glass from her hand, and drew a long, deep swallow. Even the burn of the best brandy he'd had in some time failed to temper the shock of her words. "Six hundred thousand . . ."

"Pounds." A tempting note sounded in her voice, as if she were offering a sweet to a small child or a rope to a drowning man. "And, as my husband, half of it would be yours."

"Under the laws of England, all of it will be mine," he said pointedly.

She shook her head. "Not under my terms. First of all, I am willing to divide the inheritance in half legally and have papers drawn up to that effect."

"So." He chose his words with care. "You propose to buy a husband."

"I hadn't thought of it that way at all." She huffed. "The benefits are not exactly one-sided. You will gain a great deal from this arrangement. The funding to improve your estates. Impressive dowries for your sisters. The Earl of Shelbrooke will once again take his proper place in society."

Richard stared at the brandy in his glass. There was so much more to it than that. "To what end?"

"What do you mean?"

His gaze caught hers. "Why do you think a man wishes to restore his property? Regain his good name?"

Confusion shone in her eyes. "Why, I—"

"He does it so that he has more to pass on to his children, to his heirs, than bad debts and a tarnished reputation. Under the terms of this marriage, there will be no children." He shook his head and went on.

"I had always planned on marrying some day. I have simply not had the time nor the means to devote to the search for a suitable wife. If I agree to this proposal, you are purchasing not merely a husband but a life and a future. *My* life and *my* future." He drained the last of the brandy and set the glass on the table with a deliberate motion. "Under such constraints, I must respectfully decline your offer."

He nodded, turned, and started toward the door.

"Wait." Desperation sounded in her voice, and he paused. "You must understand. I loved my husband dearly. I have always vowed I would not marry again without love."

He waited in silence.

"But I don't have time to fall in love. I don't know if I could. I don't know if I want to."

"I can't agree to the kind of marriage you want, Gillian."

"I know many people marry for reasons other than love and," her voice faltered, "have children and are happy together. Perhaps, if you would agree to an engagement, for the next two months . . ."

"And then?"

"And then . . . as we get to know one another . . . possibly affection . . ."

He turned and considered her carefully. Perhaps he wasn't the only one with deep, dark secrets. "Why are you so determined to claim this inheritance?"

"Why?" Caution edged her voice.

"You're the daughter of a duke. An Effington— one of the wealthiest families in the country. Why would a woman in your position be willing to even consider sharing the bed of a virtual stranger for the rest of her days?"

She hesitated for a moment, then her chin jerked up defiantly. "It's a great deal of money."

"Not for an Effington."

"Even for an Effington." She stared for a moment, then sighed in annoyance. "Goodness, my lord, you do ask a lot of questions."

"You've said that before."

"And I'll say it again," she snapped. "Very well." She picked up the decanter, refilled his glass, took a healthy sip, then held it out to him. He shook his head. She shrugged, took another drink, and set the snifter down.

"We are all born with certain expectations, our lots in life as it were. My brother was born to be the next Duke of Roxborough. It's his fate and his duty and what he's been trained for all his life. As a woman, my duty was to make a good match. And I did." She crossed her arms over her chest and met his gaze directly. "Only my husband decided *his* duty was to his king and his country. He was killed in Spain."

"I am sorry."

"So am I," she said simply. "It was not as life was supposed to be." A pensive look flashed in her eyes, then vanished. "He had not yet inherited his title. I was left with nothing. My family gives me a substantial allowance, but I would prefer to be independent. No." Her jaw clenched, and determination shone in her eye. "I *long* to be independent. I cannot abide the idea that I am, to be blunt, a poor relation. I cannot stand the fact of my own helplessness."

She swiveled and paced the width of the room. "Do you have any notion what it's like to realize you've done all that was expected of you in life but life has not turned out at all as expected?"

"I have a vague idea," he murmured.

"And to further realize that, regardless of your finances, because you're a women, you have no true choices?"

"There you have me," he said under his breath.

"No way, save marriage, to improve your lot?" Frustration rang in her voice. "A woman without money in this world can accomplish little of worth. And, worse, she has no way to help others accomplish anything. Oh, I can have my salons, such entertainments are fairly inexpensive you know, and introduce artists and writers to potential patrons, but I haven't the funds to help them myself."

"Like Lady Forester helps?"

She pulled up short and stared. Then, without warning, she burst into laughter. "That was not what I had in mind."

"Thank God," he said wryly. "So you want to be a patron?"

"Not exactly."

"Then what?"

She shook her head. "I'm not entirely sure. At the moment, it's little more than a vague, elusive idea. And rather too ill-formed to mention."

"Tell me anyway." He stepped to her side. Her scent, a vague, provocative mix of subtle florals and spice, wafted around him, and his stomach tightened.

She stared up at him as if deciding whether or not he was worthy of her trust. "It's far-fetched, probably impossible, and very likely more than a little foolish."

"I'm well acquainted with foolish ideas."

"Then perhaps I will tell you in time." A teasing smile lifted the corners of her mouth. "When we're married."

Richard cupped her chin between his thumb and forefinger and gazed into her blue eyes. "I will not marry a woman who does not want me in her bed. I will not be a husband in name only. Do you understand?"

She swallowed hard. "Yes."

"Very well, then." Once again he resisted the urge to kiss her. To seal their agreement. And perhaps their fate. He stepped away. "I will call on you soon with my decision."

She nodded silently, a bemused expression on her face.

He turned and strode out of the room and out of the house, not slowing his pace until he was a good block away.

Blast it all, what was he going to do? If he was half as smart as he'd always thought he was, he would have accepted her proposal at once. He was, of necessity, a practical man, and his hesitation was not at all practical. Her offer was the answer to his prayers. It would solve all his financial problems, ensuring his future and the futures of his sisters.

In addition, marriage to the daughter of the Duke of Roxborough would go a long way in restoring the respectability of his title and his family name. Certainly his own actions in the last few years had

started that process, but restoring the honor of the
earls of Shelbrooke was as arduous a process as
restoring their fortune.

What in the name of all that's holy had possessed
him? What stubborn and previously unknown facet
of his personality could explain his idiotic disregard of six hundred thousand pounds, eight ships,
more or less, and a great deal of land in America?

Was the idea of *that kind of marriage* so repug-
nant? And in truth, would it be *that kind of marriage*
for long? He'd never had a great deal of trouble
gaining the affections of women in the past, although admittedly his skills were a bit rusty. Still,
once wed, affection would certainly follow. Perhaps even love.

Love? Now there was an unsettling idea. Besides,
he'd never particularly considered love an integral
part of marriage. He'd never particularly considered love at all.

But desire, that was something he well understood. And he'd known the moment he'd looked
into her eyes, that he wanted this woman. And
wanted her to want him. They would suit well together.

It was more than likely pride that held him back.
Damnable pride. It was the only thing he still had
in abundance. The only thing he hadn't been forced
to rebuild from nothing. And the very thing that
had kept him before now from seeking out an heiress with an impressive dowry and substantial income.

Yet even now he didn't want to be bought like a

prize specimen of cattle purchased only for appearance. Or acquired like a new work of art meant only for display.

And he wanted the woman he married to want more from him than his name.

He grimaced to himself. It was the height of irony that this woman who once considered him too far beneath her for notice would now turn to him for salvation. Of course, he doubted she even remembered the incident. It was long ago and of no real significance in her life. Richard had barely recalled it himself until tonight.

He had danced with her at a ball during her season, ignoring the fact that she was all but officially betrothed to her future husband. Everyone in London knew it was a love match from childhood. He cringed at the recollection of his suggestive comments, spurred by recklessness and a great deal of drink. His exact words now thankfully escaped him, but the disdain in her eyes lingered in his memory.

She'd been right, of course: he'd been unworthy of her notice. He'd been the worst sort of scoundrel—following in his father's footsteps.

He was not the same man now.

Probably why he was at the top of her bloody list.

He had two months to convince the lovely lady she wanted to be his countess in more than name alone. It would not be easy. She'd obviously built walls around her feelings. After all, no woman alive could talk about the death of her husband, even one that had occurred eight years earlier, with the same lack of emotion Lady Gillian had shown. What kind of man could break down those barriers?

Oh certainly, with the sterling qualities that had propelled him to the top of her husband list *he* could, no doubt, in time. He'd been quite accomplished in the fine art of seduction before circumstances had forced him to become the type of man who had attracted her in the first place. Yet another odd twist of fate. His life seemed to be filled with ironies these days.

Pity, there was so little time. He could already foresee both of them trying too hard in the weeks and days until her birthday. Too many strained moments with too much at stake.

Would he stand a better chance if he wasn't at all a suitable candidate? If he didn't have strength of character and a sense of honor? If all he had was passion?

A passion born from a love of life. It's extremely compelling. Almost irresistible.

He stopped in his tracks.

Weren't women always pining after men completely wrong for them? Didn't that account for the attraction of rakes and rogues?

Perhaps the key to the cool and serene Lady Gillian was not held by a man with those noble qualities that had placed him at the top of her husband list. A man respectable and dependable and solid.

A man one might well choose as a spouse but never as a lover.

Perhaps the man who could truly reach beyond her walls was not the man he was today.

But the man he used to be.

Chapter 3

"I cannot believe you went ahead with this."
Robert, the Earl of Weston, slumped back
in the brocade wing chair he had claimed as his
own years ago and drummed his fingers on a side
table, looking, if possible, even more morose than
usual. "Without so much as discussing it with us."

Christopher, Viscount Cummings, leaned against
the mantel, arms crossed over his chest, and surveyed her with an expression only slightly less
glum than Robin's. "And without even allowing us
the pleasure of witnessing the event. It could have
been quite entertaining."

"Precisely why I did not want you present," Gillian said. "As for discussing this with you, as you
recall, I did just that." She stalked to a nearby sideboard, pulled open a drawer, snatched up two
sheets of paper, and waved them at the men. "And
this was your response."

The two exchanged glances, and Gillian grit her teeth. Any other time this silent communication between Robin and Kit would have amused her. Today she was not in the mood for anything from these childhood friends but blind loyalty and unwavering support.

"We didn't realize you were serious," Kit muttered.

"If I wasn't serious why would I have asked each of you to provide me with lists of potential husbands?"

Kit traded another quick glance with Robin. There was something in that look . . .

"Good Lord. I should have known." Gillian glanced at the papers in her hand. "These were a joke, weren't they?"

Kit shifted uneasily.

Robin avoided her gaze. "Not entirely, but—"

"They certainly make sense now." She held the lists before her, her gaze skipping from Robin's precise hand to Kit's barely legible scrawl. "I wondered why, with all the men in London to choose from, there were only a handful of names here."

"Well, what did you expect?" Irritation rang in Robin's voice. "We don't think this is a good idea. And quite frankly, what you want in a potential husband is not entirely easy to find."

"It's not like going to Tattersall's and selecting a prime bit of cattle," Kit huffed. "Besides, we've never looked at men in terms of their suitability for harness before."

"But look at who you've named here." She drew

her brows together in disgust. "Why, the Viscount Reynolds is far too well known at the gaming tables—"

"And therefore always needs money." A smug smile creased Kit's face. "A perfect choice."

"Not for me." She studied the lists. "The Marquess of Dunstable has nine children—"

"And wants a wife," Robin pointed out.

"He wants a governess," Gillian snorted. "At least he already has an heir."

"Yes, well . . ." Robin cleared his throat. "Have you considered that at all, Gillian? The possibility of children?"

"Believe me, it is a prime consideration," she said under her breath.

"Then—"

"But not one I wish to discuss at the moment. This"—she slapped the papers—"is what I want to talk about. Look at the rest of these names."

She shook her head in disgust. "This one is old. This one fat. I simply couldn't abide a man whose only passion in life is food. Here's one with a notorious reputation, and I am in no mood to reform a rake."

"Come now, they aren't all unacceptable." Robin rose to his feet and moved to her side, plucking the list from her hands. "What's wrong with Lord Runley?"

She rolled her gaze toward the ceiling. "The man's an idiot. He hasn't the sense God gave a sheep."

"Or Lord Harkin?"

She stared in disbelief. "He barely comes up to my chin. In addition, if I am forced to spend a lifetime looking down at the top of a man's head, I prefer it be a head of hair."

Kit shrugged. "A minor detail."

"You're not looking for a husband," Robin said wryly. "You're looking for a saint."

"A saint who needs money." Gillian folded her arms over her chest. "Shelbrooke will serve nicely."

"Even if it appears he's not the rake he once was," Robin said, "Shelbrooke is hardly a saint."

"The devil is more like it. It's unnatural the way he's never seen at the gaming tables anymore. His name hasn't been linked with any woman at all for years. I see him at any number of social occasions, but he keeps to himself. With his dark looks and brooding manner he reminds me of one of those long-suffering poets you always seem to have around." Kit narrowed his eyes as if this fact alone was enough to condemn the man. "He's not to be trusted."

"He's not nearly as brooding as you might think," Gillian said under her breath. "If you both believe Shelbrooke is such a bad idea, why did you suggest him at all?"

"I didn't know he was on Robin's list," Kit said quickly.

Robin cast him an irritated look. "I had to name someone who at least appeared suitable."

"Oh? Did you run out of men who were old or fat or stupid or totally unacceptable?" Gillian raised a brow.

"I thought they were *all* unacceptable," Robin said.

"Up to and including Shelbrooke." Kit shook his head. "Who in his right mind would have imagined you'd actually approach the man, let alone propose marriage?"

"It's not as if I'm looking for a love match." She heaved a frustrated sigh. "It's a convenience, nothing more than that. This marriage is simply a means to an end."

"The end being a great deal of money." Robin studied her carefully. "I must admit I am disappointed. I never thought *you* would succumb to this kind of temptation."

"Then you thought wrong." The tension of recent days sharpened her tone, but it couldn't be helped.

It had been a scant week since her great-uncle's solicitor had called on her with news of her inheritance. She had never met Jasper Effington, the youngest of her grandfather's three brothers. All three had left England years before her parents were born, to make their fortune in America. And make it they did, in shipping and other pursuits.

The two older brothers had married and had families to inherit their fortunes. Jasper's wife had died childless, and he had never remarried. Gillian knew few other details of his life. According to his solicitor, her great-uncle had wished his considerable wealth to go to her because he had well understood the limited expectations of the youngest sibling in a family and further knew they were even less for a woman.

However, Jasper was not quite as beneficent as to leave his holdings to an unmarried woman, even a widow. His bequest carried the stipulation that she be married by her thirtieth birthday.

"I doubt Charles would approve," Kit murmured.

Robin shot him a quelling glance. "Charles would expect her to go on with her life."

"I have." A pang of regret stabbed through her.

And gone on rather well, she'd thought, until Jasper's bequest had brought back the feelings of sorrow and anger she'd believed she'd put to rest with her husband eight years ago.

Charles, Kit, Robin, and she had grown up together, forming a lasting friendship long before they realized the difference between boys and girls and their lots in life. The bonds forged in childhood remained even now. But while Kit and Robin were her dearest friends, it was Charles who had captured her heart. They'd married after her first season, and the joy of their time together lingered so strongly in her memory that no other man had ever seriously attracted her interest.

To this day, one of Gillian's deepest regrets was not fighting Charles's decision to purchase a commission in the army, but they had both been young and convinced of their own invulnerability. To her everlasting despair they had been wrong.

"I have gone on with my life," she said again, wondering exactly who she wished to convince.

"Marrying a man like Shelbrooke is scarcely

what Charles would have had in mind," Kit said loftily.

"No, we know what he would have preferred." Robin paused and nodded sharply at Kit, who sighed and, with a show of reluctance, stepped to his friend's side. The men stared at her as if they were about to meet their doom and she was the executioner.

Robin drew a deep breath. "Charles would have expected one of us to step forward."

"Bravely." Kit squared his shoulders. "And without regard for the consequences."

"Consequences?" Gillian stared and tried hard not to laugh. They looked so . . . so . . . resigned.

"Indeed." Robin's chin lifted. "Marriage."

"Shackled." Kit sniffed. "For life. Or what would be left of it."

For a moment she considered letting them both dwell on the dire fate they fully believed she would deliver them, but they were, after all, her dearest friends. "I don't expect either of you to marry me."

Matching expressions, not unlike those of men pardoned from the gallows at the last moment, passed over their faces. They were so predictable and frequently annoying, but she loved them as if they were her brothers. In truth, she was closer to these two than to her own brother. Their mutual relief brought her the first real smile she'd had all day.

"It's going to be difficult enough as it is without having one of you directly involved. Besides, how could I possibly choose between you?"

Robin stepped forward earnestly. "We would do it though, Gillian. If that's what you wanted. Either of us."

"Not me. I would have regained my senses far short of the altar." Kit shook his head. "I love you Gillian, and I always will, but not even for you would I voluntarily—"

"Kit, before I'm forced to blush at the flattering nature of your comment, do be still," she said dryly.

"See." He nodded at Robin. "And that's exactly why I wouldn't. It's bad enough being around her now. It's like having an overbearing sister always telling you to straighten your cravat or mind your table manners or dance with horse-faced females no one else will go near. At least I can still escape to my own home."

Robin frowned. "You don't have a sister."

"I don't need one. I have Gillian."

"Well, we won't have her for much longer if she goes through with this ridiculous scheme." Robin's eyes narrowed. "Shelbrooke does not seem the type of man to allow his wife to continue to go her merry way in the company of two unmarried men regardless of how long they have been friends."

"Nonsense, Robin," Gillian said with a conviction she didn't quite believe. "My marriage will not change our relationship one bit."

"We shall see," Robin said thoughtfully. "I don't know him personally, only by reputation, and I suppose he may well be a decent sort. He definitely isn't the same bounder his father was. Or, for that matter, he once was."

"His coats are always shabby," Kit said as if this alone was a sin too great to forgive.

She'd noticed, of course. Everything about his appearance was not quite up to snuff. In many ways, she thought it spoke well of the man. He obviously wasn't squandering what little funding he had on himself.

Robin shook his head. "It's obvious why Shelbrooke would agree to this marriage—"

"He hasn't actually agreed," she said quickly. "At least not yet."

"I'm sure he will," Kit said darkly.

"Nonetheless"—Robin glared at Kit, and the other man shrugged—"what I still don't understand is why you're willing to go to such lengths to acquire this inheritance."

"It's a great deal of money," she said defensively, knowing full well the reason sounded little better today than it had last night.

Robin and Kit stared expectantly, and she wanted nothing more than to punch them both the way she had on occasion when they were children.

"You two, of all people, should understand. And I must say I'm disappointed." She balled her hands into fists and willed a note of calm to her voice. She wasn't ready to tell either of her old friends that her plans went beyond simple independence. Especially since those plans were still little more than the vague, and probably foolish, idea of repaying a debt. "You would never question the desire of a man to achieve financial independence. Why do you question mine?"

"Because we know you," Kit said pointedly. "Because you've never hesitated to give your opinion of those who marry only for money or titles or to further their positions in the world."

"You married Charles because you loved him," Robin said. "You've always said you'd only marry again for love."

"Circumstances have forced me to reconsider my position."

"I can't believe your family approves of this." Robin studied her carefully. "What does your brother think of this outrageous condition to your inheritance?"

"He doesn't know. No one in my family knows, and they will not be told." She pinned Robin with an unyielding look. "You will not mention this to anyone." She turned to Kit. "Neither will you. If Shelbrooke and I can reach an agreement, I would prefer the world, including each and every member of the Effington family, to believe this marriage is for no other reason than—"

"Love?" Kit's tone was mocking.

"Affection," she said in a no-nonsense tone. "Or whatever other reasons people marry for."

"I'll hold my tongue, but until the moment you wed I will not cease to express my opinion as to the foolishness of your decision." Robin shook his head. "Mark my words, Gillian, you will regret this."

"Perhaps, but I shall regret it in a state of sweet

financial freedom." She smiled pleasantly. "Enough of this. Since we were speaking of Thomas, come see the landscape he sent me. He's never been particularly interested in art, but this is excellent." She crossed the room to the painting.

Robin and Kit dutifully stepped to her side and murmured appreciative comments. It was indeed a striking work, with muted greens and shafts of golden sunlight. An idyllic depiction of the English countryside. The way life should be. This was an artist who poured his heart and soul into his work.

One could say the painting expresses not the soul of man but the soul of God.

A shiver ran up her spine, and without thinking, Gillian crumpled the lists in her hand.

"You look like hell." Thomas Effington, the Marquess of Helmsley, lounged in an aged, threadbare chair and swirled the brandy in the glass held loosely in his hand. "Did you work all night again?"

"Not all night," Richard said absently and dabbed an infinitesimal dot of azure blue on the canvas before him. "I dozed a bit before dawn."

"And were back at your easel the moment the sun was up."

"Um-hum." Richard stepped back and studied the painting with a critical eye.

"You're working too bloody hard."

"I have little choice," he murmured. "I needed to finish this." It was a half-truth at best. Oh, he did wish to complete the painting: the sooner it was in the hands of a dealer, the sooner he would be paid. There were a half dozen other unfinished works that demanded his attention as well. Besides, work always cleared his mind and helped him think. And he had a great deal to think about.

Thomas heaved a frustrated sigh. "I still don't see why you insist on remaining anonymous. You could be the darling of the ton."

"I would prefer the Earl of Shelbrooke not be the *pet du jour*, thank you very much." Richard picked up a turpentine-soaked rag and wiped his brush. "Besides, from what you've said and the gossip I've heard, plus the sizable sums my paintings are starting to command, success is already within reach."

"Perhaps, but not your reach," Thomas said pointedly. "The artist gaining growing acclaim is Etienne-Louis Toussaint."

"At your service, my lord." Richard swept an overly dramatic bow.

"If people knew Toussaint was in reality the Earl of—"

"All would be lost." Richard tossed the rag and brush onto a battered, paint-speckled table. "We've had this discussion before, and my views have not changed. If anything, my desire to keep my identity secret has strengthened."

Thomas adopted the stubborn expression Richard knew all too well and braced himself for yet another round of debate. "Still, now that Toussaint's paintings are becoming all the rage—"

"Even more reason to remain hidden," Richard said mildly. "Come now, Thomas. Think for a moment. Earls gamble. Earls hunt. Earls ride." He snorted in disdain. "Earls squander their families' money and destroy their good names, yet no one in society gives it a second thought.

"However, earls do not go into business to earn an honorable living. Earls do not emigrate to uncivilized countries to seek their fortunes. And under no circumstances do earls paint. It's what little girls still in the schoolroom or elderly female relatives do to fill their empty hours." He raised a brow. "Society views such activities much the same way it views the writing of poetry by marquesses."

"I haven't published anything," Thomas muttered and shifted uncomfortably in the chair.

Richard grinned. "And you've told no one about your efforts, have you?"

"No, but my writing is an entirely different issue altogether from your painting."

"Oh? How is that?"

Thomas raised his glass in a mock salute. "Your work is excellent. My poems reek."

Richard laughed but could not bring himself to deny it. Thomas had written poetry since their schooldays, and in spite of his continuing efforts, had not shown significant improvement through the years.

"Still, if my writing was any good, I would not hesitate to shout it from the rooftops."

"Yes, but you are a marquess and heir to the Duke of Roxborough, with all the wealth and power of the Effington family at your disposal. You can do as you please. I, however, have a name and a reputation to restore. I am dependent on the good will of the *ton* for that as well as for its money. Do you honestly think the work of an earl could command the prices of a mysterious Frenchman?"

"Perhaps not."

"There is no perhaps about it. My work would never be taken seriously if my real name was attached to it."

"Then it is as much your pride that keeps you silent as anything else."

"Damnable pride," Richard said with a wry laugh. He could joke about it with Thomas, but it did rankle that the same skills praised in an unknown artist would be seen as little more than dabbling in a member of the upper classes. "Besides, I quite enjoy the history we've—or rather, you've—concocted for Etienne-Louis."

"I have done a remarkably fine job." Thomas grinned and took a sip of his drink. "Not that it was all that difficult. A well-placed comment here. An observation there, and—"

"Voila." Richard adopted an exaggerated French accent. "We have Etienne-Louis Toussaint, the only surviving son of a noble French family slaughtered in the revolution, who was spirited out of the country by loyal servants. Now he spends his days painting with the passion of his forebears, and his nights, ah, *mon ami*, his nights—"

"That was a brilliant touch." Thomas's grin widened.

"Brilliant, indeed. For a man who has never been

seen in person, his reputation as a lover is approaching legend."

"Thank you." Thomas shrugged in an overdone show of humility. "One does what one can. I must admit, it has been a great deal of fun, particularly when I overhear women discussing the charms of the irresistible Etienne-Louis. Pity I don't hear similar comments about the Earl of Shelbrooke. Isn't it about time you looked for a suitable match?"

Was Thomas aware of his sister's legacy and the conditions it carried? Richard wouldn't put it past Thomas to maneuver his friend into a marriage with his sister that would benefit them both.

"The last thing I need in my life right now is another female. Between my sisters and my aunt, I have more than enough women to deal with. Besides, a woman who is both suitable and willing to overlook my financial shortcomings is difficult to find." Richard paused. If indeed Thomas was aware of Gillian's inheritance, there was no more opportune moment for him to mention it. But his friend remained silent, and Richard suspected he knew nothing of his sister's proposal. "Enough talk of women, Thomas, now come here and look at this."

Thomas pulled himself to his feet and crossed the room to stand beside Richard. For a long moment neither man spoke.

"You have a great talent, my friend," Thomas said softly. "Your skills improve with every work. It's excellent."

"Excellent? It's magnificent."

"Your modesty is as overwhelming as your talent."

"Modesty is pointless when you live your life hidden in the shadows of another's name."

"I wish you'd let me speak to my sister. She wields a great deal of influence and would never betray your secret." Thomas's voice was a shade too casual.

In light of everything else that had occurred last night, Richard had nearly forgotten his shock at seeing one of his works in Gillian's possession. He matched Thomas's manner of studied indifference with his own. "Ah yes, the lovely, widowed Lady Gillian. However, as I said, I have no need for another woman complicating my life at this point, even if the lady in question could be of great benefit. I will repeat once again that I do not wish you to approach your sister on my behalf." He raised a brow. "You are honoring my wishes, aren't you?"

Thomas hesitated, and Richard bit back a grin. "Well . . . certainly."

"You would never speak to her about my work?"

"No . . . never."

"Or suggest she invite me to one of her salons?"

"Absolutely not," Thomas said staunchly.

Richard studied him carefully. "Then you did not prompt her to invite me to a gathering last night?"

"Last night? No, of course not." Thomas frowned. "Did you go?"

"Well, yes but—"

"She invited you? And you went." Thomas's expression brightened. "I say, what luck."

"Why?"

"Well, it's obvious . . ." Thomas hesitated. "Exactly *whom* did she invite?"

Richard crossed his arms over his chest. "The Earl of Shelbrooke. The invitation came through my solicitor."

"I swear I had nothing to do with it."

"I believe you." He turned his attention to the last of the brushes still needing cleaning but watched Thomas out of the corner of his eye. "It was a rather interesting evening."

"Was it?"

"Rife with fascinating discussion, entertaining guests, and the occasional odd coincidence."

"Oh?" Thomas said uneasily.

"You, of all people, can imagine my surprise when I discovered one of my landscapes on display."

"One of your paintings?"

"The presence of the painting plus my unexpected invitation, well, you can see why I wondered if my secret had been revealed."

"Of course." Apprehension colored Thomas's expression. "And was it?"

"Not at all. But I was shocked to hear a bit of information I never anticipated." He leaned toward Thomas as if he was about to reveal a well-kept confidence. "Did you know Lady Gillian has a brother other than yourself?"

Thomas's brow furrowed in confusion. "What on earth are you talking about? Gillian has no other brothers."

"No?" Richard widened his eyes in mock surprise. "But she must."

"Why?"

"Well it's obvious, old man." Richard straightened and pinned Thomas with a firm look. "If she has only one brother, then the brother who sent her my painting must be you. And we both know you would never disregard my wishes and do that."

For a moment Thomas stared, looking for all the world like a man with the axe still in his hand ready to deny the chopped tree at his feet. "Damnation, Richard." He downed the rest of his brandy. "You never would have known if she hadn't invited you to her salon. Who could have foreseen that?"

Richard raised a brow.

"Very well, I confess." Thomas strode to an ancient, wobbly table littered with an array of paint jars, rags, and various other supplies and plucked a bottle of barely passable brandy from the confusion. "I had to do something. You simply cannot keep on like this."

"Thomas." A warning sounded in Richard's voice.

He ignored it. "No, this time you listen to me. You spend every day and most nights painting in this hellhole—"

"Come now, it's shabby but it's not that bad. Besides, you own this hellhole."

"That doesn't make it any more acceptable," Thomas snapped. "When you're not painting you're attending the occasional social affair simply to observe subjects for your portraits—"

"Who pay very well," Richard murmured.

"Of course they do. You paint from that remarkable memory of yours that conveniently fails to note overlong noses or mottled complexions." He refilled his glass and held the bottle out to Richard. "And when you're not here you're in the country trying to do something completely absurd like assist your tenants with harvesting—"

"Planting at this time of year." Richard removed several brushes from a glass, wondering vaguely if he didn't have an actual snifter somewhere, dropped them on the table, then crossed the room and accepted the bottle.

"Regardless. You're in the fields or pouring over ledgers or trying to mend the roof of Shelbrooke Manor—"

"Someone has to." Richard shrugged and poured the brandy.

"Yes, but that someone needn't be you." Thomas drew a deep breath. "Gillian can introduce your works—"

"Toussaint's works."

"*Your* works to the people who could most benefit your career. Your paintings will be in demand. You could charge whatever you wish." He aimed his glass at Richard. "And you'll have the money to hire someone to fix the blasted roof or do anything else you want."

"Very well."

"Very well?" Thomas's eyes narrowed suspiciously. "What do you mean, *very well*? I've offered to involve Gillian before, but you've always rejected the idea in no uncertain terms. Why aren't you objecting now? What are you up to, Richard?"

"Not a thing. I've come to my senses, that's all. You're right: the Lady Gillian can be a great help to my endeavors." *What would Thomas say if he knew just how much of a help his sister really could be?*

"I'm right?" A slow grin spread across Thomas's face. "Of course I am."

"So." Richard pulled a long swallow of the brandy and tried not to compare it to the fine liquor he'd sampled last night. "Tell me about her, this sister of yours?"

"Well . . . she's a sister. You understand, *you* have sisters." Thomas shrugged. "I don't know exactly what to say. She's quite smart and somewhat pretty, even at her age—"

"Very pretty."

"Stubborn and strong-willed, but then, she's an Effington."

"Why hasn't she married again?" Richard asked as if the answer was of no importance.

Thomas stared into his glass. "She loved Charles very much. Had loved him from the time she was a child. It was really quite impressive." He looked up. "She was devastated when he died and not herself for a long time. My parents worried that she'd never be the same again.

"She was, of course, eventually, although she is somewhat more reserved now than she was then."

Thomas shook his head. "One never knows what Gillian is thinking or feeling. At least I never do. Maybe her friends—"

"Weston and Cummings?"

Thomas nodded. "The three—four, including Charles—practically grew up together. I've often wondered if they're among the reasons she hasn't remarried."

Richard swirled the brandy in his hand, the pale amber coating the sides of the cheap glass. "I understand her husband had not yet inherited."

"Bloody piece of bad luck. She deserved better. She does receive an allowance from the family, but it's not extensive. Mother frets that she won't accept more. I don't understand it myself. Gillian rarely speaks of it, but I suspect she would prefer not to take anything at all."

"I see," Richard said quietly, remembering her passionate comments last night. Maybe Gillian was simply tired of her family's charity. For whatever reasons, she obviously wanted this inheritance badly.

"I should be on my way." Thomas glanced at the new painting. "I gather this isn't ready for me to take yet?"

"Not quite. It should be completely dry by the end of the week. You can fetch it up then. I expect it to bring enough to pay the staff at Shelbrooke Manor, or what's left of the staff, for a good three months."

"You could also invest in a new jacket." The marquess cast a disdainful glance at the glass in his hand. "And a better bottle of brandy."

"You don't seem to mind drinking it."

"But I do mind. I drink it only to be polite." He finished the liquor and set the glass on a table.

"The sure sign of a good friend."

Thomas was indeed his closest, in truth his only, friend, as well as his coconspirator. They had known each other from their school days but hadn't seen much of one another until after Richard's father had died. Somehow, they'd renewed their acquaintance then and now were as close as brothers.

Etienne had been born three years ago when Richard was at his wits' end trying to turn a neglected estate into a profitable enterprise. It was in fact Thomas who had originally suggested that Richard attempt to make his secret vice provide the income he sorely needed.

Now, Thomas delivered his paintings to a solicitor who in turn passed them on to a dealer in art. Payment proceeded backwards along the same obscure route. Both men were confident the convoluted process ensured Richard's continued anonymity.

"And, Thomas, don't forget this time to take the rent out of whatever is left after the dealer's commission."

Thomas rolled his gaze toward the ceiling. This too was an ongoing debate between them. "This place cost me less than what I'd spend on a good horse. I can well afford to—"

"Nonetheless, I will not—"

"I know, I know." Thomas blew a resigned

breath and strode to the door. "Very well. But you could at least permit me to find better quarters for you."

"This is adequate for my needs. And the light is excellent. Besides," he grinned, "I rather like this *hellhole*. It asks nothing from me."

It was a single large room encompassing the top floor of a mercantile building in an unfashionable but not disreputable area on the fringe of the city's business district. The room served both as studio and living quarters and was passable for a man living alone. His sisters and aunt remained in the country at Shelbrooke Manor, but Richard's work demanded his presence in London. His family had no inkling as to the source of his still meager funds, and he preferred to keep it that way.

Thomas had bought the building without telling Richard, and he insisted that the rent generated by the rest of the edifice had long ago reimbursed him for the purchase price.

"That damnable pride of yours will be the end of you yet, Richard."

"We shall see." Richard's gaze caught his. "I will pay you back for everything one day."

"I've no doubt of that," Thomas smiled. "I've also no doubt you would do the same for me should our positions be reversed." He opened the door, then turned back, his manner tentative. "So . . . how are your finances these days?"

"They'd improve if I could paint faster." Richard raised a shoulder in a casual shrug, as if it was of no consequence. "I could use a few more commissions, particularly for those portraits that ignore the more unflattering aspects of a face."

"Exactly why Etienne-Louis will be a success." Thomas laughed, and Richard joined him.

The friends exchanged a few more comments, and Thomas took his leave.

At once Richard's spirits dropped. Certainly a sale here would pay one bill, a commission there another, but even with his prices increasing, it was not enough. He raked his fingers through his hair in frustration. It seemed that no matter what he did or how hard he worked, he was not substantially further ahead now than he had been a year ago. Or two. Or five. What he needed was a great deal of money, an influx of funds all at once, not in the piecemeal fashion that so limited him now.

Gillian's proposal would solve all his problems. But he could never live with her conditions. If they married, it must be a marriage in every sense. Nothing less would serve.

Richard removed the newly completed painting from the easel and leaned it carefully against a wall. Gillian had said she didn't know if she could fall in love again. Richard didn't doubt his ability to win the lady's favors, but there was too much at stake for both of them to risk failure.

It had been a long time since the Earl of Shelbrooke had cut a wide swath through the hearts of the ladies of London. Richard now had no patience for frivolous pursuits and no desire for anything beyond meaningless physical encounters easily obtained and just as easily forgotten. Even so, surely the skills that had enhanced his amorous reputation in his younger days lingered, a bit tarnished, perhaps, from lack of use but there nonetheless.

The outrageous thought that had occurred to him last night still hovered in the back of his mind, yet it was little more than a vague idea and no doubt a poor one at that. Being the rogue he'd once been would not only topple him from her list but change her mind about his suitability as a husband. Richard heaved a heartfelt sigh. Besides, he suspected there was no turning back. His character had come too far, and in truth he regarded who and what he'd been with a certain amount of regret and more than a touch of disgust.

Gillian was no innocent straight from the schoolroom, no on-the-shelf maiden eager for a husband. She would not fall willingly into his embrace under any circumstances. Gillian may well agree to a true marriage out of desire for her legacy, but the idea of a reluctant bride twisted Richard's stomach. How to convince her otherwise would take a great deal of careful consideration.

Absently, he selected a large, prepared canvas from a stack in the corner and placed it on the easel. What he needed was a plan.

In the meantime, he also needed to work. Nothing helped him think as well as immersion in a new painting, as if the act of creation left a more practical part of his mind free to ponder whatever problem was at hand. And he did need the money. At the moment, he was not substantially closer to six hundred thousand pounds, eight ships, more or less, and a great deal of land in America.

Richard stared at the blank canvas and considered his next project. Landscapes were all the rage, and he would have no trouble selling one. Yet for some odd reason he preferred to do a portrait right now.

And odder still, only one face came to mind.

Chapter 4

⁓⁓⁓⁓⁓⁓⁓

T he incessant pounding echoed through the house.

Gillian stumbled down the front stairway, trying to grip the banister with one hand and hold her wrapper together with the other. Who on earth could be demanding entrance at this hour of the night? She peered through the shadows to the circle of light cast by a candle held by her butler at the front entry.

Wilkins fumbled with the door and muttered dire pronunciations she couldn't quite make out but had heard before through the years. For the most part, Wilkins was well trained and performed his duties admirably. Unless, of course, he was out of favor with Mrs. Wilkins, Gillian's cook. Or had indulged in one too many glasses of sherry. Or was awakened in the middle of the night.

He yanked the door open with a vengeance, although no wider than necessary, then appeared to remember his position, stiffening his posture in preparation to look down his nose at whoever had the temerity to rouse them all from a sound sleep. Wilkins was extremely good at looking down his nose and made up in haughtiness what he lacked in stature. The man barely came up to her chin and resembled nothing so much as a stout, arrogant elf.

Gillian paused halfway down the stairs and waited to see if her attention was needed or if she could return to bed. This could be nothing more than a late-night reveler mistaking her door for another. Wilkins's voice was low, his tone perfectly proper, although she couldn't catch his words.

He turned from the barely opened door and gazed up at her. "My lady, you have a caller."

"A caller? At this hour?"

"Shall I tell him you're not receiving guests?" Wilkins said as if he routinely greeted late-night visitors while wearing his dressing gown and a long nightcap.

"Since he's behind the door and has obviously heard every word we've said, that would be somewhat awkward." Gillian stifled a yawn and walked down the stairs. "But do find out who it is first."

"Very well, my lady." Wilkins sniffed and turned back to the door.

Without warning it swung open, smacking into Wilkins's rotund figure with a fleshy thud.

"Pardon me, old chap. You should watch where you stand, you know. Do take care." Shelbrooke brushed past the butler and nodded to her. "Good evening."

She widened her eyes in disbelief. "Evening was over hours ago. It's nearly dawn."

"Is it?" He grinned and ran his fingers through already tousled hair. "Imagine that. I wonder what happened to the night?"

"For most of us it was spent asleep in our beds," she said sharply.

"In our . . . bed?" His gaze met hers, and at once the innocent words were fraught with a far different meaning than she'd intended.

"Beds." She swallowed hard.

"Isn't that what I said?" He caught her hand and raised it to his lips. His jaw was dark with stubble, and she found it oddly intimate and just a touch exciting.

"No." Her voice cracked, and she couldn't tear her gaze from his. "You said bed. I said beds—more than one. Each with his own."

"My mistake." He brushed his lips across the back of her hand and her stomach fluttered. "I do hope I haven't disturbed you."

"No, of course not." His eyes were deep and intense and seemed to beckon her closer. "I couldn't really sleep anyway."

"What a shame." He released her hand, his gaze drifting over her in a far too familiar manner. At once she realized her wrapper hung open and the far too revealing nightrail she wore beneath left little to the imagination.

"What are you doing here?" She backed away,

pulling the edges of the robe tighter around her.

"I've come to give you my answer." He smiled, clasped his hands behind his back, and strolled into the parlor.

"Your answer? Now?"

"It's been on my mind," he called over his shoulder. "And I suspect it's the very reason why you were unable to sleep."

"I scarcely think so." Goodness, the man certainly made up in arrogance what he lacked in money. She stalked after him. "It was more likely a bit of dinner that disagreed with me. Or I simply might have been too tired to sleep. Or my mattress might have been just a bit—"

"Gillian." He turned so quickly that she nearly stumbled into him. "I have given your proposal a great deal of thought."

"And?" Her heart pounded in her chest.

"The biggest impediments to a marriage between us are your conditions, this marriage in name only nonsense, and my refusal to agree to it."

"Well, yes, but—"

"However, if I recall correctly, it was also your suggestion that we spend the next two months getting to know each other in a sort of trial betrothal, so to speak—"

"I didn't really—"

"—in hopes that at the end of that time you will have come to the realization that I am not completely repulsive to you—"

"I never said you were repulsive!"

"Forgive me, what I meant to say was that sharing my bed was not completely repulsive to you. That is more accurate, is it not?"

"Yes." She shook her head. "No."

"I see." He raised a brow. "Then you have changed your mind and you are ready to be my wife in every sense the title implies."

"No!" He cast her a questioning look. She shook her head impatiently. "Botheration, my lord, you have me completely confused."

"Do I?" He looked rather pleased with himself.

"Yes, you do." She turned away, squeezed her eyes closed, and pressed two fingers between her eyebrows to a point just above the bridge of her nose in an effort to stave off the dull throb she knew would begin any moment.

"Does your head ache?" Sympathy sounded in his voice.

"Not yet," she snapped, "but I expect it will shortly."

"Allow me." She sensed him moving nearer behind her, and before she could say a word, an easy touch settled on each of her temples.

She jumped and snapped her eyes open. "What are you—"

"I'm trying to help you," he said, pulling her back gently. "Relax, Gillian." His fingers moved in slow, easy circles on her head. "I do promise not to bite."

"I was not particularly worried about you biting," she murmured and kept her back straight to avoid leaning against him.

"Pity." He heaved a dramatic sigh. "There was a

time when women worried about my bite and much more. Apparently, I have reformed."

"I know." He certainly did have wonderful hands. "I know everything about you."

"Everything?"

"Everything that's important." She tilted her head to give him better access.

"Do you?"

"Of course. I would never approach a man about something as important as marriage without knowing all I could about him." Still, she had no idea he could do anything like this. Her eyes drifted closed.

"That would be foolish."

"Um-hmm." It was difficult to form a coherent sentence. She wondered if her very bones would dissolve from his touch.

"Does your head feel better?"

"Um-hmm." She relaxed, leaning lightly against him, and surrendered to the remarkable feel of his fingers on her face.

"I'm pleased I could be of assistance." His voice was low against her ear. In some part of her mind not fogged with the pleasure of his touch she realized he'd bent his head closer, noted the intimate nature of their stance and how very easy it would be for this reformed rake to kiss her neck, her shoulders, her . . .

"Now then." He dropped his hands and stepped away so abruptly that she struggled to keep her balance. A vague sense of disappointment washed through her. She ignored it and drew a steadying breath. "About our arrangement."

"Ah yes, you said you'd made a decision." She turned toward him. "And what..." He hadn't moved as far as she'd thought. In fact, he was less than a step away, far and away too close, and her eyes were level with his mouth. A rather nice mouth, actually, with lips full and firm and probably quite warm. Definitely a rake's mouth—reformed or not. How many women had that mouth kissed? Caressed? *Pleasured?*

"Gillian?" A hint of a smile curved his lips as if he knew exactly what she was thinking.

She jerked her gaze to his and barely noted the breathless note in her voice. "Yes?"

At once the amusement in his gaze vanished, and he stared down at her as if he'd never seen her before, his eyes dark and intense and as compelling as his lips. An unfamiliar ache rose inside her. She could lose her soul in those eyes. Surrender it for the feel of his arms around her. Sacrifice it for the taste of his lips upon hers.

"Gillian?" His voice was strained, as if he knew the longing that gripped her and shared it.

"Richard, I..." She swallowed. "I..."

"I think perhaps we shall suit well together as husband and wife."

"Your wife." Richard's wife.

Charles's wife.

Guilt, strong and fast and hard, swept through her, catching at her chest with the impact of a physical blow. She gasped and jerked back.

"Gillian, what—"

She wrapped her arms around herself, whirled,

and crossed the room, fighting off a mounting sense of panic. How could she even think of betraying the one man she'd ever loved? Always loved? Other men had kissed her in the years since her husband's death, but their advances had been neither welcomed nor encouraged. But never, ever had she wanted a man's kiss—or desired his touch. Or needed his arms around her.

"Gillian?" Caution edged Richard's voice.

She drew a deep breath and willed a calm she did not feel, then turned to face him with an aloof smile, as if the intimate moment between them had never happened.

"So, my lord," she said brightly, "your decision?"

He narrowed his eyes and studied her for a long, uncomfortable moment. She forced herself to meet his gaze directly.

"Very well. While I had not been in the market for a wife it is past time I wed. In addition, I would be a fool not to admit how much this legacy of yours would improve my circumstances in life. Therefore I am willing to . . . to . . ." He shook his head, a bemused expression on his face. "*Court* doesn't seem quite the appropriate word."

"Nonetheless, I do understand," she said quickly.

"And you understand the only terms under which a marriage between us will take place?"

She raised her chin and kept her voice firm. "I do."

"Excellent. There is, however, one additional condition." He paused as if considering his words. "Should we decide, at the end of the allotted time, not to wed, with you thus forfeiting your inheritance, essentially I will be left with nothing."

"As will I," she said curtly.

"Yes, well you're not quite as desperate for funds as I am, are you? After all, you do have a wealthy family that can come to your aid if necessary."

Irritation rose within her. "I prefer not to rely on my family."

"As you wish, but the option remains should you choose to take advantage of it. I, on the other the hand, can ill afford to spend the next two months attempting to seduce you—"

"*Seduce* me?"

"What would you call it?"

She frowned in annoyance. "I believe we agreed on *court*."

"Not entirely accurate," he murmured.

"Nor is it as explicit, but I do favor it over the alternative."

"Regardless of what we wish to term it, the end result is the same—either we marry and gain the legacy or we don't and I am left with nothing for my time and trouble."

"I do hope it will not be as unpleasant for you as all that." She pulled her brows together in annoyance. "You're not suggesting I compensate you for your time? Pay you perhaps?"

"Not at all." An injured note rang in his words.

Surely she hadn't offended him? Why, she was the one who should be offended. The very idea that she would have to hire someone to seduce—court— her was absurd and rude and—

"I'm insulted you would suggest such a thing."

"You're insulted?" She stared with disbelief.

"Indeed I am. If I was the kind of man who expected to be paid for seducing you—"

"You won't be seducing me!"

"—then I wouldn't be at all the kind of man who would be at the top of your list." He raised a brow. "Would I?"

"No! Of course not. At least I don't think so. Blast it all, you've done it again!" The expected throbbing pulsed above the bridge of her nose and she rubbed it vigorously.

He stepped toward her. "Would you like me to—"

"No!" She thrust out her hand and stepped back. The last thing she needed was to add the confusion triggered by his touch to the confusion brought on by his words. "Just tell me what you want."

"Very well." Again he hesitated. "Since you claim to know all there is to know about me you are no doubt aware that I am the sole support of four sisters. All but one is of marriageable age, the eldest especially should have been wed long ago. It is my fault, I know, but there has been no money for dowries. Nor is there much opportunity in the country to make a suitable match."

He pulled a deep breath. "I would be quite grateful if you should allow her, that is Emma, the oldest, to stay here with you."

Her heart went out to him. "Richard, I can't afford to sponsor a season for a young woman."

"I'm not asking you to," he said quickly. "If you

would chaperone her, procure invitations for her to the same parties you attend, allow her to participate in your salons, that will serve nicely. With luck, she will meet someone. She's rather an attractive bit of baggage."

"But if you and I don't marry, what will you do for a dowry?

"I'll think of something." He shrugged. "I always have."

It really wasn't all that much for him to ask, considering what she had asked of him. Besides, while there were any number of Effington relatives and more than a few female cousins, she'd never had a sister. Having one, even for a short time, might be fun. "I should quite enjoy having your sister here."

"Thank you." He took her hand in both of his. "Regardless of how this arrangement between us ends, you will have my eternal gratitude." His gaze bored into hers, and once again she struggled against the sensation of drowning.

"Are you going to kiss me?" she said in an unconcerned manner, belying the fluttering in her stomach.

"I have every intention of kissing you. I can think of no better way to seal our agreement." He stared for a long moment. Silence stretched between them as taut as the unexpected tension in the air, as disconcerting as the feel of her hand in his. "But not today."

"As you wish." She pulled her hand from his in an unhurried manner. She wouldn't want him to think she was relieved. Or disappointed.

The corners of his mouth twitched as if he thought exactly that and was trying not to smile. He started toward the door. "I intend to go to the country at the end of the week. I shall fetch Emma then."

She stepped after him. "How long will you be gone?"

He stopped and raised a brow. "Do you miss me already?"

"Don't be absurd. It's just that I don't know how we are to proceed with this—"

"Seduction?"

"Courtship," she said firmly, "if you are not here."

"I shan't be gone more than a day or two. In the meantime, I assume you are going to Lady Forester's masquerade?"

In spite of herself she laughed. "I wouldn't dream of missing one of Lady Forester's masquerades. One never knows precisely who or what will be unmasked. Will you be there?"

"If you are." He nodded sharply. "Until then," he said, turned, and, before she could say a word, strode from the room. She heard a murmur of voices followed by the sound of the front door closing firmly. A moment later Wilkins appeared in the doorway.

"Will that be all, my lady, or are you expecting additional guests? If so, I should rouse Mrs. Wilkins, and perhaps she can prepare refreshments." Wilkins's bland stare only emphasized the sarcasm in his voice.

She stifled a sarcastic response of her own. "No, that will do for the moment, thank you."

"Very well." He sniffed his obvious disapproval at the entire episode and took his leave, his haughty demeanor an incongruous contrast to his bobbing nightcap.

Gillian blew out a long breath and sank onto the sofa. She should have felt relieved at Richard's willingness to go along with her proposal, but until now she hadn't really realized exactly what that would mean.

Could she truly be a real wife to him, or to any man for that matter, with all the title implied? Could she really share his life? His bed? His children?

She pulled herself to her feet and paced the room. She should have picked someone else on the list. Someone not nearly as attractive, or with hands that made her want to melt, or eyes that seemed to sap her will. Someone who would have accepted the kind of marriage she had originally proposed for half of her inheritance and been more than happy.

But what of her happiness?

The question pulled her up short. The idea of her own happiness had never entered her mind. How could she possibly be happy without Charles? Why, she couldn't. Any chance at happiness had died with him eight long years ago. No man would ever, ever take his place in her heart. She wouldn't allow it. She could never love anyone else.

Love? There was an odd thought. Love played no

part in her arrangement with Richard. It was a practical matter, nothing more. Many of her friends had entered marriage without love, and many of those had turned out well enough. She could certainly do the same.

She tried to ignore the unsettling idea that sharing Richard's bed would not be at all distasteful. She'd always assumed she could never abide with any other man the kind of intimacies she'd had with Charles. But there was a moment tonight when she'd wanted . . . wanted what? She wrapped her arms around herself as if to ward off a chill.

Surely whatever she'd felt tonight had been triggered by no more than her desire to make the relationship between the two of them succeed. Wasn't she simply trying to convince herself she could indeed be the wife he wished? Trying to regard him with a certain amount of affection? Of course that was the answer. It had to be. She couldn't desire another man any more than she could love him.

Could she?

Once again, guilt washed over her. No. Any odd yearnings she'd had in Richard's presence were an aberration, nothing more. She could marry him and do what was necessary, but she could never want any man but Charles.

How very curious to realize the betrayal wasn't so much in the act but in the need.

Richard studied the miniature portrait propped before him on the easel. He'd tried his hand at miniatures in the past for their lucrative nature, but considered them more a matter of technical skill than true art. Such renderings were better suited to women accustomed to the intricacies of needlework and the use of watercolors than serious artists, although he did wonder if his disdain was due more to his own impatience with the painstaking work than to any legitimate artistic reasons. Richard much preferred to work on a grander scale.

Still, if one had to produce a painting quickly, a miniature would serve well, and a need within him at the moment demanded speed. He'd spent the better part of the night before his visit to Gillian completing this one.

Ice blue eyes stared up at him. No, not so severe as ice, but definitely cool and remote and reserved. If indeed eyes were windows to the soul, Gillian's soul was shuttered tight against intruders. Yet hadn't there been one brief moment tonight? . . .

He rubbed his chin absently and leaned back, automatically adjusting his balance on the precarious stool, his gaze locked on the tiny portrait. He wasn't entirely certain why he wanted to melt the ice in her eyes. Pride was the obvious answer. He had no wish to marry a woman who needed him only as a means to an end. No, he wanted his wife to desire him, long for his touch, yearn for his caress. It seemed little enough to ask in exchange for a lifetime.

Had Gillian ever known such desire in the long years after her husband's death? Richard couldn't recall hearing rumors about her and other men.

And Thomas would have mentioned any liaisons of his sister's, if only out of concern for her.

Had there been no one in her bed other than her husband? His stomach clenched, and he knew without a doubt the answer to his question. Bloody hell, the woman was practically a virgin. He detested virgins and, to his knowledge, had never been involved with one. One had to be exceedingly delicate with virgins—under the bedclothes and elsewhere. He far preferred experienced women.

Oh, certainly, as the world defined such things, Gillian was a widow, not a virgin. But in a practical sense, was there any significant difference between a woman who was untouched and a woman who had not been touched in nearly a decade?

Damnation. How on earth could he willingly bring such a woman, a woman who had no doubt managed to resist untold advances given her family name and her appearance, to his bed? He had no idea whatsoever and not even the vaguest inkling of a plan, far-fetched or otherwise.

A smile danced on the lips of the face staring up at him, as if the portrait itself were amused at his dilemma. He might have painted it such, but not from life. He didn't doubt Gillian saw nothing humorous in their situation. Did her pride, too, chafe at the thought of marrying for financial gain? He still didn't know why she was so eager to acquire her inheritance, although he could hardly fault her, or anyone else, for refusing to forfeit such a fortune.

His gaze slid back to the eyes of the portrait.

Painting this had been an odd exercise in futility. His time would have been better spent on something a little more profitable. But for some absurd reason—or six hundred thousand reasons, none of them absurd—her face lingered in his mind, obscuring any other scenes he might have put to canvas.

Perhaps he could present the miniature to her? Seal their agreement with a memento? Ridiculous idea, of course. Where would the Earl of Shelbrooke get the money for such a commission?

No, he couldn't possibly give it to her. She would be far too curious. It was extremely tempting, though. He did rather like her reaction to his work.

He carefully picked up the ivory by its edges and studied it. Why couldn't he give it to her? Indirectly, of course. He could have Thomas deliver it for him and simply explain to his friend that he'd painted it because she appreciated the landscape. No. Thomas would never believe that. He'd ask as many questions as his sister. Blasted family. Curiosity ran with the blood in their veins.

Why couldn't Etienne-Louis Toussaint send it directly?

Why indeed? Even though the elusive artist's work had never been sold through anything but the most surreptitious manner, there was no reason why Toussaint couldn't send Gillian the miniature, without the auspices of an agent or gallery. After all, she did like his work. And a word from her could only benefit an artist's career. What would be more appropriate than an offering of gratitude?

Really nothing more than a thoughtful token. Merely a polite gesture.

Richard grinned and resisted the impulse to laugh, yawning instead. He knew full well the same pride that kept him from accepting Gillian's offer of marriage without hesitation now compelled him to present a gift of his work. Pride was the only thing that hadn't changed with his fortunes. Admittedly, it might well be his downfall one day.

He smiled at the portrait in his hand. One day perhaps. But with any luck at all, not today.

Chapter 5

～～ ✑ *～～*

"A Greek muse. I expected nothing less."
The tall, masked gentleman swept a low
bow before her.

"Really, my lord?" Gillian extended her hand
with a dignity that belied the pounding of her
heart. She would have known Richard's voice anywhere, even in the midst of Lady Forester's
crowded masquerade ball. "A muse, you say?"

"Indeed." He took her hand and raised it to his
lips.

"But only a mere muse?" she said, surprised at
the flirtatious note in her voice. "Why not a goddess?"

"A goddess commands." He released her hand.
His eyes glittered behind his mask, and he considered her for a long moment. She wore a simple
Grecian-style gown, tied with a gold cord wrapped
around her waist and held at each shoulder by

74

gilded pins. Her hair was swept up and bound with a gold ribbon. It was the same costume she'd worn last year and the year before, but under his scrutiny tonight it was once again new and special. "A muse inspires."

"And do I inspire?" She tilted her head in a teasing manner.

His voice was at once intense. "Very much so."

Her breath caught. It was the second time today someone had claimed her as his inspiration. She'd barely given the earlier instance a second thought. But Richard's comment—

"Good evening, Lord Shelbrooke." Robin stepped up beside her.

"Lord Shelbrooke." Kit nodded, standing on her other side. Lord, she had quite forgotten about Robin and Kit. They'd accompanied her tonight, as they had for most social occasions in recent years, but for the first time in memory she would have much preferred to have come to the ball alone.

"Lord Weston, Lord Cummings," Richard said mildly.

Silence fell among the three men as if each one was assessing the respective merits and weaknesses of the others in preparation for mortal combat. It would have been a humorous sight under different circumstances: Robin dressed as a Roman soldier, Kit costumed as a French musketeer, Richard in what appeared to be the same clothes he'd worn to her salon. All three were sporting the half-masks that were *de rigueur* for male guests at Lady Forester's annual masquerade.

Gillian groaned. Thus far, the evening had been every bit as awkward as she'd expected. She'd tried to avoid Robin and Kit in the few days since she'd told them of her plans to marry Richard, though each had found time to pay her a visit in a futile attempt to convince her of the error of her decision. At the moment their disapproval was silent but obvious nonetheless.

"Interesting choice of costume, my lord," Kit said at last, inclining his head toward Richard. "What precisely are you supposed to be?"

"Precisely?" Richard spread his arms wide and glanced down at his clothes. While not exactly shabby, they had definitely seen better days. "Why, isn't it obvious? I'm a penniless earl planning to marry a wealthy heiress."

Gillian sucked in a hard breath.

Robin's eyes narrowed. Kit's widened with disbelief.

Richard laughed.

It might have been the shock of hearing his laugh, deep and unrestrained for all the world to witness. Or the looks on the faces of her two dearest friends. Or the moment Richard's gaze met hers and she distinctly caught his wink. The absurdity of it all bubbled up inside her, and she joined in his laughter.

"This is not funny," Robin said indignantly.

"Not at all." Kit's brow furrowed.

"Oh, but it is. I've never seen a Roman quite so astounded or a musketeer nearly so stunned." Gillian lowered her voice and leaned toward her friends. "And I must say you two deserve it. You've treated me like I don't have a brain in my head from the moment I first took you into my confidence, and I'm tired of it. In point of fact, I'm beginning to believe you're right in that I have indeed made one stupid decision—"

"Gillian," Robin started, "we never—"

"I say, you needn't—" Kit sputtered.

"—and that was confiding in the two of you!" She turned toward Richard and cast him her brightest smile. "My lord, it is hot and stuffy and I would like nothing better than to be escorted to a spot where I could get a breath of fresh air."

"I am, as always, at your service." Richard took her elbow. "Gentlemen."

Gillian nodded in dismissal and allowed Richard to steer her through the crowd and away from a staring Roman and an openmouthed musketeer.

"I am sorry, Gillian." Richard bent closer to be heard over the din of the throng. "I simply couldn't resist. They were so blasted protective and rather condemning and . . . Good Lord." He stopped and stared at her. "They did know, didn't they? About your legacy? I just assumed—"

"They know," she said with a sigh. "And they haven't been at all helpful."

"No?" He raised a brow. "I'm surprised they didn't offer to marry you."

"They did."

"I see." He again took her arm, and they started toward the doors at the far end of the room.

It was pointless to try to explain anything to him

here. She could barely hear herself think, and the last thing she wanted was for all of London to learn anything about her arrangement with Richard through a misplaced shout. She'd already noticed more then a few curious glances cast in their direction. She hadn't been seen in the company of anyone other than Robin and Kit in years, and Richard was viewed only as a silent figure always on the edge of a crowd.

They made their way across the ballroom packed with revelers in costumes ranging from the exquisite to the ridiculous, skirted the dance floor, and headed toward the open doors, where the festive crowd overflowed onto a gaily decorated terrace.

Lady Forester's home was well suited to grand entertainments, and she had arranged the evening with a theatrical flair, even out of doors. Lanterns danced on the slight breeze and led the way into the gardens below, trailing into shadow for those guests seeking a private moment. Huge flower-filled urns and swags of netting and ribbons festooned the balustrades. Everywhere servants dressed in dominos offered refreshments.

The hostess's setting extended to her guests. Men were expected, if not required, to wear masks. She was not quite as strident in her requirements for female guests, however, stipulating only that they carry a mask and not necessarily wear it. Gillian's dangled from a tie at her wrist. Lady Forester was ever aware of the possibility of mussing an elaborately concocted hairstyle and even more acutely aware of the need to have a mask close at hand should a guest require anonymity for whatever reason.

"The crush is barely less out here," Richard muttered and scanned the area. "This way." He escorted her to the stairs leading down into the garden. A stone pathway encircled a large pool and gently trickling fountain. Paved walks branched off at precise intervals. Larger-than-life marble statues stood like white, silent sentinels over the grounds. Just off the first turn, a stone bench sat half hidden by a huge marble figure, providing discretion for privacy but not secluded enough for an illicit rendezvous. "Do you think anyone will notice us here?"

"I think everyone will notice the two of us everywhere. Especially going into the gardens. Lady Forester's gardens have a formidable reputation." She smiled and leaned her back against the statue. "All manner of amorous activities are reputed to take place here."

"Need I worry about compromising your reputation?"

"I really haven't much of a reputation. Not like . . . well, any number of women I could name."

"Why not?"

"Why?" She stared in disbelief. "Goodness, Richard, you do ask the most unexpected questions."

He shrugged. "I am simply trying to learn all I can about you. You're a beautiful woman. You spend much of your time surrounded by writers and artists. Why is it you haven't succumbed to the lure of a well-turned phrase or a seductive brush-stroke?"

"Seductive brushstroke?" She laughed. "You certainly do know how to turn a phrase."

"And I am scarcely trying," he said with a grin. "But I do find it hard to believe no poet has ever written of the stars in your eyes—"

"An 'Ode to Gillian' perhaps?"

"No artist has sought to capture your spirit on canvas."

"On canvas?" Odd that he should mention that. Just today she'd received a miniature portrait of herself from the French artist whose landscape she'd so admired. She'd planned on bringing it with her tonight to show Richard and perhaps get his opinion. It would have given them something to talk about other than themselves, but at the last moment she'd decided against it. There was something about the tiny image that struck her as rather personal. A feeling, more than anything else. Still, it was a strange sensation, and she wasn't quite certain how Richard would react to it. The man did seem to be remarkably perceptive. There was time enough to show him the miniature at a later date. "Don't be absurd."

"So there have been no artists," he said lightly, "no poets—"

"No."

"No composers, no politicians—"

"No. Richard—"

"No butchers, no bakers—"

"No! No one! Honestly, Richard." She heaved an

exasperated sigh. "I haven't . . . what I mean to say
is . . ."

"You have no reputation."

"Exactly," she huffed. "Are you happy?"

"Blissful. Although," he shook his head in mock
distress, "we should probably consider *my* reputation."

"Yours?"

"I used to have one, you know," he said
staunchly. "And damned impressive it was, too.
But look at me now. Out in a disreputable garden
with a woman with no reputation whatsoever. And
not a soul to give it a second thought because I'm
considered quite reformed. A man of honor no less,
topping your list of husbands.

"I can hear the whispers now: she'll be safe with
him." A mournful note sounded in his voice.
"What a sorry end I've come to."

"It's not that bad. Why tonight alone you have
laughed aloud and emerged from the shadows of
the room. I daresay everyone in the place is spec-
ulating about us at this very moment."

"Do you think so?" he said hopefully.

She bit back a laugh and nodded somberly. "I
do."

"Then I have nowhere to go but up." The teasing
note in his voice vanished. "And bloody hell, I cannot stand this another minute."

Unease stabbed her. "Richard, what are you—"

With a swift movement, he ripped his mask off
like a man escaping from a prison. He pushed his
hair away from his forehead, tilted his face up to

catch the breeze, and pulled a deep breath. "That's much better. I detest masks. I cannot abide things pressing on my face." He shuddered. "Do you think Lady Forester will have me ejected for taking it off?"

Gillian narrowed her eyes and adopted an overly thoughtful manner. "Perhaps. It could indeed be an unforgivable offense. I've heard her say there is nothing quite as attractive as a man of mystery."

"Hence her passion for deep, dark secrets."

"As well as other things." She smiled and shook her head. "She may be right, though. What is more mysterious and exciting than a man with secrets? Or a man whose face is hidden? He could be anything. A pauper, a prince, a—"

"He could be dangerous."

She lifted a shoulder in a casual shrug. "I imagine that simply adds to the excitement."

Richard propped his foot on the bench, rested his forearm on his thigh, and clasped his hands. "Do women typically wish for such excitement?"

"Lady Forester is not at all a typical woman."

"Neither are you." He studied her intently. "Then do *you* wish for such excitement?"

"Me? I've never especially thought about it. I can certainly understand . . ." Did she long for excitement? For a man of mystery? A stranger with secrets? Dangerous and irresistible? The possibility had never arisen. She shook her head. "No, of course not."

"No, you prefer to know all there is to know about a man before you propose marriage."

"It seemed wise at the time," she murmured uneasily. It did sound rather harsh and calculating when he said it.

"And extremely practical." He nodded thoughtfully. "Why didn't you accept Weston or Cummings? You've known them all your life."

"Oh, I could never do that to either of them," she said quickly.

"However, you could do *that* to me?"

"I didn't mean it quite the way it sounded. Perhaps I simply know them too well. They're like brothers. Besides," she laughed softly, "at this very moment I suspect Kit is flirting with a rather attractive shepherdess he remarked on earlier and Robin is trying to determine whether or not he should actively pursue a wife or if he can put it off for another year."

"They do care for you, though."

"And I for them, but . . ."

"And I suspect either of them would give you the kind of marriage you want."

"The kind of marriage . . ."

"In name only." His eyes smoldered.

"Yes, well . . ." She avoided his gaze and stepped away from the statue. She pulled a deep breath and turned to him. "That's not to be, is it?"

"It's entirely up to you." He shifted his foot off the bench and moved toward her. Her heart thudded in her chest. Was he going to kiss her? Panic surged through her. She couldn't tear her gaze from his.

"Is it?" She choked out the words, her throat

abruptly dry. Without thinking she moistened her lips. His gaze flicked to her mouth, then back to her eyes.

"Isn't it?"

She wanted to run. Turn and flee into the night. But she couldn't seem to move. Couldn't seem to breathe.

He lowered his face to hers, his lips a scant brush from her own. "Gillian."

"Yes?" she whispered. Perhaps it would be best if he did kiss her and got it over with right here and now. Surely then she would know if she could be the kind of wife he wanted.

"I was wondering."

"Yes?" She braced herself.

"I find I'm quite parched. Would you care for a glass of champagne?"

"Champagne?" Her voice rose. "You're offering me champagne?"

The corners of his mouth quirked upward. "Unless there's something else you'd prefer."

"No," she said, her tone surprisingly sharp. With relief? "Nothing at all."

"Very well then. You'll be here when I return?"

"Of course."

"Excellent." He started to leave, then paused. "Gillian, I—"

"Yes?"

"It's of no significance at the moment." He flashed her an arrogant smile, turned, and retraced their steps. She watched until he disappeared up the stairs. Blasted man. Why hadn't he kissed her?

Of course, it was best that he hadn't. It was far too soon. She barely knew him. Barely knew herself. Still, once again, her relief was mingled with an odd sense of disappointment.

She hadn't seen him since his early morning call yesterday, but he was never far from her thoughts. Nor were the conflicting emotions that rushed through her with a mere glance of his dark eyes or touch of his hand. Or the promise of a kiss.

She clasped her hands behind her back and paced before the bench.

Since their last encounter she'd done nothing but think long and hard about their arrangement and their possible future together. In the part of her mind reserved for logic and practical matters she'd come to the realization that wanting Richard, even perhaps someday loving him, was not truly a betrayal of what she'd shared with Charles. Indeed, she'd spent so many years trying not to dwell on the past that the brief time they'd spent together seemed often little more than a lovely dream.

Her emotions were something else altogether and not as easily resolved. She couldn't deny the sense of guilt that clutched at her heart and tensed her shoulders and sent a rush of panic through her whenever Richard came too close. No man had triggered such feelings in her before. She was as self-assured and confident as ever when they bantered and their comments were lighthearted, but the moment their words took on a deeper meaning, the moment his gaze bored into hers, she was as uncertain and nervous as a green girl. She'd thought her reaction to him was simply because of their situation, their need to marry, but she now suspected there was much more to it all than that.

Was it indeed guilt? Or was it fear?

She stopped abruptly and stared unseeing into the night. Not once in the last few moments with Richard had Charles so much as entered her mind. Did her feelings have little to do with her husband and everything to do with herself? Was Charles simply a convenient excuse to avoid—what? Life?

Or Richard?

There was something about the man that drew her to him as surely as a leaf caught in the current of a waterfall.

Inevitable. And exciting?

Despite what she'd told him, did she want excitement? Did some part of her long for a man of mystery? Certainly Richard was not mysterious, but he was nothing she'd thought he was. And wasn't that in itself exciting?

And terrifying?

Was fear any easier to overcome than guilt? She wrapped her arms around herself and tried to stop the trembling that swept through her. Realizing the truth made it no easier to manage.

How had she gotten into this mess? All she'd wanted was her inheritance and, with it, independence and the ability to fully pay a debt of honor. Now she wasn't entirely sure which prize would be the greater.

The legacy or the man.

*   *   *

Blast it all, he should have kissed her. Had wanted to kiss her. Why hadn't he?

Because when he'd gazed into her eyes he'd seen the terrified look of a trapped animal. Because he'd never forced his affections on any woman.

Because he wanted her to want him.

He stalked up the terrace stairs and slowed, searching for the distinctive black cloak, tricorn hats, and white masks that marked the Venetian costumes worn by the waiters. There had been a dozen of them just a few minutes ago. Had they all disappeared?

He blew a long breath and circled the edge of the terrace. To make matters worse, Gillian hadn't even mentioned the miniature. He knew she'd received it: he'd refused to pay the boy he'd hired to deliver it until the youth returned with a signature of receipt from Gillian's morose butler.

He spotted a servant bearing a tray of champagne and gestured to him. At once the man started in his direction.

What if she didn't like it? What if she thought it was a poor likeness—or worse, badly done? How could he find out?

The waiter wove his way through the crowd toward him, deftly avoiding one guest after the other. An odd, dreamlike figure in the black cape and white mask.

He certainly couldn't come right out and ask her. After all, Toussaint had sent her the portrait—not Shelbrooke. Pity Toussaint couldn't ask her. He supposed he could send a note.

The waiter reached him and presented the tray. Richard reached for the glasses and paused, his hand hovering in midair.

"Is something amiss, milord?" the waiter said.

Behind the mask, beneath the cloak and the hat, the waiter could be anyone. A pauper, a prince . . . a painter? This was a masquerade ball and costumes were a necessity. A requirement. Of course, it would mean donning a damnable mask. And there was always the possibility of recognition. Still, occasionally a man who could not publicly acknowledge his accomplishments needed to know if a woman he admired, admired him as well. Or at least his work.

Certainly, there were risks. To his pride and his secret. But it might well be worth a bit of risk.

"Not at all." Richard favored the man with his most amicable smile. "In fact, everything may be far better than I could possibly have hoped for."

Chapter 6

This was insane.

Richard ignored the annoying thought even as he acknowledged its truth. Up to now, his role of Toussaint had been impersonal, with minimal risk. This act tonight was something else altogether. He adjusted the irritating mask one last time, drew a steadying breath, and stepped out of the shadows.

Gillian paced in front of the bench, exactly where he had left her. She glanced up at his approach.

What was he going to do now? He hadn't thought this through, hadn't considered any course of action beyond borrowing the servant's costume. At least he'd had the presence of mind to take the waiter's tray along with his attire.

Her gaze dropped to the lone glass it bore. "Did Lord Shelbrooke send you?"

He nodded mutely.

"I did expect him to bring it himself," she said under her breath. "I assume he has been detained..." She accepted the champagne and started to turn away, then paused and smiled politely. "Thank you."

It was a pleasant dismissal but a dismissal nonetheless and not at all what he'd had in mind. What did he have in mind? How on earth was he going to proceed? Or rather, how would Toussaint proceed?

Gillian was pacing the length of the bench, already deep in thought. Richard and Thomas had concocted a life for Toussaint, but Richard had never imagined actually pretending to be the man. If he was to act the part of Toussaint he would have to become Toussaint at least for tonight. The son of a noble French line, arrogant in his heritage. An artist supremely confident of his talent.

She swiveled back and stopped short. He hadn't moved. Her brow furrowed slightly. "Yes?"

A man adored by women.

"Was there something else?" She took a cautious step backwards. At once he realized the attire of a domino was charming and clever amidst the crowd in the ballroom or on the well-lit terrace, but here in the shadows of the gardens the white mask was stark, the black cloak forbidding. A romantic figure no longer, he was now a disconcerting, even threatening, vision.

He deepened his voice and adopted a heavy French accent. "You need not be frightened of me, madame."

"I'm not." He could see the lie in her eyes and wondered how long it would take for help to arrive if she decided to scream for assistance. "Now, I really must—"

"Permit me to introduce myself." He drew a deep breath and tossed the tray onto the bench.

"I scarcely think—"

"I am," he bowed with an exaggerated flourish and what he hoped was a distinctly Continental flair, "Etienne-Louis Toussaint."

"I cannot imagine . . ." Her eyes widened. "The artist?"

"None other."

"You're quite good." Admiration sounded in her voice.

"Indeed I am," he said smugly.

"And modest as well." A slight smile lifted her lips.

He shrugged. "Modesty is an affectation I cannot afford. I must be free to throw aside the shackles of convention if I am to create great art." *Shackles of convention?* He groaned to himself.

"I see." She studied him for a moment. "And was the miniature you sent me great art?"

"You are an expert in such matters, madame, what is your opinion?" he said as if her answer didn't matter.

"It was nicely done."

"Nicely done?" Indignation swept away his accent, but only for a moment. "Nicely done is what one says about a child's first drawing of a pony."

"Oh, it's much better than a drawing of a pony." Amusement colored her tone.

"I am so pleased you think so, madame," he said dryly.

"It's quite an accurate likeness, given that I did not sit for it."

"I am an excellent observer of life, and I have seen you many times. In a carriage on the street, on a horse in the park, across a ballroom." *Nicely done? Accurate likeness?* What kind of comments were those? He wasn't entirely sure what he'd wanted her to say, but this certainly wasn't it.

She sipped her wine thoughtfully. "It struck me as an extremely personal work."

He drew himself up. "A good portrait should be quite personal. It should make one looking at it say, Mais oui, it is she. I sought to capture not merely your beauty but your soul."

She laughed lightly. "You have no knowledge of my soul."

"Ah, but I do. The world of artists is an intimate one. All who you so graciously introduce to potential patrons have said much about the charms and intelligence of the Lady Gillian. Your actions reveal your soul. As do your eyes."

"Do they? And you could see my soul in my eyes from across a ballroom? You have remarkably good vision. Unless," she studied him carefully, "have we met?"

"You would never forget such a meeting."

"No doubt." Her smile softened her words. Her

gaze traveled over him. "Still, in that costume you could be anyone."

"I could indeed." But for the moment, he was Toussaint. "I could be a king or a peasant but, alas, I am merely Etienne-Louis Toussaint."

"Merely?" Her eyes twinkled.

He ignored her, clasped his hands behind his back, and slowly circled her. "Tell me, madame, do you think then that it does capture your esprit—your spirit?"

"Perhaps," she said slowly. "Perhaps a bit too much."

"How can it be too much?"

"I really don't—"

"Is it too much to put the stars of the heavens above in the eyes when you see them there?"

"I'm not saying—" She turned to follow him.

"Is it too much to paint lips with the hue of ripe cherries as though a bite had just been taken, if that is what you observe?"

"Monsieur, I—"

He stopped in front of her. "Is it too much to color flesh with the tones of summer so that one feels the image itself would be warm to the touch if indeed that is what you imagine?"

"Yes," she said firmly. "It does seem rather too much. I have no quarrel with the liberties taken by artists as a rule. I well understand the nature of creative expression. And most miniatures are no more than keepsakes. But the manner in which you painted it is, well, somewhat intimate."

"How do you mean, 'intimate'?" He stared down at her.

"I'm not entirely certain. I only know when I look at it . . ." She shook her head impatiently. "It reveals more of me than I wish to have revealed. It is a measure of your talent, I know, but it is quite unnerving." A puzzled look showed on her face. He was a mere inch away, yet she stood her ground. "Are you certain we haven't met?"

"Only in my dreams, ma chérie."

Her eyes widened at the endearment, and she laughed. "Monsieur, I am not your dearest—"

"That is my eternal loss."

"Nor will I ever be." Her gaze was unflinching yet relaxed, her stance unyielding yet nonchalant, as if their discussion was nothing more than a mild and familiar flirtation.

"Are you so certain?" His voice carried an unexpected intensity.

Why didn't she back away? She'd never let him get this close without a touch of panic in her eyes. Or rather—she'd never let the earl get this close.

"Yes, monsieur, I am quite certain." No, there was nothing even remotely like panic here—only the self-assured gleam of a woman of confidence. "I am well aware of the fickle nature of men who reserve their passion for their work. And I am not foolish enough to risk my heart on such a man."

"I did not know we were discussing matters of the heart." How far could he take this farce?

"We aren't."

"Ah, but we were speaking of passion." How far

would she let him? "And I am Etienne-Louis Toussaint. Have I not a reputation for passion for more than my work alone?"

"A reputation rivaled only by your talent." She brought her glass to her lips and gazed at him over the rim. "I find one quite interesting and the other not at all."

"You wound me deeply," he said in a low tone.

"Oh, come now." She drained the last of her champagne and smiled. "I suspect it would take more than a mere set down to temper your confidence."

He clapped his hand over his heart. "My life's blood is flowing from my veins with every word from your lips."

"Nonsense. Only your arrogance is injured, and that is a minor pain."

He huffed. "You are a hard woman, madame."

"Not at all. I am simply practical." Her gaze searched his eyes. With the mask in the shadows, surely she wouldn't recognize them. His heart beat faster at the thought, and he took a backward step. "And somewhat curious as well."

He nodded sagely. "About the passion."

"About your attire." She stepped to the bench and set down the glass, then turned toward him. Her gaze traveled over him curiously. "Why are you dressed like the waiters?"

"Why?" *Why?* "It is not an unusual costume for a masquerade." He shook his head in mock dismay. "You can only imagine my distress when I arrived to discover I was attired not like a figure of the carnivals of Venice but as a servant. What was I to do? I should not wish to offend our hostess by discarding my cloak and mask."

"And does the tray accompany the costume?"

"Merely an excuse to approach you."

"I see." She paused. "I didn't know you were acquainted with Lady Forester."

"Acquainted may not be the right word," he murmured. He'd never actually met the lady, but it was a simple matter to procure an invitation to the ball.

"Odd, she's never spoken of you. And she rarely keeps secret those she has agreed to sponsor."

"I did not say she was my patron." Damnation, he certainly didn't want Gillian to think he was Lady Forester's latest amorous foray into the world of art. "She is perhaps more discreet than one would expect." Or did he?

"Perhaps." She leaned back against a statue and lifted her mask to her face. "Lady Forester requires masks for this occasion to allow those who should not be seen together to be discreet when slipping away. Together. It's most considerate of her and, I believe, quite appreciated. Yet she has never been particularly discreet in her own liaisons."

"I, however, am most discreet."

"Are you?" She paused and considered him. "Even without a mask?"

"We all wear masks of one sort or another, madame," he said cautiously.

"Surely, you can take this one off?" She shrugged in an offhand manner. "I did warn you as to my

curious nature, and I do wish to see the face of
Etienne-Louis Toussaint."

He would have liked nothing better than to rip
the irritating mask off and fling it into the dark, but
he could bear it for a while longer. It was well
worth the discomfort to be in Gillian's company. A
Gillian far different from the woman who wished
to marry Richard. Besides, he rather enjoyed the
banter between them. "For you and for you alone
I would but, regretfully, I cannot."

"Why?"

Why? He groped for a response. "Why?"

"Yes, why?" A wicked smile danced on her lips
as if she knew he had no answer.

"I am an artist, madame," he said slowly, his
mind racing for something, anything, she would accept. "I deal in . . . perception. Illusion."

"Illusion?"

"Indeed, the illusion created by a brushstroke on
canvas." That sounded reasonable. The words came
a bit easier. "Viewed from a distance, a painting
seems complete. Perfect. But upon close inspection
one sees each stroke, each dab of color, each nuance
of the artist's hand." He shook his head in feigned
regret. "Illusion is as fragile as fine crystal. And
shatters as easily."

"What illusion does your mask preserve?"

"Why, the illusion of Etienne-Louis Toussaint, of
course."

She laughed with delight.

Her sheer Grecian gown and the white marble
statue towering above her caught the glow from the

light on the terrace, and for a moment reality was indeed obscured by illusion. For the merest instant, marble merged with flesh. The lines and shadows of woman and stone flowed into one as if the two belonged together. Mined from the same quarry. Carved from the same block. Part of the same whole. It was a trick of illumination, nothing more; still, it cast a spell that caught at his artist's eye. Or his heart.

"I wish to paint you," he said without thinking.

She lowered her mask. "But you have. My soul as well as my face, I believe."

"A miniature." He snorted in disdain. Excitement roared through his veins in anticipation of a new project, this new project, overpowering the voice of reason cursing in the back of his mind. "An exercise in technique, nothing more. I want to do a real portrait. I want you to sit for me." He would paint her in this dress with a marble statue behind her. A mythical shadow of a very real woman.

"As lovely as the thought is, demand for your work is growing, and I simply can't afford your prices." She sighed. "Pity, I have never sat for an artist before."

"Then I must be the first. I have no doubt a buyer will be found." His voice was deceptively casual. "A lover perhaps."

"I don't . . ." She hesitated. Was she thinking of him? Of Richard? Or her husband. She straightened and lifted her chin slightly. "Perhaps, someday."

"Excellent. I shall make the arrangements at

once." He stepped toward her, stopping within arm's reach.

She gazed up at him, speculation in her voice. "What kind of arrangements?"

"Paints." There was no fear in her eyes now. "Brushes." She wasn't the least bit nervous at his nearness. "Canvas." He could easily take her in his arms.

She raised a brow. "Don't you have paints, brushes, canvas?"

"But of course," he murmured. His gaze slid to her mouth. What would she do if he kissed her? Slap his face? Flee into the night? Or would she allow his kiss? Respond to it? To him?

"Then I don't understand what kind of arrangements are necessary."

Or would she dismiss it as amusing and meaningless? An insignificant moment in a garden at a ball. Nothing more.

"Monsieur?" A teasing smile quirked her lips.

"I shall contact you soon. Madame." He nodded sharply, turned, and started off, the need to escape her presence almost overpowering.

"Monsieur," she called after him, and he slowed. "Will you take your mask off for me when I sit for you?"

He swiveled toward her. "And destroy the illusion?" He pulled the tricorn from his head and swept an overly dramatic bow. "We shall see, madame." He turned again and strode down the path.

"We shall indeed." Her voice and laughter trailed after him.

The moment he was certain he was out of sight he ducked behind a hedge into a narrow space between the plantings and the high wall of the terrace, brushed the hat off his head, pulled back the hood, and yanked the mask from his face. He ran his fingers through his hair and drew in great gasps of air. Blast it all, he hated masks.

Will you take your mask off for me when I sit for you?

Bloody hell. He sank back against the bricks. He hadn't thought about that. Hadn't thought about anything at all when he'd proposed to paint her portrait. In that one moment, he'd been too caught up in a desire, as hard and urgent and unrelenting as anything he'd ever known, to truly capture her on canvas. An impulse unchecked by reason, by sanity.

Damnation, he thought he'd conquered his impulsive nature years ago, just as he'd conquered his penchant for gaming, for whoring, for rash and reckless behavior. For five long years, everything he'd done had been well considered, practical and rational, with his aim always on the future. Even his paintings had been produced with an eye toward the market. Why then had he succumbed to impulse tonight, not once, but twice, without a second thought as to the consequences?

It was Gillian, of course, and his own misplaced pride. He wanted her to like his work and wanted to hear her say it. And more, he wanted her to want him for other than the inheritance their marriage would bring. And with every moment spent in her company he wanted it more. But whenever he came too close, in deed and in words, she withdrew. Possibly from an odd feeling of betrayal that made no sense to him: her husband was dead and buried, after all. Possibly from fear. At least that's what he'd seen in her eyes.

She certainly wasn't afraid of Toussaint.

He pushed away from the wall and absently took off his cloak, an absurd idea forming in his mind.

Gillian was well used to dealing with artists like Toussaint. She had been relaxed and unconcerned and had apparently enjoyed their lighthearted conversation. She had been flirtatious in the manner of a woman who knew there was no risk to her emotions whatsoever. Even her assessment of the miniature and its personal nature had been puzzling to her, not frightening.

It was ridiculous to even consider the possibility, but if the Earl of Shelbrooke courted her in a typical manner, while someone else, perhaps a mysterious French artist with a notorious reputation, sought her favors in a more provocative fashion, one of them might well succeed. She was on her guard with Richard but did not consider Toussaint so much as a mild threat.

Was there a woman in the world who could resist an amorous assault on two fronts? Especially from men she viewed as completely different from one another? Richard topped her husband list. Toussaint wasn't on the list at all. The artist was more the man he used to be than the man he was now. The kind of man women found appealing even as they knew such men were wrong for them.

And once her affections were engaged, he could reveal the truth to her. Since the earl and the artist were one and the same, what would be the harm? Why, they'd probably laugh about it. It would be a story to tell their grandchildren one day.

She had already agreed to sit for him. That would require spending a great deal of time together. He had no idea how he would manage to paint her portrait and still keep his true identity concealed. He absolutely refused to wear that irritating mask again. No doubt he would come up with something. He always did.

He drew his brows together thoughtfully. It was a relatively simple plan, surely destined for success, yet he wondered if it wasn't too simple. If there wasn't a flaw in it that he failed to see. Impatiently, he pushed the disquieting idea away. It was the only plan he had at the moment, and the rewards, both financially and personally, were far too great to leave to chance.

He folded the cloak over his arm, bent, and picked up the hat. He'd return the costume, then find Gillian. It was past time he shared a dance with the woman he was to marry. A slow smile grew from somewhere deep inside him, and he wondered who would be the first to seal their fate with a kiss.

Richard or Toussaint?

Gillian watched Toussaint's cloaked figure disappear in the direction of the terrace, shook her head in amusement, and sank down on the cold bench.

What an intriguing encounter. Toussaint was as arrogant and self-important as any other artist of her acquaintance, filled with an overblown sense of his own worth. And, just like the others, he had a need for praise that belied his conceit. Oh, they all hid it with bravado and swaggers that were typically smug, but the longer one observed them, the easier one recognized the signs of the artistic temperament. Toussaint was no different. *Nicely done* would never suffice for a man of his nature.

What did he look like without the costume? He was tall, that couldn't be hidden. It was apparent by the way he moved that he wasn't fat or old. But what of his face? His refusal to remove his mask and all that nonsense about illusion indicated there was something he wished to hide. Did he have hideous scars? Or warts? Perhaps he was merely quite ordinary. If she did indeed sit for him she'd surely find out.

And wasn't there something odd about his voice? His accent was pronounced and a bit too prominent, as if he were trying to emphasize it. He probably thought it enhanced his reputation. After all, if the rumors about him were true, he'd left France at least twenty-five years ago. Toussaint would not be the first artist to create an exaggerated background of mystery and romance to increase interest in his work. With the exception of his remarkable talent, Gillian, and the rest of the world, really knew nothing at all about the man.

Although he was most certainly French. She chuckled to herself. Who but a Frenchman would be brazen enough to suggest her portrait would be purchased by a lover?

Richard.

His face popped unbidden into her mind. Would he be her lover eventually? She clasped her hands in her lap and stared at her entwined fingers. Her husband? Certainly, if all went well. The thought was at once frightening and . . . what? Wonderful?

"Forgive my delay." Gillian glanced up. Richard strode toward her carrying a glass of champagne in each hand. "I was unavoidably detained."

"Were you?" She smiled and rose to her feet, paying no heed to the tiny thrill that raced through her at his approach. "I was beginning to wonder if you had abandoned me."

"Never." His voice teased, and he handed her a glass. His gaze dropped to the empty crystal on the bench. "But I see you haven't been entirely alone."

"A waiter brought champagne," she said without thinking and wondered why she hesitated to tell him about her meeting with Toussaint. Richard had a great appreciation of art and would no doubt enjoy meeting the man. Still, some cautious voice inside her urged restraint.

"A waiter?" He raised a brow.

She took a long sip. "Um-hum."

"Odd. I hadn't noticed any of the waiters going into the gardens."

"This one did," she said brightly.

"A stroke of luck then." He drew a long swallow

of his wine. "Interesting how Lady Forester has them all attired as dominoes. It's impossible to tell one from another."

"I hadn't noticed," she murmured.

"Indeed. Why, anyone could be hiding behind those masks." He considered her for a moment. "A pauper. A prince."

"Perhaps." She cast him a sharp look. He couldn't possibly know. "But more than likely simply a servant."

"More than likely." He shrugged in dismissal. "Would you care to dance?"

Her heart raced at the thought of being in his arms. She forced a lighthearted note to her voice. "Why, my lord, a dance following our sojourn in the gardens? What will people say?"

"A great deal, I suspect. Especially since I plan on more than one dance, and, furthermore, I firmly intend to occupy your attention for the remainder of the evening."

She studied him for a moment. "You realize that will be tantamount to declaring your intentions?"

"I do." He stared down at her and held out his hand. She drew a deep breath and placed hers in his.

A moment later they entered the ballroom and crossed to the dance floor. She was acutely aware of the speculative stares that followed their progress. A waltz began, and he took her in his arms. Strong and hard and unyielding.

He held her no closer than propriety dictated, yet she was engulfed by his presence, his warmth. His gaze locked on hers and all else faded away. They whirled across the floor, her steps in perfect harmony with his. As if they had danced together before. As if they had danced together always. As if they were one.

She was aware of the music, aware of their movement, but dimly, as if in a dream. She existed only in the reality of his embrace, the intensity of his dark eyes. Her blood pulsed, her breath caught, and she couldn't tear her gaze from his. And she didn't want to. There was nothing in her world save him and her, and she lost herself to the emotion sweeping through her. Desire? Need? Fear?

Whatever was happening between her and this reformed rake was as foreign to her as a gentle stream was to a raging, flood-swollen river. It had been so very long since any man had made her feel anything, let alone filled her with conflicts and terror and . . . anticipation? At once frightening and delicious.

She was scared of him, of herself, of the two of them together and what the future could hold. She'd admitted as much, accepted her fears and doubts. And in his arms, she realized acknowledging the truth wasn't enough.

Now, she had to face it.

Chapter 7

Richard's horse gingerly picked his way up the gravel drive, in truth more rut than rock these days. Pristine lawns long gone to seed encroached on the edges of the lane as if to swallow it whole. Gardens that had welcomed visitors in years past now sported only weeds and the occasional blossom too stubborn to give way to neglect and the passage of time.

In better days, an enterprising gardener in the employ of a far more prosperous Earl of Shelbrooke had laid out the grounds to draw the eye upward to the top of a slight rise and Shelbrooke Manor. The grand house had overlooked the countryside in the manner of a benevolent stone queen surveying her domain. Now, she was as run-down as her surroundings, an old lady weary of struggle with little more than pride keeping her upright.

Richard clenched his jaw, anger firing his blood

as it always did on this first sight of the manor. He remembered it from his childhood before he had left for school. Before his mother's death. Before his father's passion for drink and gaming had very nearly lost it all.

As always, his fury mixed with a grudging gratitude to his irresponsible parent. Richard had been well on his way to treading his father's path. If not for the obligations thrust upon him with his sire's demise and whatever sense of duty passed to him through his mother's blood, he would have fared no better with his life than the previous earl.

And, as always, his anger fueled his determination as well.

A peal of laughter and the bark of a dog sounded in the distance, and Richard couldn't resist an answering grin. At least his sisters had retained their spirit. Of course, they were all too young to remember when life here had been substantially different. And it wasn't as if they lived as beggars in the streets of London, never knowing where their next meal would come from. They still had a roof over their heads, such as it was, and their family name, thanks to Richard's efforts, had regained some measure of its former respect. Even their finances were slowly improving.

He reached the broad stone steps that swept up in a graceful curve to the front entry and slid off his horse. When he was a boy, there would have been someone near at hand to take the reins. In its grander days, the estate would have provided employment for more than a hundred servants in the house and stables and grounds. There were no-where near that number when Richard had come into his questionable inheritance, and he'd let most of those still in service go, retaining only old Ned, who attempted to keep the house from falling down around their heads, and his wife, Molly. Shelbrooke Manor was as much their home as it was his.

Tenants remained as well, farmers who fared lit-tle better than he but kept food on the table for their families and, in lieu of rent—his—with a paltry amount left for market. Production could be vastly increased, but improvements to the land and im-plementation of the latest in agricultural methods were costly. The fortunes of all who inhabited the estate, be it in the manor or in the cottages, were as tied together today as they had been for gener-ations. And it took funds to improve their lot.

Richard looped the reins over the saddle and strode up the steps. The horse wouldn't go far. He too was home.

He reached the wide wooden door, weathered from years of protecting those within from rain and cold and whatever else threatened. He grasped the big brass handle and pushed. The door swung open with a protesting creak.

"Richard!" The call mingled with the incessant bark of an overexcited dog. He braced himself and turned.

A large, dripping, brown-and-white fur ball bounded toward him, followed by his youngest sis-ter, just as exuberant and nearly as wet. The dog skidded to a stop at the bottom of the steps and started up the stairs.

"Henry," Richard said sharply.

The beast stopped short and stared up with what could only be described as adoration in his brown eyes. His body quivered with barely suppressed joy and the impetus of a madly wagging tail.

"He just wants to welcome you home. He misses you, you know." Becky halted beside the dog and grinned. "So do I."

"As I miss you, little sister." He smiled down at her. At age sixteen she still had more hoyden than miss in her. Her dark hair was mahogany red, and with every passing day she showed the promise of exceptional beauty. A blessing or a curse. "I would hug you, but—"

She laughed and pushed a wet strand of hair away from her face. "I was trying to give Henry a bath."

"Or he was giving you one." A whiff of wet dog assailed his nostrils. "Apparently he needs bathing."

Becky wrinkled her nose. "Henry has an alarming tendency to roll in the most vile things he can find."

As if in response to the criticism, Henry chose that moment to shake himself. Water and its accompanying pungent scent sprayed in a wide arc.

"Now, now, Henry." Becky grabbed his collar and pulled him farther from Richard. "Stop that this instant."

"Rebecca!" An indignant yell sounded from someone still out of sight.

Richard raised a brow.

Becky widened her eyes innocently. "She wanted to help."

Jocelyn rounded the far corner of the house and stalked toward them. "Blast it all, you were supposed to hold on to the damnable . . ."

She pulled up short, and her demeanor changed abruptly. At once her manner was proper and dignified, and she strolled toward them. Becky rolled her eyes toward the heavens. Jocelyn was barely a year older than Becky, and, while all his sisters shared a similarity in height and features, they couldn't have been farther apart in temperament. At this distance, Richard was certain Jocelyn didn't recognize him. She'd never been able to see clearly past a distance of about fifteen feet, but she disdained even the mere suggestion of spectacles. She too would be a beauty far sooner than he wished and, in contrast to Becky, was well aware of it.

Jocelyn drew closer, pursing her lips in a well-practiced pout. "Rebecca, you didn't tell me we had a visitor."

Becky glanced at Richard and grinned. "We don't."

Jocelyn paused and squinted. "Richard?"

"Were you expecting another gentleman caller?" he said dryly.

Becky snorted. "Hardly."

"Not expecting, merely hoping." Jocelyn sighed dramatically and reached the bottom stair. She kept a wide berth between herself and Henry, who ignored her in favor of sniffing something interesting in a crack in the stone. She climbed the steps and placed a sisterly kiss on Richard's cheek. "I—we—will never meet any acceptable, or even interesting, gentlemen exiled here in the country. Why can't we come live with you in London?"

"I don't want to live in London," Becky said quickly. "I'm quite happy right here, thank you."

Jocelyn shot her a withering look. "Then you can stay."

Richard bit back a groan. It was an ongoing point of dissension. Where Becky would have been content to spend her life in the country, Jocelyn could not wait until the day she could travel to London. Even the reality of their finances did not diminish her burning desire for a season in town.

"Richard." She hooked her arm through his and gazed up at him, her eyes wide and pleading. Her lashes fluttered, her voice lowered. "Please."

"Good God, where did you learn to do that?" Shock rang in his voice.

"To do what?" Her honey-colored eyes, a shade darker than her hair, opened even wider, if possible. Richard knew full well he had to do something to come up with the dowries to ensure good marriages for all the girls, but his first priority was of necessity his oldest sisters. He'd thought, or perhaps had hoped, that he had a bit more time to find suitable matches for the younger pair. Apparently he was wrong.

"*You* haven't been home for weeks," Becky said

pointedly, "and *she's* been listening to Aunt Louella."

"I should have known," he muttered. Since the day Lady Louella Codling had moved into Shelbrooke Manor to care for her dead sister's children, she'd filled the girls' heads with talk of London and the season, dashing suitors and glittering balls. Fortunately, in Jocelyn alone had Louella's stories found fertile ground.

"Aunt Louella is simply trying to prepare us for our proper positions in life," Jocelyn said loftily. "Not that anything she could do could possibly help you."

"Perhaps I don't need as much help as you do," Becky smirked.

Jocelyn wrinkled her nose. Becky stuck out her tongue.

"As always, it's good to be home," Richard sighed. "However, I can only stay for the night."

"Richard!" the sisters wailed in unison.

"Business, my dears." The girls traded glances, abruptly united against a common enemy. Were they up to something? He brushed the thought away. He had no time for their nonsense. "Now then, Becky, do something about that beast and then join us inside. I assume the others are about somewhere?"

"Emma, Marianne, and Aunt Louella are in the drawing room. Mending." Jocelyn said the word as if it were obscene.

"Excellent. I need to speak to everyone, and I would prefer to do it at once."

Again, the sisters exchanged looks. They were definitely up to something. Unholy allies. But in what? He shuddered at the thought.

"What about?" Becky narrowed her eyes in suspicion.

"Patience, my dear. Get rid of the dog." He smiled, turned, and stepped into the house, leaving behind the murmur of curious voices. At least they weren't screeching at one another, although admittedly he usually found their bickering more amusing than annoying.

He strode across the wide front hall between flanking staircases that rose to a gallery overlooking the entry, and tried to ignore the discolored rectangles on the walls where paintings had once hung. He turned into the west corridor and headed to the small salon.

His two oldest sisters and his aunt sat amid baskets of clothes, bent over needlework in what was probably a vain attempt to make well-worn clothing last a bit longer.

"Good day."

"Richard." Emma tossed aside the fabric in her hand and stood. He crossed the room and enfolded her in an affectionate hug. With her dark hair and dark eyes, she was the sister most like him in appearance and, these days, manner as well. Practical and matter-of-fact, she well understood the realities of their lives, and the household accounts were entrusted to her in his absence. She drew back and studied his face. "We hadn't heard from you. We were worried. Are you quite all right?"

"You haven't been here for a month," Aunt Louella said through tight lips. "You're supposed to come every week."

"We thought perhaps you'd been kidnapped by pirates." Marianne grinned and pushed the spectacles that had slid to the tip of her nose back into place. Fairer in coloring than Jocelyn but every bit as pretty, Marianne had no concern for appearance. Her light blonde hair was typically an unruly riot of curls around her head, her clothing always a bit disheveled. She lived in her books and her poems and her own dreams.

He laughed and stepped to her. "Nothing so adventurous, I'm afraid." He bent and brushed his lips across her forehead. "Simply too busy to get away."

"He says he has something to tell us," Jocelyn proclaimed as she walked into the room.

"Something serious?" Emma frowned. "Not bad news, I hope."

Becky appeared in the doorway. "You haven't discovered more of father's debts, have you?"

"Not at all. It's something rather pleasant, I should think." Of course, Jocelyn wouldn't think it was pleasant at all. Neither, he suspected, would Emma. Marianne was far too absorbed by her own world to particularly care where she lived, and he still had a few years before he needed to deal with Becky.

"Do we have money again?" Jocelyn cried with delight.

"Can we get another horse then?" Becky said.

"And a better carriage," Aunt Louella sniffed. "This one is barely held together."

"The roof first, Aunt," Emma smiled.

"And books that haven't been chewed on by mice," Marianne said wistfully.

"And clothes, Richard. Something fashionable. Made by a real modeste. Maybe even from Paris." Jocelyn grabbed her skirt and stretched it out on either side. "Not these old rags that we've made ourselves and remade over and over."

"Something pretty would be nice." Becky nodded thoughtfully, and Richard realized even Becky was nearly grown.

Marianne's voice rose eagerly. "In bright colors."

"White is appropriate for a girl who is as yet unmarried, regardless of her advancing years," Aunt Louella said primly. Emma and Marianne traded long-suffering glances. "Although pale pastels are permissible."

"And silks and satins," Emma said. "I saw a pattern in the village—"

At once the room erupted in excited feminine chatter. Richard stared, a sinking sensation in his stomach. It wasn't so much that he had to deflate their excitement, although he did regret the need to do just that, as it was the fact that his prospects for providing them with what they wanted, what they deserved, on his own were slim. "No, no, it's nothing like that."

The optimism on their faces vanished, snuffed out with the finality of a breath upon a flame, and guilt washed through him. He had it within his power right now to guarantee them a move to London, grand seasons, substantial dowries, and all the new clothes they could wear in a lifetime.

All he had to do was marry Gillian under her terms and everything they needed, everything they wanted, would be assured. Didn't they deserve that much and more?

Didn't he?

"It was rather too much to expect," Emma said with an overbright smile. She nodded at Marianne, who stood, as if on cue, and moved to her older sister's side. "Still, since the subject of our finances—"

"Or lack of them," Jocelyn muttered and stepped to stand beside Emma.

"—has been broached." Emma squared her shoulders. Becky joined Marianne. "We wish to discuss the situation. There are questions we should like answered."

Richard stared. His sisters stared back, the same determined expression on each lovely face. There was a resolute air about them, and at once he realized this was no impulsive encounter but a confrontation planned and plotted. They faced him like an opposing army determined to conquer and unwilling to take prisoners. He was outnumbered. He glanced at his aunt. She alone remained seated, her hands busy with her mending, a curious smile of anticipation on her face. He didn't like that smile any more than he liked the looks on the faces of his sisters.

"Very well then," he said slowly. "Ask your questions."

The girls exchanged glances. Emma raised her chin. "We all remember what it was like here in the years before father's death. When the only time he came home from London was to select another painting to sell—"

"Or a horse," Becky added.

"Or anything else that would finance his losses at the gaming tables," Marianne said.

"He would have sold one of us had the opportunity presented itself." Jocelyn's voice held a touch of bitterness, and he could scarcely blame her. "He put a pretty face on it but we all know he was about to sell Emma when he died."

"Jocelyn," Emma snapped. It was known, yet rarely discussed aloud, that their father had indeed been negotiating a marriage for Emma to a wealthy, elderly lord. The man had been willing to pay off most of the earl's debts in exchange for the hand of the then barely seventeen-year-old girl. "That scarcely matters now."

"Richard should know," Marianne said, her tone even and without condemnation. "It's not as if he was here at all back then."

Once again guilt stabbed him. He'd been far too busy living his own decadent life to note what was happening at Shelbrooke Manor. He'd been at school when his mother had died and, in the years that followed, had seen little reason for more than an occasional trip to the country. No, he'd been too busy squandering funds he didn't have, confident that his promissory notes were backed up by the family fortune. In truth, the first debts he'd managed to pay off were those of his own making.

"I know," he said quietly.

It was in fact that very arrangement that had made him realize how dire his family's situation had become. The creature his father had promised Emma to had approached Richard the day of the funeral, demanding Richard live up to the agreement.

The lord was more than three times her age and wealthy enough, but Richard had heard disturbing rumors about his preferences when it came to the fairer sex. Indeed, there were questions about the nature of the deaths of his two previous wives.

Granted, at that time Richard knew little of his sisters' lives, in truth did not know his sisters at all, but the idea of a relation of his bound to the despicable man's perverse whims snapped something inside him. In a moment of perfect clarity he'd realized that Emma's future, the futures of his family and himself, were in his hands and his alone. "I regret I didn't know before—"

"That's neither here nor there at the moment," Emma said quickly. The two of them had agreed years ago not to bring up the topic, although Richard wondered now if they should have at least told the rest of the family he was aware of the alleged betrothal. And had taken steps to end it. "It's no longer of any significance."

"Isn't it?" Jocelyn crossed her arms in a gesture

of defiance. "Isn't that the heart of what we wish to ask him?"

"How do we know you won't sell one of us to the highest bidder?" Becky's eyes flashed. "Or do something else every bit as wicked?"

"Becky," Emma snapped.

Shock coursed through him. "How can you, any of you, think such a thing? I've spent the last five years trying my best—"

"You can't blame them, us, for wondering, Richard. For being concerned—"

"If a son is like a father . . ." Aunt Louella murmured.

"Haven't I done all I can to improve our lot in life? Your lot in life?" He ran his fingers through his hair, angered as much by the implication of his aunt's comment as by the basic truth, and the fear, deep inside, that they could be right. "Blast it all, is that what this is about? Is this what has you worried?"

"No." Emma slanted a quelling look at her sisters. "We know you would never do that. However—"

"We want to know about the money, Richard." Marianne's firm gaze pinned his.

Emma drew a deep breath. "We want to know where you get it."

"Although it's scarcely a significant amount," Jocelyn muttered.

Becky nodded. "And it doesn't appear to be at all regular—"

"You do seem to be paying off father's debts," Emma said.

"In addition to supporting us." Marianne shrugged. "Not well, but—"

"Well enough for the moment," Emma added. "Even so . . ."

"We're afraid—" Becky said.

"That is, concerned—" Emma cut in.

"That you're doing something"—Marianne hesitated, then plunged ahead—"illegal."

"Immoral," Emma said.

"Illicit," Becky chimed in. "And the last thing we want is to see you thrown into prison."

"Or hung," Jocelyn said darkly. "What will become of us then?"

For a moment, Richard could only stare in stunned silence. He'd given up his admittedly wicked, but nonetheless enjoyable, ways in exchange for watching every penny. He lived in rooms that no decent gentleman would consider. He worked well into the night until his eyes stung with the fumes of turpentine to produce paintings aimed toward sales and not the joy of creation, and he dabbled in society only as an observer. He'd given up gambling and drinking to excess and, for the most part, women.

The rest of the world considered him completely reformed and honorable. He'd gained a certain amount of respect and even trust. From everyone but his sisters. Bloody hell, he'd even climbed to the top of Gillian's damnable list of husbands!

He forced a note of calm to his voice. "And what,

dear sisters, would you say if indeed I was involved in something illegal or immoral or illicit?"

The girls looked at each other, then each and every gaze focused on him. Their confrontational demeanor disappeared, replaced by determination and something more. Courage?

"Naturally we would wish you to stop," Emma said quietly.

"Would you?" He raised a brow. "And what would become of you then?"

Jocelyn had the good grace to cringe at hearing her words thrown back at her.

"I can go into service." Calm resignation sounded in Emma's voice. "I can get a position as a governess."

"As can I," Marianne said firmly.

Jocelyn cast a pleading glance at the older girls. They nodded in response. Her voice was grim. "I can probably find a husband who doesn't care about such things as dowries." She heaved a heartfelt sigh. "The butcher's son is looking for a wife and seems somewhat taken with me."

"Somewhat?" Becky snorted. "But even I wouldn't encourage that." She leaned toward Richard. "He has warts."

"He's a very nice young man," Emma said sharply.

"If you like warts," Jocelyn said under her breath.

Richard studied them for a moment. "And what of you, Becky? What are you willing to do to keep me from the hangman's noose?"

"I could marry, I suppose, although in fact I think I'm too young for that. But," her gaze met his, "we could sell the horse. He's rather old and tends to be a bit cranky, but we could get something for him . . ." A wistful note sounded in her voice.

Richard's anger dissolved. Aside from Aunt Louella, and she scarcely counted, he was all the family they had left. Apparently they were willing one and all to sacrifice whatever was needed to keep him out of trouble. The knowledge touched something inside him.

"I am impressed, dear ladies, and I do appreciate your offers, but they are not necessary." He grinned slowly. "I am doing nothing illegal, illicit, or even immoral. I have become eminently respectable and redeemed my reputation to the point where, if I am anything at all presently, it is simply quite boring."

Their expressions didn't change.

"Blast it all, what is it now?" Annoyance drew his brows together. "Obviously, there's more." Once again the sisters exchanged looks. "Out with it then."

"We want to know . . ." Emma paused as if summoning strength for a question she hated to ask. And feared the answer. "If your money comes from gambling."

"Apparently winning occasionally," Jocelyn said grudgingly.

"But gaming nonetheless." Marianne's gaze was troubled.

Abruptly any remaining annoyance vanished. He should have known his silence about his activities would arouse suspicion eventually. Certainly, in the first few years the girls had paid no attention to his attempts to juggle creditors in London, and he'd been with them in the country more often than he was in town. It wasn't until he'd started painting that he'd stayed away from the manor more and more.

He couldn't blame them for their fears. They'd grown up with a father whose infrequent visits home had only been to collect yet another family heirloom or valuable to sell and finance his games. On rare occasions, he'd brought token amounts for necessities, but more often than not his return to Shelbrooke Manor had marked the disappearance of treasures rather than the disbursement of funds.

"The blood of the father in the veins of the son," Aunt Louella murmured.

Richard bit back a sharp response. Louella was a termagant, but he could scarcely fault her, either, for her suspicions.

"I can assure you"—he shot his aunt a pointed glance—"all of you, that I do not frequent the tables and have not set foot in a gaming hell for longer than I can remember." He grinned wryly and shrugged. "Haven't the money."

The very room itself seemed to breathe a sigh of relief, as if collective breaths had been released.

"As to what I have been doing," he directed a firm look toward Emma, "there is nothing wrong with it whatsoever." His gaze slid to Marianne. "Payment is simply a bit erratic." He met Jocelyn's eyes directly. "It is quite respectable. However," his attention turned to Becky, "circumstances and profitability dictate I keep much about it private. Do you understand?"

Louella sniffed.

Emma nodded. "Of course."

"Certainly," Marianne said with a puzzled smile.

"Well, I don't understand." Jocelyn planted her hands on her hips.

"Neither do I." Becky mimicked Jocelyn's actions.

Richard laughed. "Pity, but you shall have to live with your confusion." He narrowed his eyes, his lighthearted tone belying the serious nature of his words. "And you shall have to trust me."

Emma stepped toward him. "We do, Richard. It was just—"

"Well, I do." Marianne returned to her chair and plopped into it, the movement sliding her glasses to the end of her nose. She grinned up at him. "Now I, for one, want to know what you wished to tell us."

"Me too." Becky settled herself on the arm of Marianne's chair.

"So do I, I suppose." Jocelyn flounced across the room and sank down beside her aunt on the settee. "Although I can't see what could be so fascinating if Richard hasn't managed to make our fortune yet."

Richard suppressed a grin. Jocelyn had a good heart even if she tended to be a bit centered on her own interests. It was Aunt Louella's fault for all her talk about the past and the days when the Shelton family fortune was unquestioned.

"Yes, Richard, do tell," Emma said. "What is it?"

"I have an . . . acquaintance, a friend actually, who has agreed, for the remainder of the season in London, to take one of you under her wing—"

"A friend?" Aunt Louella said with a raised brow.

"Which one of us?" Jocelyn's eyes widened.

"A female friend?" Louella's eyes narrowed.

"Who is going to London?" Jocelyn jumped to her feet.

"What kind of *female friend?*" Louella pressed her lips together tightly.

Richard directed her a pointed stare. "She is of good family, the daughter of a duke, and a widow. Highly respected, with an unblemished reputation."

"Why would someone like that agree to such a thing?" Emma murmured.

"Perhaps she's a very good friend." Marianne's eyes twinkled. "Perhaps she's more than a mere friend."

"No doubt." Louella snorted.

"Is she, Richard?" Becky jumped to her feet. "Is there more to this than friendship?"

Emma's brows drew together, and she considered him thoughtfully. "One would think there would have to be if she is willing to sponsor a season for one of us."

"Who is she sponsoring?" Jocelyn's voice rose.

"No, no." Richard shook his head. "She's not precisely going to sponsor—"

"A London season would be rather exciting," Marianne said wistfully.

Emma smiled. "Wouldn't it?"

Richard tried again. "Not the entire season—"

"Balls and routs," Marianne's voice was wistful.

"And masquerades and rides in the park." Becky wrinkled her nose. "Not that we have anything to wear to such things."

"Mother's old clothes are still in the attic," Marianne pointed out.

Emma shook her head. "They are sadly out of style."

"But of good quality," Marianne said. "The fabric should be—"

"Who cares about the blasted fabric!" Jocelyn stamped her foot. "Who are you taking to London?"

At once five pairs of eyes pinned him. Regardless of what he said now, there would be disappointment. He drew a steadying breath. "Emma."

"Me?" Emma's eyes widened.

Richard nodded. "You are the oldest."

"But the only true purpose of a season in London is to make a suitable match, and I'm not at all certain I wish to find a husband." Emma's shoulders dropped in resignation. "I'm somewhat older than is usual for a first season."

"She's practically on the shelf," Jocelyn wailed. "A season would be wasted on her."

"Nonsense," Richard said firmly. "Emma has more than earned this opportunity."

Emma shook her head. "I daresay I—"

"No, my dear, you deserve it." He moved to her and placed his hands on her shoulders, his gaze trapping hers. "Through most of your life you've taken the place of parent here. You've managed this household in my absence and done it far better than I could have. Now, we have the chance to allow you to at least sample a bit of what would have been your due if life had not turned out as it had."

"But I can't leave the manor." Indecision sounded in Emma's voice, and at once Richard knew she did indeed want to go. "Who will—"

"I will." Confidence sounded in Marianne's voice. "I'm perfectly capable of taking your place. After all, you won't be gone forever."

"Unless she finds a husband." Becky's grin matched Marianne's. "A husband with a great fortune preferably."

"If the idea is for one of us to make a good match," Jocelyn said, clasping her hands together and smiling innocently, "perhaps we would be better served by sending someone else."

Emma's eyes flashed with laughter, and Richard held his tongue. Jocelyn's opinion of herself was no surprise, but what Richard couldn't understand was why the rest of his sisters didn't realize they were just as lovely. He stepped away from Emma and considered Jocelyn thoughtfully.

"Why, you may have something there." He

folded his arms over his chest and drew his brows together. "What would you suggest?"

"Well, let me think." Jocelyn's voice held a current of suppressed excitement, like a rapid stream eager to break through a dam. Richard stifled a grin. "It's not that Emma isn't pleasant enough in appearance, but she said it herself." Her voice dropped as if she were revealing a distressing secret. "She's really rather old. One-and-twenty."

"As old as that," Richard said solemnly. "Then perhaps Marianne should go?"

"I'd love to go to London," Marianne said.

"Marianne is but a year younger than Emma," Jocelyn said quickly. "And she's such a bluestocking, why, she'd scarcely notice if she were here or in London."

"I'd notice." Marianne's tone was wry.

"That could be a problem." Richard shook his head and sighed dramatically. "What a pity. Here I have the opportunity to bring one of you to London, yet there seems to be an impediment to everyone I suggest. I don't imagine you have any way to solve this dilemma?"

"Me?" Jocelyn's expression mirrored the feigned surprise in her voice. Becky snickered, and Jocelyn shot her a sharp glance. "I can't really . . . I mean I don't think . . . well, I suppose I could be prevailed upon to go."

"You?" Richard stared as if the idea was completely unexpected.

"I'd be willing to do it." Jocelyn glanced around

the room and added quickly, "for the sake of the family, of course."

"Of course," Richard murmured. "How thoughtful of you."

"Then, may I go?" she said eagerly. Apparently Jocelyn was the only one present who had no idea her ploy to go to London was futile.

He smiled pleasantly. "No."

Her expression fell. "No? As simple as that? Just no?"

"Very well," Richard grinned. "Absolutely not."

Frustration colored Joceyln's face. "Why n—"

"Because, my dear." Louella got to her feet. "Emma is the oldest and should have had a season long ago. This arrangement of Richard's, as precarious as it sounds, is better than nothing at all."

Jocelyn huffed. "But it isn't at all fair. Emma doesn't even want to go."

"In point of fact, I rather like the idea." Emma's eyes sparkled, and Richard realized that he, too, had assumed his oldest sister had little desire to go to London. Once again, he was wrong. Apparently he didn't know women, especially his sisters, as well as he'd always thought he did.

"Nonetheless." Louella pinned Jocelyn with a no-nonsense stare. "There will be no more discussion about it. I agree with your brother's decision."

"There is a first for everything," he said under his breath.

Louella cast him a sharp glare, then turned her attention to Emma. "Now then, my dear, we must see to your bags. The rest of you can come along and help." She and the girls started for the door.

"No more than one bag," he said. "I don't plan on taking the carriage, so we shall have to share my horse."

Emma stopped, her chin tilted in a stubborn manner. "I will bring my paints, Richard."

He groaned. It was a continuing dispute between them. Emma had a fine hand with watercolors, but she longed to work in oils, and that he would not allow. Oils were for professional artists, men intending to sell their work. Watercolors were quite respectable for a proper lady. Even so, he'd prefer she give it up altogether. Regardless of what he did to eke out a living, there was no place in that odd world for his sister.

"I will not leave them behind."

"Very well," he snapped. "Bring the blasted things."

Emma smiled and left the room behind Louella. Marianne and Becky followed, trailed by a sullen Jocelyn.

"Jocelyn." He caught her hand and pulled her around to face him. "Do try to understand my reasoning."

"I do," she sighed. "It's just . . . have you ever wanted something so badly it hurts?" She gazed up at him with all the intense emotion of youth in her eyes.

"Perhaps." His heart went out to her. "I will make you a promise here and now. Should all go as I hope, you will come to London next year and have your season."

She studied him for a moment. "Do you mean it?"

He nodded solemnly. "I do."

"And if all doesn't go as you hope?" She considered him carefully.

"If it doesn't . . ." Richard shrugged in surrender. "I shall still do everything in my power to assure you of a season."

She stared in suspicion. "And I have your word?"

"You do." He nodded solemnly.

"Very well then. I shall hold you to it." She smiled with satisfaction, swiveled, and swept out of the room.

He stared after her, his smile fading. Damnation, the last thing he needed was one more practical reason to marry Gillian. No matter what else was at stake, nothing was as important to Jocelyn as a season in London. Now he'd gone and given her his solemn vow.

And there wasn't the slightest chance she'd ever let him forget it.

Chapter 8

"Then I shall see you tomorrow evening?" Richard held Gillian's hand and gazed into her eyes.

"Yes." In spite of her best efforts, her voice had a disturbing, breathless quality. "As I said, I've arranged a small dinner party. I thought it would be best to start with something simple before throwing Emma full tilt into the social whirl of the *ton*. There is a ball the night after and another—"

"What of tonight?" Richard's voice was intense.

"I am . . . engaged this evening." Her first sitting with Toussaint was tonight. His note arranging the details had been delivered by a somewhat grubby boy, according to Wilkins. Now she had no way to reach the artist and rather regretted agreeing to the appointment.

"Engaged?"

"Yes." The heat of his hand crept up her arms

133

and flushed through her body. How could any man have such warm hands? Was the rest of him as warm?

"Should I be jealous?" A teasing light shone in his eyes.

"I don't know. Are you?" She tried to match the lightness of his tone, but somehow her words held a deeper meaning.

"Always." He pulled her hand to his mouth and placed a kiss in her palm. Her breath caught. His gaze never left hers. "Until tomorrow, then."

"Tomorrow," she said softly.

He released her and stepped through the open door. She closed it slowly, turned, and leaned against it, needing support for legs abruptly too weak to hold her upright.

Richard had left for the country yesterday morning to fetch his sister and had returned late this afternoon. It had been barely two days since she'd last seen him at Lady Forester's masquerade. Barely two days since they'd spent most of the ball together and she'd laughed more than she'd suspected possible, never imagining she'd enjoy the simple pleasure of any man's company as much. Barely two days since he'd held her in his arms and danced in a manner at once proper and intimate, charged with emotions she'd never dreamed she'd know again.

And in those two bare days, every minute, every hour, she'd thought of nothing but him.

What was happening to her? Was her desire for a simple, convenient marriage, nothing more than a means to an end, evolving into desire of a more profound nature? Was the fluttering in her stomach, the weakness in her knees, the quickening of her pulse whenever he so much as entered the room symptoms of her own fears? Or was she afraid of something she'd never considered?

Was she falling in love?

She pushed aside the idea and straightened, refusing to give it another thought. She simply had no time at the moment. Gillian shook her head and walked into the parlor. Emma stood on the far side, studying one of the many paintings that graced the walls.

For a moment, Gillian considered her thoughtfully. Emma was as tall as Gillian and with coloring that echoed her brother's. How had he described her? Oh yes, *an attractive bit of baggage*. She was indeed. Regardless of her age, with the proper clothing, Gillian was certain this particular sister would not go unnoticed by the unmarried gentlemen of the *ton*.

"Do you like art?" Gillian crossed the room.

"Very much. We used to have a great many paintings at the manor, but," she shrugged in a matter-of-fact manner, "father sold them."

Gillian stepped to her side. "What a shame. I find there's nothing that makes me feel better about life than losing myself in the viewing of a beautiful work."

"As if you could simply step through the frame and into a whole new world," Emma murmured.

"Exactly." So, the eminently practical Emma

Richard had described was not quite so down-to-earth as her brother thought. What else didn't Richard know about his sister?

"These are wonderful." Emma leaned closer to the landscape that had captured her attention. "Richard says you know a great many artists."

"And poets, writers, and musicians. And more than my fair share of politicians as well."

"It must be very interesting."

"It is for the most part. The politicians can be a bit trying."

Emma nodded absently and stepped to the next painting, the work done by Toussaint. "Richard used to paint, you know."

"No, I didn't." Surprise coursed through her. "He's never said a word."

"No, he probably wouldn't. It was a very long time ago. I daresay he hasn't touched a brush in years." Emma glanced at her. "As I understand it, father decreed painting was no way for a future earl to spend his time. I only know about it at all because I found some of his paintings after father's death. Molly told me—"

"Molly?"

"Our maid." Emma smiled apologetically. "Our only maid. She's been with us for as long as I can remember. At any rate, she said mother encouraged Richard to paint. But after she died, father forbid it. They had quite a row about it. Apparently father said some awful things to him, although Molly never told me precisely what. I suspect that's one of the reasons why we rarely saw him after mother's death. And then of course, father was different after that too . . ."

She nodded at the landscape. "This work reminds me a little of Richard's. Of course, he wasn't nearly this good."

So Richard was once an artist himself. No wonder his observations were so perceptive.

Emma peered intently at the painting, as if studying the technique. Gillian had seen similar expressions on the faces of artists perusing the work of peers. Did the creative urge run through all of Richard's family? "Do you paint?"

"Watercolors," Emma said absently. "I should like to paint in oils but Richard doesn't feel they're appropriate for a woman."

"Oh?"

"No. He says women don't have the temperament for oils, for great art. He says women are more suited for the less serious nature of watercolors."

"He does, does he? How very interesting." Interesting indeed and more than a touch annoying. "Well, Richard is wrong."

Emma laughed. "I've always thought so, in this particular case anyway."

"Yes, but I can prove it." Gillian paused for a moment. Surely it would do no harm to share her secret with Emma. Already she quite liked the young woman and was confident she would understand, at least when it came to this particular subject. "Come with me. I want to show you something."

She led Emma up the stairs to her own chamber and threw open the door. A series of four paintings, rather average in size, hung on the wall opposite the entry, the only art in the room.

Emma gasped.

From their position in the doorway, the works seemed to be created of light instead of mere paint. As if the late afternoon sun shone through them, from them, rather than streaking in through the windows on the adjacent wall.

"They're magnificent." Awe sounded in Emma's voice, and she moved toward them.

Gillian smiled with satisfaction. "They are indeed."

When first seen from the entry, they appeared to be simple scenes: two of the rich English countryside, and one each of the sea and a rocky coast, with only that amazing illusion of illumination marking them as created by the same hand and setting them apart from the ordinary. But Gillian knew that as one drew closer, the images became distinct. They were indeed landscapes, but of no scenery seen on earth. Highly idealized, they depicted life as it should be, fraught with an ethereal quality and a sheer joy that had touched her soul from the first moment she'd laid eyes on them.

Emma stopped a few feet from the wall and stared. A reverence reserved for all things holy sounded in her voice. "They're brilliant. I feel as though I should hold my hands out before me to see if light falls on them."

Gillian laughed softly. "It won't. I've tried."

Emma fell silent, lost in contemplation of the works and the emotions they would surely trigger. Gillian well remembered her first sight of the paintings during a time when she'd wondered if her own life had ended with her husband's. A time when she'd often wished she had the courage to make certain it did in reality as well as in spirit.

"They were painted by a woman, weren't they?"

Gillian nodded. "Yes."

Emma's gaze didn't waver from the paintings. "Who was she?"

"I don't know a great deal about her. Only that she was originally from a noble family and apparently gave up all ties to pursue her art. She died alone and penniless years before I found these. I bought them from a dealer who claimed he had purchased them from a relative, although I doubt the veracity of that story. In spite of their brilliance, I paid next to nothing for them." Gillian smiled humorlessly. "They were painted by an unknown woman and therefore the dealer considered them of little value. He was happy just to get them off his hands.

"He didn't even know her name. Neither do I. There are initials in the corner, but I've never been able to make them out."

Emma glanced at her curiously. "These mean a great deal to you, don't they?"

"Yes, they do." Gillian hesitated. Robin and Kit had seen the paintings but she'd never told them why they were so important to her. Of course, they'd never asked. Never suspected that their value to Gillian went beyond aesthetics. She hadn't told anyone of her true feelings and wasn't entirely sure why she trusted Emma, but she did. Perhaps it was because she was a woman. Or an artist. Or, more likely, both.

She drew a deep breath. "When Charles, my husband, died, I'd thought I died as well. In truth, I wanted to. At first I couldn't do anything but weep and then I couldn't do anything but sleep and finally . . . I couldn't seem to do anything at all. I was rather mad at the time I think."

Gillian wrapped her arms around herself. "My family and two dear friends, you'll meet them tomorrow, were wonderful through it all. Eventually they made me understand I had to continue with my life although I didn't have any desire to.

"But I pretended, for them really, and made a good show of it. I went to balls and gatherings and said all the right things, but it always felt as though I was an apparition, a ghost, at once there and not there. I existed but wasn't really present." She pulled her brows together. "Does that make any sense whatsoever?"

"I think so." Emma nodded thoughtfully. "Please go on."

Gillian's thoughts traveled back through the years. "I found myself being drawn increasingly to concerts and galleries. I discovered I could escape my life for a few hours in music and even more in art.

"When I stumbled upon these, quite by accident, mind you, they touched me in some odd way." She stared at the seascape in front of her. "They seemed somehow vibrant and, well, alive. More alive than I was.

"I still can't tell you exactly how it happened." Gillian paused to pull her thoughts together. "I looked at these paintings and I could smell the scent of the sea and feel the spray of the ocean or the freshness of spring in the country. One moment I was living as though in a dream and the next I had awakened. The world around me was once more solid and real and I was alive again as I hadn't been since Charles's death."

Emma studied her silently.

Gillian forced a light laugh. "It still sounds quite mad, doesn't it?"

"Not at all." A slight smile lifted the corners of Emma's lips. "We each handle grief in our own way."

Gillian raised an amused brow. "You're rather wise for one so young."

"I'm practically in my dotage, according to at least one of my sisters. Besides," Emma shrugged, "I've seen what grief can do."

Of course Emma would be well acquainted with grief with both her parents dead. Regardless of how much of a scoundrel her father had been, his loss would still affect his children. Gratitude welled within her at the knowledge that her own parents were alive and well.

"So did you begin your salons to assist artists?"

"In part. I felt as if I had a debt to repay. I would very much like to lend my support to female artists, although those who attempt to display their work publicly are rare. I only know of a few, and even they have left England to work in Paris." She nodded at the paintings. "She probably died as much from poverty and neglect as anything else."

"It's a pity women with talent like this can't make their own way." Emma shook her head. "It must be impossible to create works of this nature without knowing where your next meal will come from or if you will keep a roof over your head."

"I don't know how she managed to survive at all," Gillian said softly.

Emma turned and folded her arms over her chest. "Why don't you do something then? For women like that?"

Gillian heaved a frustrated sigh. "First of all, I have no idea what I could do. Secondly, anything truly beneficial would take money."

Emma's eyes widened. "But I thought . . . that is, I assumed you were quite wealthy."

Gillian chose her words carefully. "I have the prospects of a substantial fortune. But at the moment, I have little more than what you see here."

"Oh dear." Emma's forehead furrowed as if she was considering this detail, which Richard had obviously failed to mention.

Gillian stepped across the room, perched on the edge of the bed, and waited.

Emma's gaze met hers. "What is your relationship with my brother?"

This was not the question Gillian had expected, and she wasn't entirely certain how to respond.

Still, the truth was usually best. "I plan to marry him."

"Do you?" Emma's voice rang with surprise. "Why?"

"Why?" Gillian laughed. "For any number of reasons. He's an honorable man with a good head on his shoulders and a not altogether unattractive head at that. In addition, while his title was perhaps a bit tarnished, it is old and noble, and he has managed to make it respectable once again."

"Well thought out, my lady, but," Emma shook her head, "your reasons sound as much like those one would use to hire a good solicitor as to choose a husband."

"Well, I—"

"Does he love you?" Emma walked toward her. "Do you love him?"

Do I? She raised her chin firmly. "I don't know."

"I see. I never expected something like this. How very interesting," Emma murmured. "I wonder what the others will say?"

"Let's keep it to ourselves for the moment, shall we?" Gillian said quickly. "Nothing is certain as of yet."

"As you wish." A thoughtful light shone in Emma's eyes, and Gillian wondered exactly what the girl was thinking.

"Now," Gillian rose to her feet, "I should show you to your room." She turned, but Emma reached out to stop her.

"If perhaps we shall be related someday, you

might well wish to refuse my request." Emma's tone was cautious.

"What request?"

"While I'm here, in your home, do you think . . . would it be possible . . ." Emma pulled a deep breath and released her words in a rush. "Would you allow me to paint?"

"In watercolors?" Gillian raised a brow. "Or something perhaps more, oh, shall we say, unsuited to the temperament of women?"

Emma laughed and nodded eagerly.

"I have an attic room that gets excellent light. It could be used as a studio." Gillian grinned. She rather liked the idea of helping Richard's sister do something he disapproved of, since that disapproval was ridiculous in the first place. She'd never imagined he would be so narrow-minded. It was the first thing she'd learned about him that she didn't like. "I'm certain I can afford a few canvases and paints—"

"Oh, I have paints. Richard thinks they're only watercolors, that I've given up, but . . ." A blush of embarrassment at deceiving her brother swept up Emma's face.

"Then all we need is canvas." Gillian hooked her arm through Emma's and headed toward the door. "This should be great fun. I've never had an artist under my roof before. I've never been able to watch one work before."

Emma glanced back at Gillian's paintings. "What a shame she didn't have someone to provide a roof for her."

"Indeed—" Gillian stopped short and stared at Emma. "What did you say?"

Confusion colored Emma's face. "Nothing really, only that it was a shame she didn't have—"

"Someone to provide a roof for her," Gillian said slowly, a dozen ideas tumbling through her head like pieces of a puzzle. "Or for others like her."

"Others?"

"Women. Artists." At once the pieces fit. The puzzle solved. "That's it, Emma. That's exactly what I can do if I get this inheritance."

"What inheritance?"

"The details aren't important at the moment." Gillian waved away the question. "Suffice it to say, it's an inheritance that will truly allow me to repay my debt." Excitement raised her voice. "With money I can provide a place for artists, female artists, to work without having to worry about mundane things like room and board. I can purchase a house or, better yet, a mansion. Here or maybe in the country. Maybe a manor or a hall—"

"Or a castle?" Emma's eyes twinkled.

"Perhaps." Gillian laughed. "It's perfect. Absolutely perfect. And you shall be my first beneficiary."

"Thank you, my lady." Emma grinned and bobbed a curtsey, obviously caught up in Gillian's excitement. "I shall be honored."

Gillian curtseyed back and laughed. "The honor is all mine."

Emma joined her laughter, and Gillian wondered

if this was what it would be like to have an artist in the house. Or a sister.

"It's a wonderful idea. I see but one possible obstacle to your plan."

Gillian opened her arms wide in an expansive gesture, her voice as exuberant as her mood. "There are no impediments, no problems we cannot overcome. What is this paltry obstacle?"

Emma smiled wryly. "Richard."

Chapter 9

"**E**ntrez."

Gillian pushed open the door at the top of the stairs with a touch of trepidation. Perhaps it hadn't been entirely wise to come to Toussaint's studio at night. But she hadn't been so foolish as to come alone. Wilkins waited at the bottom of the stairway, still muttering dire predictions about what happened to ladies who frequented neighborhoods like this after dark.

In truth it wasn't all that disreputable an area of the city, simply business in nature rather than residential. And it was not in Toussaint's best interests to allow anything to happen to her.

Even so, it was comforting to know Wilkins was there should she need him, although how much help he would be if called upon was questionable.

Gillian pulled her cloak tighter around her and stepped into the studio. The sharp smell of turpentine hung faint in the air. It was, if possible, even darker in here than it had been on the stairs. A few candles on the far right side of the huge room illuminated a chaise. Stars shone in the night sky framed by high windows running the length of the walls on either side. The rest of the space was consumed by shadows, but she had the impression of a vast, empty area. She suspected the artist's studio took up the entire top floor of the mercantile building.

"Toussaint?" she said hesitantly even while acknowledging that it was a bit late for caution.

"But of course, madame. I am pleased you did not choose to disappoint me. I was afraid you would not come." Toussaint's voice echoed from across the room. She could make out the dark figure of a man, but his features were indiscernible.

"You must admit, it's a bit odd. A sitting at night like this." She closed the door behind her, taking care not to shut it completely, and stepped further into the room. "I've never heard of such a thing."

"Ah, but I must use the light of day for work for which I am commissioned. This portrait is—how do you say—speculative and as much for the joy of creation and the beauty of the subject as for anything of a more practical nature." It might have been the mysterious setting, or even a trace of nerves on her part, but his thick accent seemed somewhat heavier tonight than she'd remembered.

"Perhaps you would be more comfortable ... Est-ce que vous préfériez parler français?" she asked.

"Huh?"

Huh?

"Je m'excuse," he said quickly. "But I did not quite understand your question. A thousand apologies, madame, but your accent . . ." Condescension colored his tone.

"My accent is impeccable," she said coolly.

"Perhaps to the English, but to a true Frenchman . . ." She could hear the dismissive shrug in his voice.

"Then I gather you would prefer not to speak French?"

"Forgive me once more, but the language I speak is not the same as that which comes from your lips, as lovely as they are."

"Very well." Her tone was a bit sharper than she'd intended. She was rather proud of her ability with languages, and to have this man tell her otherwise was more than a little annoying. "I have no wish to offend you."

He chuckled. "I fear it is I who have offended you. It was not my intent. I can only think your overwhelming kindness has affected my senses and turned me into an ungrateful idiot."

"Nonsense," she said, mollified. "It is your language, after all, and you no doubt have a better grasp of it than I." Although she would have wagered a great deal on her fluent command of French. Still, he was the expert, and she merely a gifted student. "Now then, what next?"

"Did you wear the costume as I requested?"

She nodded and slipped out of her cloak, draping

it over a battered chair. The Grecian gown might have struck someone else as odd, but she rather liked the idea of being painted in this particular dress.

"Excellent. Then if you would be so kind as to take your place."

"On the chaise, I presume."

She started toward it, noting the lack of other furnishings. From what little she could see, there were several tables stacked so full with jars and bottles and other accoutrements of the artist's trade that they seemed in imminent danger of collapse. What were probably canvases leaned against the walls in piles a half dozen deep, whether pristine or works in progress she couldn't determine. The dim outline of a sagging bed lurked in one corner of the room.

The chaise was the only acceptable piece in the place, and it, too, had seen better days.

She perched stiffly on the edge of the recliner and clasped her hands in her lap, abruptly at a loss as to what he expected of her. She squinted into the dark recesses of the room and could make out Toussaint moving between an easel and a large screen. A five-branched candelabra sat on a rickety table in front of her and slightly off to the side, obviously placed to cast light on her face and perhaps intended to make him more indistinct as well.

"Relax, madame, it will not hurt a bit."

"I am not anticipating pain," she said with a laugh. "I simply have no idea what to do now. How to hold my head, where to put my hands, should I smile or appear serious or—"

"The look in your eye is as you wish. As for the rest of you . . ."

He explained how he wanted her to pose. Within moments, she was in the position he'd directed, reclining slightly, the lines of her body echoing the lines of the chaise. She rested one elbow on its rolled arm, her bare feet peeked from beneath her white gown. His manner was brisk and matter of fact, and her unease vanished.

Nothing to this point had been even remotely personal. He seemed to regard her with no more interest than he would a bowl of fruit. Even when he'd asked her to remove her shoes it had been for aesthetic reasons. While under other circumstances she would never have considered it, Toussaint was an artist and a certain amount of forward behavior was to be expected. In fact, the man issued commands rather than made requests.

"I wouldn't have been at all surprised if he'd asked me to remove my clothing as well," she muttered to herself.

"Did you say something, madame?"

With a start, Gillian realized she'd spoken aloud. "No, not at all." She stared at his dark figure. "How can you see to paint me from over there?"

"I see you quite well. The candles illuminate your face and features. And I have another here to work by."

"Well, the light is directly in my eyes. I can hardly make out anything beyond the reach of my arm." He chuckled, and immediately his intentions were clear. "I should have suspected as much the moment I received your note. You're going to continue this ridiculous masquerade of yours. You're not going to let me see your face again tonight, are you?"

"I think not, madame." Amusement sounded in his voice.

"Why on earth not?" she said with surprise. "I thought surely once I was here—"

"Ah, but you forget I am a master of illusion. In my art and in my person. I find I like it very much." He settled onto a stool behind the easel. "Did you not say it yourself: what is more mysterious and exciting than a man whose face is hidden? Or a man with secrets."

"Yes, I suppose I did." She vaguely remembered saying something of the sort in Lady Forester's garden, but she thought she had said it to Richard. Apparently not.

"And what man would not wish to be exciting to a woman such as yourself?"

"I really haven't thought—"

"Then you must permit me my secrets."

It was not as if she had any choice in the matter. Toussaint had made certain of that. Between the canvas supported on the easel and the positioning of the screen, Toussaint could have a clear view of her yet still remain in the shadows. Only when he shifted could she see so much as a black silhouette. Short of running across the room to confront him directly, which she refused to rule out altogether, there was little she could do.

"If I must." She wasn't entirely sure if she was

amused, intrigued, or irritated by this game of his. Perhaps it was a combination of all three. Still, what would be the harm in playing, at least for the moment? If nothing else, he was right: there was something exciting about a man whose face was hidden. "Do you have secrets, then, other than your face?"

"Untold," he murmured. She could hear the slight swish of charcoal on canvas. Apparently he had already started to work.

She waited. And apparently, he worked in silence. Pity she couldn't. "What manner of secrets?"

"The usual," he said absently.

Again she waited. This game wouldn't be at all enjoyable if he was the only one allowed to play. "And what are the usual?"

"Everyone has something they prefer the world not know. Typically about the past. Their heritage. Or their families."

"Families? Really?"

"Oui. Insane aunts in the attic. Bastard heirs. Disreputable parents. Scandalous liaisons." He rattled off the list as if he was paying no attention to his words, obviously preoccupied with the canvas before him.

She counted to ten in her head and tried again. "Are those your secrets?"

"Yes, madame, they are indeed mine. Each and every one." He huffed an impatient sigh. "I have not one but three insane aunts and as many bastard brothers all fighting for a share of my vast inheritance which was amassed by a father who was, in truth, a pirate. My legacy includes a castle in the mountains of Switzerland and the imperial crown jewels of Russia. Now that you know all there is to know, hold your tongue, s'il vous plaît!"

"Very well. You needn't be so overset about it." She paused and bit back a smile. It may well be his game, but she had no problem playing by her own rules. "You didn't mention scandalous liaisons."

Silence came from behind the easel. She wanted to laugh, giggle like a girl still in the schoolroom.

"I did not mention murder either," his voice was level, "yet the evening is young."

She tried not to laugh, but an odd, strangled sound burst from her, and she could barely choke out the words. "I am sorry. I shall try, but I simply cannot sit here, not being able to see beyond the light, for the next hour or two without saying a word."

"Very well, madame," he said with a note of resignation. "I shall make you a bargain. If you will refrain from chatter for the next few minutes and allow me to concentrate, I shall permit you to speak and even join you in discussion of whatever you wish."

"Anything at all?"

"Of course not." Surrender sounded in his voice. "Nearly anything. Is it agreed, then?"

"As you wish."

Long, silent minutes passed, and Gillian tried not to fidget. She was not used to enforced idleness, to sitting still with nothing to do but think. And there was only one thing to think about. One thing on her mind, always on her mind.

Richard.

With each minute in his presence she grew more certain she could be the wife he wished. She could share his bed, have his children. Indeed, there were moments when she wanted just that. Wanted him.

Then why did she recoil like a frightened fawn whenever he came too close? Why did fear grip her stomach and tighten her throat? Surely she wasn't afraid of caring for him, even loving him? She'd known love before, and it was wonderful. Wouldn't it be just as wonderful with Richard?

Was she falling in love with him?

The question she'd dismissed earlier now demanded consideration. It would be much easier to be his wife in every sense of the word if she loved him. But would love on her side alone be enough?

Love was not part of their agreement, and she wondered if it would ever be. It was pride on Richard's part that demanded this condition to their marriage. Nothing more than that. Even so, she knew he wanted her. Knew by the look in his eye and the way he held her in his arms that his desire no longer had anything to do with her inheritance and was not merely part and parcel of his intention to seduce her. Still, it wasn't love, and with Richard she suspected the likelihood that it ever would be was slim.

Could she love a man who didn't love her? It was one thing to commit to a marriage that was nothing more than a convenience and quite another to offer your heart to someone who wasn't particularly interested in such things. Is that what she was afraid of?

Regardless, she was determined to wed Richard, and these thoughts of love were nothing more than a distraction. Why, wasn't there already desire on her part, or at least the beginnings of desire? Wouldn't that be enough? And the blasted man hadn't so much as kissed her yet. What would happen when he did?

Would those lips that had up to now only brushed her hand be as equally gentle against her mouth? Would he tease her lips with his own until her resistance dissolved and she melted into his embrace? Or would his mouth be demanding, insistent, an assault on her senses and her soul? Would his arms pull her so tight against him that the heat of his body would sear her flesh? Would he tear off her clothes in a mad rush of passion at long last unleashed and make her his without a thought as to time or place?

And would she meet his desire with her own? Would she counter his need with hers? Run her hands over the hard planes of his body with an urgency she'd never known? Abandon herself to the pleasure of touching him, of him touching her? Would she claim him as her own without a thought as to the future or the past? Would she—

"You have lied to me, madame."

Gillian jumped, her mind jerking back to her surroundings. Good Lord, what had she been thinking? Heat flashed up her face.

"Lied?" She smoothed the fabric of her gown

with a trembling hand and struggled to regain her composure. "What makes you think I've lied?"

"You said you did not have a lover."

"I don't," she said quickly.

"No?" Skepticism rang in his voice. "A woman does not look as you do unless she is thinking about a man."

"Don't be silly." She ignored a sudden need to fan her face. "I was thinking nothing of the kind."

"Then you must have a dog."

"A dog?" She shook her head in confusion. "Why do you say that?"

"It has been my experience with Englishwomen they are as attached to their dogs as to their men." He chuckled. "Sometimes more."

"And sometimes a dog is more worthy of attachment," she said pointedly. "However, I do not have a dog nor do I have a lover and you, monsieur, are quite impertinent."

"But of course. It is my nature. It is why women find me charming and most irresistible."

She laughed in spite of herself. "Do they now?"

"You have not heard the stories? The tales told of Etienne-Louis Toussaint, master painter and lover extraordinaire?" He clucked his tongue in mock dismay. "I am most distressed."

"You shall have to work harder, then. It's not at all easy to maintain a reputation like that."

"To my regret and my eternal joy. Now, madame," his voice lowered, "tell me of this man who is not your lover."

"I most certainly will not. I am not in the habit

of discussing matters of a personal nature with people I scarcely know. Besides, I thought you wished
for silence."

"Only at the start of a work. I can now divide
my attention without concern. You did agree to discuss anything."

"I agreed to let *you* discuss anything," she said
quickly.

"And I wish to discuss the gentleman who oc-
cupies your mind." He paused for a moment. "Do
not worry that I will reveal what you confide in
me. Those who sit for portraits often speak of
things they would not otherwise mention. If I were
not to hold my tongue, I would quickly find myself
at a loss for clients. What is said between artist and
subject is as sacred as that which passes between
priest and penitent."

"Rubbish. I don't believe that for a moment." She
laughed. "And by your own admission you are no
priest."

"No. But I give you my word what passes between us stays between us. And my word, too, is
sacred."

"Still, I really don't—"

"If you are concerned about embarrassment
when next we meet, do not be. You do not know
my face. We could pass on the street and you
would be none the wiser. There is much to be said
for anonymity." He paused as if sensing her indecision.

Could she trust him? It was absurd to consider
confiding in him, even though she realized she

longed to discuss her feelings with someone. Surely the temptation was due to nothing more than her surroundings at the moment. The lull of the dark room. The lure of the faceless stranger. Her relaxed position on the chaise, even her bare feet all created a sense of sanctuary. Secure, safe, and private. Perhaps it was akin to a confessional after all.

"I suspect as well, madame, you have no one else to confide in."

She hadn't thought about it, but he was right. She'd always shared everything with Robin and Kit, but on the subject of Richard they were impossible. She refused to face their continuing disapproval, and she had no other close friends. She'd grown more and more independent of her family in recent years, and while she loved them all dearly, they didn't know of the legacy, and she preferred to keep that knowledge to herself for the moment.

Her cousin Pandora would understand, but from the gossip Gillian had heard, Pandora was occupied with her own intriguing dilemma. And while Gillian suspected she and Emma would prove to be great friends, they did not know one another well enough yet for confidences of this nature. In addition, Emma was Richard's sister, and her loyalties would lie with him.

"You are perceptive, monsieur, I will grant you that," she said quietly.

"And discreet."

"I do hope so."

What harm could there be in talking to him? The

worst that could possibly happen is that he would reveal her situation to the rest of the world, and he would scarcely do that. She could be of great benefit to his career, and he would be a fool to betray her. Toussaint was definitely no fool. He had also given his word, and there was nothing to lead her to believe he would not keep it.

She drew a deep breath. "There is a man."

"Ah, you see? There is always a man." He laughed softly.

"I plan to marry him."

"Do you? Yet you say he is not your lover, and since you are not of an age where such matters are arranged . . . I do not understand."

"It's a rather . . . well . . . unusual circumstance." She thought for a moment. "I don't especially understand it myself. It's become so much more complicated than I ever expected."

"Complicated? What is more complicated than that between a man and a woman, yet what is more simple as well."

"It did start out simply enough." She quickly outlined the details of the legacy, the resulting list of husbands, her choice of Richard, prudently omitting his name, and his conditions for the marriage. "So, there you have it."

"It is indeed an unusual story." He fell silent, obviously considering her words. His own were measured. "Have you then decided to be the wife he wishes?"

"Yes." She shook her head. "No." Frustration welled inside her. "I don't know. One moment I will, I want to, and the next I can't. It's terribly confusing."

"Confusing?"

She groped for the right words. "It was, as I said, in the beginning a simple matter. A marriage strictly for the purposes of gaining my inheritance. A marriage in nothing more than name. Then, of course, he wouldn't agree to that, and frankly, I do understand why and I don't blame him. But in the process of his seduction—"

"I thought it was a courtship?"

"Yes, of course." She waved off his correction. "That's what I meant. I don't know why I said seduction." Richard's dark, intense gaze flashed through her mind, and she knew full well why she'd said seduction. "At any rate, I seem to have all these odd feelings whenever I'm anywhere near him."

"I see. Then perhaps you have made your decision after all?"

"No, no, not those kind of feelings. At least not entirely." She pushed herself upright and stared in his direction. "What overwhelms everything else when I'm with him is . . . well . . . fear."

"I cannot work if you do not stay in one spot," he murmured.

"Sorry." She settled back into position. "Please don't misunderstand me. I'm not scared of him specifically, at least I don't think I am. What I mean to say is he's not the kind of man who beats children or kicks dogs—"

"Hah! I knew there would be dogs."

She ignored him. "He's an honorable man. A good man."

"A good man?" Toussaint scoffed. "How tedious. And how boring."

"Not at all," she said staunchly.

"If he is so *good*"—Toussaint said the word as if it were obscene—"then what are you afraid of?"

"I only wish I knew."

He didn't respond, and she wondered if he was mulling over his words or working.

"Toussaint?"

"You are a widow, are you not?"

"Yes," she said cautiously.

"Then it is not the act of love that frightens you."

"Of course not." Indignation colored her tone. "I am an adult. I have been married, and I am well aware of what transpires between a man and a woman."

"But, if rumor is correct, you have not been free with your favors since the death of your husband."

She stifled a sharp reply, annoyed as much by the accuracy of *ton* gossip as his temerity in repeating it. She kept her voice cool and slightly amused. "Your impertinence is not quite as charming as you've been led to believe."

"Ah, but again you lie, madame." He chuckled. "If you did not enjoy my insolent nature you would have left long ago."

"I could very well leave now." And she should probably do just that.

"You could." A shrug sounded in his voice. "But you will not."

"Why on earth not?" Of course she could.

"You admitted it yourself. I am the only one you have to confide in. In addition, we have neither solved your problem nor finished your portrait. In fact, we have scarcely begun on both."

"I doubt you can resolve my dilemma. Particularly since I am not at all certain precisely what it is."

"Then perhaps your fear is indeed of the act of love." He paused. "Or love itself."

Irritation washed through her. "Nonsense. On both counts." She sat up, found her shoes beside the chaise, and slipped them on. "But I think I've had quite enough for one night, and I shall indeed take my leave."

"Because you cannot face the truth."

She stood. "And what truth is that?"

"You plan to marry a man who has never taken you in his arms. Never swept aside your sensibilities with his touch, his caress. Never so much as kissed you as a woman like yourself should be kissed."

"I never said he hasn't kissed me," she snapped.

"Has he?"

"That's none of your concern. This discussion has gotten completely out of hand." She started toward the door.

"Perhaps you are afraid when he does, you will feel nothing?"

She sucked in a hard breath. Was he right? Was that what she was so afraid of? No. The very idea was ridiculous. The one and only thing she knew at this point was that when Richard finally did kiss her she would feel a great deal. "That's quite enough. This conversation is at an end."

She stalked across the room, snatched her cloak from the chair, stepped to the door, and yanked it open. At once his footsteps echoed hers. His hand reached from behind her and slammed the door shut. She gasped, and he gripped her shoulders and held her still.

His voice sounded beside her ear. "Do not turn, ma chérie—"

"I'm not your—"

"Listen to me." His tone was low and intense.

She tried to break away, but he held her tight. "Let me go."

"You are a lovely woman who has been without a man too long."

"I'll scream if you don't release me at once."

"I would love to hear you scream." He held her firmly against him. "You need a man who will make you cry out with pleasure. Who will claim not just your body but your soul."

"No!"

"And that, my dear madame, is what you fear."

"It is not!" Was it?

"No? Then why are you not afraid of me? We are together, alone, in the night."

"I don't know." But even now, held tightly to him, she wasn't afraid, when she probably should have been.

"Don't you? I could have you now. Here. And

you would not resist." His lips brushed against her ear.

"I would!" Would she?

"You do not fear my touch. I know it. I feel it in the way your body molds against mine." He shifted behind her, and she could feel him hard and lean and strong. "You know it as well."

"I know nothing of the sort." But he was right: she wasn't at all scared.

"Why are you not afraid?"

"I don't know!"

"Why?"

"I don't—" Her blood pounded in her ears. "Because you pose no threat to my heart!" she blurted, stunned by her own admission.

"Are you so certain?" He brushed his lips against her neck and she stiffened but couldn't bring herself to pull away.

"Yes." His body was hot against her back and, in an odd way, welcoming, and even, somehow, familiar.

"Why? Because I am not a good man? Because I am not on your silly list? Because you run no risk of caring for me?" His voice softened, whispering against her neck. A shiver ran through her. "Because I am not the kind of man who would take his time to seduce you."

"You're not?" she whispered. What was happening to her?

"I would not waste one precious moment with you on such nonsense." He nuzzled the curve where her neck met her shoulder, and she bit her lip to keep from crying out.

"I have to go," she murmured. It was obviously lust surging through her. Nothing more than that. Plain and simply physical need. By God, Toussaint was right: it had been far too long since she'd been with a man. "You have to stop. Now."

"Why? You are not yet married. Not even betrothed." He slipped the sheer fabric of her gown down her arm, bared her shoulder, and kissed it until she marveled she could still stand.

Part of her mind cried out in protest, ignored by her traitorous body that screamed for more. Much more. In another moment, any denial, any objection would be futile.

He lessened his grip and ran his hands along her arms, and she shuddered with the realization that for the first time since her husband's death she wanted a man in her bed. And at the moment, she wanted this man. This faceless, anonymous stranger who triggered sensations she hadn't known she'd missed, hadn't known she'd wanted, until now.

"No!" With the last vestige of resistance in a mind weakened by numbing desire, she jerked out of his arms, yanked open the door, and flew down the stairs.

His confident voice followed her. "You will return, madame."

"No," she called over her shoulder.

Why not?

She paused and turned to stare at the still open door. She had nothing to fear but her own lustful desire, and that she could surely curb. She squared her shoulders. *Why not indeed?* "Perhaps. But only for the portrait. Nothing more."

She swiveled and started back down the stairs, pulling her cloak on over her shoulders as she went. Wilkins stared up at her as if she had lost her mind. Perhaps she had.

Toussaint's laughter echoed in the stairwell. "We shall see, madame, we shall see."

Richard closed the door and grinned. That had certainly gone well. He started toward Gillian's portrait. Very well indeed. His step slowed, and his grin faded. Perhaps too well?

He sank down on the stool before the canvas and stared at the rough charcoal drawing. What in the hell had really happened tonight? He ran his fingers through his hair impatiently and recounted the events of the evening.

It had started out well enough, although he'd thought all was lost when she'd spoken to him in French. Damnation, why hadn't he paid more attention to his studies years ago and learned the blasted language? Still, he'd managed to recover nicely. He grinned at the thought of her indignation when he'd slandered her accent.

Gillian had been a good subject once she'd agreed to keep quiet, providing him with more than enough time to sketch her form lying on the chaise. Indeed, with every line the excitement of a work in progress, a work he knew would be his best, had grown within him. It had proceeded extremely well as long as he'd been immersed in what he was doing, as long as he'd viewed her as nothing more than a model.

But the moment he'd started on her face, he was lost. He'd studied her for a time, stared at her, without her noticing that the quiet sound of charcoal against canvas had ceased. Of course, he had arranged the room to make certain he would remain in the shadows and she would see him as nothing more than a silhouette. Even so, it had been apparent by her expression that she'd no longer been aware of her surroundings. Of where she was or who she was with.

He'd wondered at the time, or perhaps hoped, he was what was on her mind. If he was the one who had put that dreamlike expression in her eyes and the flush on her cheeks. If when she'd parted her lips and licked them slowly, she had been thinking of him. It had been all he could do to keep from racing across the room to take her in his arms.

He swallowed hard and stared at the face on the canvas. Quick, unfinished strokes of black that hinted at what was to come.

He'd managed to keep himself in control and had even succeeded in sustaining that silly accent. Who would have thought an accent adopted for a brief meeting in a garden would be so difficult to maintain during an hour in a studio? He'd nearly forgotten it altogether in those final moments at the door.

He picked up the charcoal and started to work,

refining the vaguely formed image. He didn't need her here to continue: her face was as vivid in his mind as if she stood before him.

Those final moments at the door.

Whatever had possessed him to follow her? To hold her so tight against him that he could feel every curve of her body through that scandalous wisp of a dress. Feel as well the warmth of her skin. Each breath she took. The beating of her heart.

What would have happened then if she hadn't pulled away? He'd wanted her with an intensity that even now shocked him, and he knew she'd wanted him as well. And that too was shocking. *She'd* wanted *him?* Or was it Toussaint she'd wanted?

She certainly hadn't withdrawn from Toussaint's arms. No, there had been no fear in her manner when Toussaint had embraced her. In fact, while not entirely eager, her resistance had been minimal at best. Annoyance tightened his grip, and his strokes on the canvas were hard and swift.

Was it that nonsense about her heart, about love that made the difference? Surely she didn't want love from Richard? From him? Blast it all, she was right, this was damned confusing. Her behavior. His reaction. And just who was reacting to whom?

With Toussaint there was no question of love. Was that why with Toussaint she had nothing to fear? No reason to retreat or withdraw?

Still, a little fear wouldn't be uncalled for. A bit of resistance would be only proper. Hell, the woman was practically putty in his arms. Or Toussaint's arms.

He blew out a long breath. Well, that was his plan, wasn't it? His so-called two-prong attack? What woman could resist both the advances of an English earl and a French artist? It was as clever as any military strategy ever devised by Wellington or Napoleon.

No, his plan was still sound. Should she surrender to Toussaint, it would only serve to prove to her that she had nothing to fear from him, from Richard. Prove that she could share his bed without losing her heart.

He drew his brows together in irritation. Is that what he wanted? Of course. He had no interest in love. Oh, he'd started to care for her and certainly seemed to think about nothing else but her, and the idea of her inheritance was no longer as important as it had been, but love? Hardly.

Once again the English were battling the French, and surely once again the English would win. He ignored the nagging thought that, once again, it could be a long and bloody war.

Chapter 10

Gillian wondered just how improper it would be to send her guests home and Emma to her room so she could at last be alone with Richard.

She surveyed the small group now gathered in her parlor. Richard and Robin stood debating the merits of the latest actions of Parliament. Emma sat on a nearby settee dividing her attention between the political discussion and Kit beside her. Thus far the evening had gone surprisingly well, all things considered.

Oh, certainly Robin had been of no help, politely challenging everything Richard said, whether he was commenting on the current state of governmental affairs or the fine spring weather. Fortunately, Kit had been far too busy gazing wide-eyed at Emma to join in Robin's sport.

From the moment Kit had walked in the door, he'd been unable to keep his eyes off the girl. Of course, she did look quite fetching with her hair properly dressed and wearing the gown Gillian had loaned her. Emma's own clothes had been her mother's and were sadly out of fashion. Gillian had thought Richard would need to come up with at least a few pounds to clothe his sister appropriately, but as she and Gillian were of a similar size and height it might not be necessary.

In point of fact, if the purpose of any season, no matter how modest, was to find a husband, Emma might well have achieved that already, if Gillian were to judge by Kit's manner and the dazed look in his eye. Gillian was at once delighted by the development and, oddly, just a wee bit annoyed.

Emma was accepting Kit's attentions with an air of cool amusement. Gillian couldn't help but be impressed. Richard's sister may well be straight from the country, but she had all the poise of a young woman with several seasons to her credit. When it came to matters of the heart and the art of flirtation, Emma had nearly as much natural talent as she did for painting.

They'd set up a studio of sorts earlier in the day, and Emma had already thrown herself into her work. Gillian wondered if she should bring the girl to her next sitting with Toussaint to observe his work. Besides, Emma's presence would serve more than one purpose.

Richard did not appear to notice the unexpected attraction between his sister and Kit. No, for the first time since she'd come to know him, he was living up to his public reputation. He was rather abrupt tonight, reluctant to make conversation and continually cast her the most annoying looks, as if he was trying to see inside her. Why, the man was positively brooding. Given last night's sitting with Toussaint and Gillian's intentions toward Richard this evening, it was most unnerving.

She'd thought about the encounter with the artist all day, dismissing the feelings she'd experienced at the end of the evening as nothing more than a physical response to the embrace of a man skilled in seduction. Still, it was hard to ignore them completely. She'd never considered herself prone to passion, and to have such reactions to a man whose face she'd never seen was disturbing.

But what truly preyed on her mind were her admissions. Was she indeed afraid of losing her heart to Richard? Was she afraid of what she might feel in his arms? In their few brief encounters she'd already felt a great deal.

But what if it was nothing more than the same physical longing she'd experienced with Toussaint? What if she wasn't afraid of losing her heart but afraid of not losing it? Afraid of feeling nothing at all beyond desire? If she was going to marry the man, it was past time to find out. Regardless of what was at stake, could she spend the rest of her life with a man she didn't love?

"Robin," she said abruptly, "I do hate to call an end to this lovely evening, but it is getting rather late."

A wry smile lifted the corners of Richard's

mouth. It was neither late nor, in truth, had it been all that lovely.

Robin looked at her with an assessing eye. "Very well. Kit?"

"It doesn't seem late to me," Kit murmured, his gaze never leaving Emma.

Emma rose to her feet, and Kit stood at once. "Lady Gillian is right. It has been an exceedingly long day." She held out her hand.

Kit took it and favored it with a lingering kiss. Gillian tried not to grin. "I do hope to have the pleasure of seeing you again."

Emma blushed.

Robin rolled his eyes and started toward the door. "Come along then, Kit." Kit followed reluctantly. Robin stopped and directed a pointed stare at Richard. "Are you coming, Shelbrooke?"

"In a moment," Gillian said quickly. "We have some matters to discuss."

Richard raised a brow. "Apparently not, Weston."

Robin's eyes narrowed. He studied Gillian thoughtfully, then nodded. "I see. I will bid you good evening then." He turned and stalked from the room.

"Good evening." Kit cast a last longing look at Emma and trailed after Robin. Wilkins's voice was heard in the hall, followed a moment later by the sound of the door opening and closing.

Emma's gaze met Gillian's. There was an attractive flush in her cheeks, and her eyes sparkled. "He certainly is a pleasant gentleman, isn't he?"

"Pleasant?" Richard snorted. "He's a flirtatious rake and you'd be well advised to keep your distance."

"Richard!" Emma's eyes widened.

"Nonsense," Gillian snapped. "He's somewhat high spirited, but he's quite honorable, very nice, and one of my dearest friends. In addition, he has a respectable fortune and title and would make Emma an excellent match."

"An excellent match?" Richard's brows drew together.

"Do you think so?" Emma said in a dreamy manner.

"I do indeed." Gillian nodded and smiled. "And I have never seen him look at a woman like this before. I think it's an excellent start."

"It's not a start." Richard's voice rose. "It's not a start at all. It's an end. I have no intention of allowing my sister to have anything more to do with the man."

"Oh dear," Emma murmured.

"Your intentions scarcely matter." Gillian planted her hands on her hips. "She is one-and-twenty and there is not a great deal you can say about it."

Richard glared back. "There most certainly is. As long as she enjoys my protection—"

"Perhaps, but at the moment one could make the argument that she is not precisely enjoying your protection, as she is living under my roof." Gillian smirked.

"It is rather late after all," Emma said, inching toward the door.

"And since she is under my roof, my approval is the only thing she needs to concern herself with. At the moment, I see nothing wrong with allowing her to see whomever she wishes and do as she pleases."

"Your approval?" Richard sputtered. "I scarcely think you are any judge of character when it comes to scoundrels like Weston."

"I'm an excellent judge of character." Indignation washed through her.

"Hah!"

"I should probably be going," Emma said uneasily.

Gillian crossed her arms over her chest and stepped toward him. " 'Hah'? What do you mean by 'hah'?"

"Only that your so-called ability to judge character remains to be seen," he said with a lofty air.

"By whom?" Her voice rose with ire.

"By me." His tone was firm, as if this was the end of the discussion. She resisted the immediate impulse to scream in frustration. Or smack him.

"I chose you, didn't I? Was that a mistake?" Her voice rang with challenge.

"That too remains to be seen," he said smugly.

"It does indeed." Her gaze locked with his.

"Well, I certainly wouldn't use your positioning of me at the top of your list as an example of your excellent assessment of a man's nature." He glowered down at her.

"What list?" Emma said curiously.

"So far, I'd say your behavior has been damnably proper." She stared up at him. "So apparently I was right."

"Isn't that what you wanted? What you selected? A man who behaves properly, honorably, respectably." His eyes narrowed. "A man who doesn't want anything more from you than your bloody inheritance?"

"Yes, but that's not what I got, was it?" She was losing control, and right now, she didn't really care. The man was infuriating. "What I got was a beast who wants more than my money. He wants me in his bed. He wants—"

"What?" Richard roared. "What do you think I want from you?"

"I should definitely retire." Emma fled from the room, flinging the doors closed behind her.

Gillian refused to pull her gaze from Richard's. "Look at what you've done now, you've scared her."

"The way I scare you?"

"You don't scare me," she snapped. It was true. She was far too angry to be scared.

"Something does."

Irritation swept away caution, and she spoke without thinking. "Why haven't you kissed me?"

"What?" Confusion colored his face. "What does that have to do with anything?"

"You didn't answer my question." She stared up at him. "You haven't even tried to kiss me. For a man who claims to be trying to seduce—"

"Court," he murmured.

"Seduce! Although I scarcely think nuzzling my hand on occasion can be considered seduction. Why, you've not put any real effort into this seduction of yours."

"Indeed I have." His tone was wounded, as if she'd maligned his manhood.

She snorted.

"I didn't think you especially wanted me to kiss you or anything else," he replied. "Every time I'd so much as hold your hand . . ." He shook his head. She didn't think she'd ever seen a man look quite so puzzled. "I thought . . . well, the way you—"

"Kiss me, Richard." She wasn't the least bit afraid, and she had to know what, if anything, she'd feel when he did. Would it be fear? Passion? Love? Or nothing at all? This was obviously the right moment to find out. "Now."

His eyes flashed. Was he too angry to kiss her? "Are you certain this is what you want?"

"Yes, yes." She gestured impatiently. "Do go on."

The corners of his lips twitched. Or was he amused? "If you insist."

He lowered his head, and she closed her eyes. His lips met hers, warm and gentle, and heat flashed through her. It was an excellent beginning. She strained upward, and without warning, he was gone.

She snapped her eyes open. He raised a brow. "Well?"

"Well what?" Disbelief sounded in her voice, but

she couldn't help it. Surely that wasn't the best he could do? Her heart sank.

"Well, how was it?"

"It was . . ." *Brief, short, diminutive.* Not that she could possibly tell him that. She forced a weak smile. "Pleasant."

"Respectable." He nodded solemnly.

"Yes, I suppose." It was, in fact, scarcely worth mentioning. What if it was the best he could do?

"Then you're disappointed?"

"Not at all," she said quickly. "At any rate, I'm scarcely a judge of such things. I can't recall the last time I asked a man to kiss me." Still, she had an excellent memory and a fairly good idea of what to expect. Disappointed was as appropriate a word as any. Good Lord, his perfunctory peck barely counted as a kiss. "I did expect . . . something . . . well . . ."

"Not quite as restrained?"

"Perhaps. You do have a reputation, after all."

"I did have a reputation, remember," he said pointedly. "I have reformed. That's why I head your list."

"Pity," she said under her breath. What if he'd reformed too well? What was she to do now? This so-called kiss of his hadn't proved anything at all. It had been far too reserved, too proper, and entirely too short.

"Now then, if there's nothing else, I shall take my leave." He nodded, turned, and strode toward the door. Very formal, quite correct, and yet . . .

Damn it all, she had seen it in his eyes: he was amused!

"Richard!" He stopped in his tracks. His shoulders shook. "Are you laughing?"

"Nothing of the sort." His voice had an odd inflection. Like a man about to choke or struggling to hold himself in check.

"There isn't anything to laugh about."

He turned to face her, biting on his bottom lip so hard that she wondered he didn't draw blood. "There isn't?"

"Not at all."

"Perhaps you're right." He nodded slowly and crossed his arms over his chest. "I suppose there isn't anything remotely comical in our situation?"

"I see nothing to so much as draw a smile."

"You don't think it's even mildly amusing that you, a well-respected lady, would propose marriage to me, someone you have considered far beneath your notice, for the sole purpose of acquiring your legacy?"

"No," she huffed. "It was a necessity and I resent your saying that I considered you beneath my notice."

"Didn't you?"

"Perhaps, once, but that was years ago."

"Forgive me then. Time and circumstances have changed us both." He stepped closer, his teasing manner gone. "However, to continue, you don't believe my refusal to agree to the kind of marriage you want and your subsequent suggestion that we spend the time until your birthday getting ac-

quainted well enough for you to concede to share
my bed to be the least bit humorous?"

"No, I don't."

"It doesn't strike you as rather farcical that I have
played your game in a perfectly proper manner?
That I have done everything within my power to
set you at ease?" His voice hardened. "That I have
racked my brains trying to determine why you look
like a frightened rabbit whenever I come near
you?"

"No." She drew the word out slowly. He was
rather near her now, close enough to reach out and
touch. Close enough for him to pull her into his
arms. She wasn't afraid, although her insides were
churning in a distinctly uncomfortable manner.

"Why do you want me to kiss you?" he said
abruptly, his tone heavy with unasked questions.

She stared up at him, a hundred responses flying
through her head. Not one of which came to her
lips.

"When I kiss you, Gillian, really kiss you, if I kiss
you, it shall be at a time of my own choosing." His
gaze bored into hers. Anger flared in his eyes. "For
my own purposes and not because you need to
prove anything. To me or to yourself."

Her breath caught in her throat. "I don't need—"

"You do," he said sharply. "I can see it in your
eyes. Whether you need to prove that you can be
my wife without sharing the kind of affection you
shared with your husband—"

"I can," she snapped. "I can be the wife you

want, in every way you want, and I've decided I will. We shall be married at once."

"Shall we?" Sarcasm dripped from his words. "And thereby secure your inheritance of six hundred thousand pounds, eight ships, and a great deal of land in America. Do you realize, my lady, what the word is for a woman who gives herself to a man for money? Even so great a fortune as this?"

Shock shot through her. Her head snapped backward as if she'd been slapped. Without thinking, she drew her hand back and let it fly.

He caught it with a firm grasp just inches from his face and twisted it behind her, pulling her hard against him.

"Release me at once!" Her chest heaved, and she couldn't catch her breath.

"No!" He held her tighter against him and stared into her eyes, remorse on his face. "I am sorry, Gillian. I never meant—"

"Don't!" The word was little more than a sob, and she hated the weakness of the sound. She tried to wrench free, but he held her tight. She drew a deep breath and forced a cold tone to her voice. "Don't waste your apology. I don't want it and I won't accept it. You as much as called me a wh—"

"Don't say it! I was angry and—"

"And now I'm angry." Her chin jerked up, and she glared.

"—and frustrated as well, and, I don't know, tired perhaps of not knowing what you wanted of me." His gaze searched her face. "And, I suppose, even hurt." He released her hand but kept his arms around her. "Forgive me, Gillian."

The tone in his voice called to something deep inside her, and she stilled.

"Please." He drew her closer and brushed his lips across her forehead, holding her silently for long moments.

She knew she should pull away. He deserved as much. But she couldn't seem to move, to leave his embrace. "Hurt? What do you mean?"

"It's not easy to know a woman wants you for nothing more than your name. I daresay it's nothing more than my own damnable pride and it didn't seem to matter as much at first, but I don't want to be only your means to a fortune." His lips whispered along the side of her face to the line of her jaw.

"You don't?" His touch was soothing and sensual, and her anger faded to something altogether different.

"I want more from you than that." His lips moved lower on her neck.

Reason vanished, and she wanted more. She tilted her head back, the sensation of his mouth against her skin intoxicating. His caress was assured yet light and teasing, and delight shivered through her. Her eyes drifted closed. She could focus on nothing but his touch.

"Do you?" Her hands crept up his arms and she gripped the fabric of his coat.

"I do." His tongue dipped into the hollow at the base of her neck and lower, to the valley between her breasts. One hand splayed across her back, strong and possessive. The other trailed lower across her derriere and up her side. Slowly, inevitably, until his fingertips grazed her breast through the fabric of her gown.

"What do you want from me, Richard?" she murmured

His thumb rubbed across her nipple, and she gasped. She felt her bodice slip downward and cool air on her bare breasts. He cupped one in his hand, his mouth moving to claim it. Teeth and tongue teased and toyed. A sweet, awful ache gripped her, and she dug her nails into his arms, if only to keep herself standing on legs threatening to buckle beneath her. He turned his attention to her other breast and suckled until her mind fogged with desire.

"I want you to want me."

He pushed her dress lower, gown and petticoat falling to puddle on the floor at her feet, and he sank to his knees before her. His lips never left her skin, and everywhere his mouth touched her flesh burned and her blood pounded and she yearned for more. His hands skimmed down her legs, over her stockings, and in some still lucid section of her mind, she noted how odd she must look in her slippers and stockings and nothing more. His hands moved up her legs to her inner thighs, long, slow caresses, and she held her breath, waiting for him to reach the throbbing between her legs. Wondering if she would die of longing before he did. Or of joy when he did.

He shifted, wrapping an arm around her, his fingers trailing up and down her buttocks. His tongue continued its exploration of the sensitive skin on her stomach. His other hand slid upwards. She was afraid to move. Afraid he'd stop. Afraid he wouldn't.

He reached the curls between her legs, and his fingers slipped past, over her, slick and hot. She moaned with pleasure. He rubbed back and forth, to and fro with a gentle, easy pressure until she thought she'd swoon from the sheer bliss of it. His fingers slipped inside her, and she tensed at the invasion and the exquisite sensations.

She gazed down at his dark head and tunneled her fingers through his hair.

"I do want you." She could barely whisper the words, her voice so low she didn't know if he could hear. She wasn't sure she wanted him to. And didn't care.

He drew back and stared up at her. "Are you certain?"

"Yes." She nodded and slid to her knees in front of him. Her gaze locked with his. She pushed his jacket over his shoulders, and he shrugged it off. "I am." She yanked impatiently at his cravat. His hands cupped her bottom and drew her toward him. She struggled to pull his shirt free until he released her and jerked it over his head. "Quite certain." His chest was broad, his muscles defined, emphasized by a smattering of dark hair that drifted lower to disappear in his trousers.

She splayed her hands across his chest and reveled in the look of him and the feel of his bare skin beneath her fingers. He sucked in a shocked breath and grabbed her hand, pulling it to his lips. Her gaze met and locked with his.

Perhaps it was a moment of utter clarity. Perhaps complete insanity. Or it might have been his gesture, simple yet touching, but something inside her, long held in check or merely ignored, shattered. At once her arms were around him and she rained kisses on his neck, his throat, his shoulders. He tasted of heat and spice and aching desire. He pulled her tighter against him, and they tumbled down onto the carpet. She ran her fingers over the sleek, smooth planes of his back, and lower, sliding her hands beneath the fabric of his trousers. She needed to touch every part of him, taste every bit of him. And needed his touch in return.

He rolled away to discard his trousers. Irrational loss gripped her, and she started to sit up. Then he was back, gathering her into his arms, and she knew at this moment that she wanted nothing more than to mold her body to his, merge her heat with his and welcome him into her. His erection pushed hard against her stomach. She entwined her legs with his, and they rolled together until she lay on top of him.

He slid her down along the stretch of his body until her legs straddled his and the hot, solid length of him nudged between her legs.

His touch broke through her haze of desire, and she hesitated.

"Gillian?"

She pushed herself up and stared down into his eyes, glazed with passion and touched with concern. "Richard, I . . . well, I'm not sure how to say this, but I . . . that is I haven't . . ."

"Since your husband," he said quietly.

She nodded.

"Do you want to stop?"

A warm glow that had nothing to do with her body and everything to do with her heart flooded through her. She smiled slowly. "The last thing I want to do is stop. I just wanted you to know. It's been rather a long time, and I'm not terribly experienced and—"

He laughed. "I do appreciate the warning."

"I just don't want you to be disappointed."

He pulled her against him and rolled over, reversing their positions. His eyes burned with desire, and he gazed into hers as if he was looking for something elusive. A question unspoken. An answer unknown. "I could never be disappointed with you."

He guided himself into her with a care that caught at her heart. She was tight but wet and wanting. He slid slowly, firmly into her, his gaze never leaving hers. His body joined with hers as if they were made each with the other in mind. Merged with hers as if they were half of the same whole. Filled hers as if she were empty and waiting for him alone.

And still his gaze locked with hers.

He started to move, a gentle rhythm, undemanding. She tightened around him, matched her movements to his, and wrapped her legs around his waist. He plunged deeper, and she met his thrusts with her own, and they moved as one. Hot tension curled within her, urging her on. The muscles of his back strained under her hands, and she clung to him as though holding on for her very life. Her very soul.

Faster and harder they moved, and she knew nothing of the world surrounding them save the feel of him inside her and the spiraling ache that encompassed her very being. She marveled that she would know such pleasure and endure and still want more. Need more. And when she knew she would surely die from sheer rapture, a taut flame of bliss within her exploded. She cried out, and her body jerked beneath his and shook in waves of delicious release. He buried his head in the crook of her neck and groaned, his body shuddering in unison with her own.

Minutes passed, or maybe hours, and they lay still, wrapped in each other's arms, savoring what had passed between them. She didn't want to move, didn't want to lose the shelter of his embrace. She could feel his heart thudding in his chest next to hers and her own beating in harmony.

At long last he raised his head and smiled down at her. "I was not disappointed."

"Nor was I." She grinned. "Although I did note the carpet is a bit threadbare and not at all comfortable and should be replaced as soon as possible."

He laughed. Then, slowly, with a reluctance that

matched her own, he withdrew from her and got to his feet. She sat up and studied him. She was not embarrassed at all to be sitting on her floor in nothing but her stockings, wondering precisely when she had lost her slippers. Not the tiniest bit abashed at staring at a naked man in her parlor. Of course she was well used to appreciating nude figures in finely carved marble for their artistic merits. And Richard was rather magnificent without his clothing and extremely artistic. He reached out his hand. She took it, and he pulled her to her feet and into his arms. And much, much warmer than marble.

His body pressed against hers. She rested her head on his chest and sent a silent prayer of gratitude for this man at the top of her list.

A knock sounded on the parlor door.

"My lady, if you are no longer in need of my services I should like to retire for the evening," Wilkins's annoyed voice called through the door.

A hot blush burned her cheeks. "Good Lord, what must he be thinking?"

Richard raised a brow. "All manner of scandalous things, I should think." He kissed her lightly on her forehead. "Each and every one of them quite true."

"Madame?" Wilkins said impatiently.

"Retire, Wilkins," Richard called. "Lady Gillian has no further need of you tonight."

Wilkins muttered something Gillian couldn't make out. She considered that for the best.

"I, too, should take my leave." Richard stepped

away from her, glanced around, located his clothes, and began to dress.

She picked up her gown and slipped it over her head, wondering at the odd and glorious turn the night had taken. She didn't regret it. Not at all.

He came up behind her and wrapped his arms around her. She leaned back against him. His voice was soft against her ear. "I should go."

"Should you?"

He nibbled at the curve where her shoulder met her neck. "If I don't leave now, I shall never leave."

Shivers coursed through her at his touch. "Then never leave."

"One day." He paused. "Perhaps."

She sighed with contentment. "One day."

He released her and she turned to say good-bye, but he was already at the door.

"Gillian." He nodded, gave her a strange, remote smile, then pulled the doors open and vanished. The outer door opened and closed, and she was alone.

She stared where he had been, and her own smile faded.

"One day. Perhaps."

What on earth had he meant by that? He wouldn't have to leave when they were married, and they would be wed now. She'd proved, rather well she thought, that she could be completely and fully his wife. Share his bed, or his carpet, without reserve. There were no further impediments to their marriage.

Or were there? Richard hadn't mentioned their

arrangement. Nor had he actually kissed her, now that she thought about it. At least not on her lips. Perhaps it hadn't been a time of his own choosing. She laughed to herself. Not that she'd noticed. Still, regardless of whether he'd truly kissed her or not, there was no doubt that he hadn't brought up their marriage. Why on earth not?

And why hadn't she?

She sank down onto the settee. A dozen thoughts tumbled through her head. She could marry him now and get her inheritance and with it financial independence. She would have more than enough to support artists like Emma and the unknown woman who had saved her soul. Richard would have the money he needed for his estates and his sisters' dowries. Everything had worked out for everyone's benefit. Hadn't it?

She'd wondered if she was falling in love with Richard and whether that was the source of her fear. But there had been no fear in Richard's arms tonight—only passion. Yet hadn't she felt precisely the same passion with Toussaint? Had the artist been right when he'd said she was afraid not of feeling too much but of feeling nothing at all?

Was passion enough to justify marriage? She hadn't wanted it, and certainly hadn't expected it, when she'd come up with the idea of marrying Richard. One could even consider what they shared something of a delightful bonus.

Did she love Richard? Or did she only want him? And could she really marry a man she didn't love? She could have done just that when this had all begun and was nothing more than an absurd solution to a difficult problem. But now . . .

It was all confusing and ironic. Gillian had always believed there was no reason other than love to marry. Her inheritance had forced her to think otherwise. Now, she was back to where she'd started.

She got to her feet and slowly crossed the room, stopping to pick up her petticoat and a lone shoe. Unanswered questions filled her head. Was it love she feared? Or was it loving Richard?

And what of Richard? Was he as confused as she? Or was there some other reason why he'd left tonight in such an odd and abrupt manner?

And what role did Toussaint play in all this? Why was his touch as intoxicating as Richard's? She'd lived her life since Charles had died without any man affecting her the way either of them did. She would have sworn what she felt for Richard was at least the beginning of love. But if it was nothing more than lust with Toussaint, was it nothing more with Richard as well?

And what would she have to do to find out?

In the meantime, she had to speak to Emma. At some point, they'd reveal her painting to Richard, but not quite yet. And if they were going to keep Emma's secret, the girl would have to be more careful.

Gillian hadn't noticed it earlier in the evening, and it was so subtle that it might well have escaped attention altogether. But at some point, when she and Richard had been alone, in those few brief moments when she'd been aware of her surroundings and her senses had been most acute, she'd noted it. The faint, but unmistakable, scent of turpentine.

Chapter 11

The jar shattered against the far wall.

"Bloody hell."

Richard impatiently pushed his hair away from his face and glared at the fingers of cobalt blue reaching toward the floor. In the early morning light the stain resembled a huge, vividly hued spider smashed against the wall by a giant hand. Even if it was fairly inexpensive, he could scarcely afford to squander premixed pigment this way. Especially since it gave him no satisfaction whatsoever.

For the first time, his work failed to absorb him completely. Failed to occupy his mind, his soul. No doubt because the subject of his work was the one thing already occupying his mind. Perhaps even his soul.

Gillian.

He kicked the stool out of his way and paced the room, refusing to so much as glance at the portrait.

At the eyes that followed him: one minute re-
proaching, the next inviting. In the back of his
mind, he acknowledged the skill needed to achieve
such an illusion, but at the moment he would have
preferred to be a talentless dabbler. It would have
been much easier.

How could he have been such a coward? Certainly he had apologized for what he'd said, but he
hadn't had the courage to acknowledge the truth.
At least not aloud. If there was a whore in their
relationship, it was not Gillian. She was only trying
to get what she should have had from the start
without ridiculous conditions attached. No, he was
the one who was willing to sell himself for profit.
Willing to wed in exchange for half her fortune and
far more than she'd ever intended.

And what did he offer her in return? His name?
He snorted in disdain, strode to a table, and pawed
through the assorted debris of his daily life. Hadn't
there been a bottle of brandy here somewhere? His
name was scarcely worth more than the effort it
took to scrawl it on a slip of paper. Oh, certainly
he was doing all he could to restore the honor of
the ancient and noble Shelton name. To return it to
a position of respect held by the Earls of Shelbrooke
before his father had ground it into the mud.

Still, hadn't the fortune his father had squandered been in truth brought to the family in the first
place by his mother? Hadn't it been his mother's
dowry and inheritance that had shored up the already sagging Shelton finances? Hadn't his father
married his mother for only one reason?

He found the bottle, pulled out the stopper, and drank greedily. Even the burn of the inferior liquor didn't wash away the bad taste in his mouth.

The blood of the father . . .

He wiped his mouth with the back of his free hand and stared unseeing at the paint stain on the wall. His father had wed for no better reason than to improve his lot in life.

. . . the veins of the son.

He gripped the bottle until his knuckles whitened. Was there any difference between his father's actions and his own?

The blue spider throbbed accusingly.

He hefted the bottle in his hand and drew back. Hadn't he been following his father's footsteps until—

Until he'd had no other choice.

Until his father's death had altered his life forever. He lowered the bottle slowly.

Until the man he'd been well on his way to becoming had been forced by circumstances to become something else entirely. Something more than his father ever expected. Something more than he himself expected.

A man at the top of the list.

An odd sense of calm descended on him. He set the bottle on the table gently, as if it were made of the finest crystal. As fragile as the realization that swept through him.

He was wrong.

He had had any number of choices at his father's death. He could have forced Emma to marry.

Abandoned his sisters altogether. Washed his hands of all of them, as well as Shelbrooke Manor and the people dependent on the estate. He could have continued his disreputable ways, surviving on credit and gaming and whatever else came along.

His father's blood flowed through his veins and, perhaps, some of his traits as well, but he was not his father. His father had succumbed to his weaknesses, allowed them to destroy his life and devastate his children.

Richard had chosen to take another path. And that was the difference between sire and offspring.

He laced his fingers behind his neck and stared out the high windows into the lightening skies of morning.

Apparently, he was a better man than he ever thought he'd be. Otherwise he would have claimed Gillian's hand last night before he'd so much as recovered his trousers. If it was pride that insisted she share his bed if they married, what was it now that made him hesitate to exact his prize? She'd obviously overcome whatever fear she'd had, and there was no doubt she'd wanted him. Wanted him with the same surprising intensity with which he'd wanted her. Wanted her even now, if the truth were told. Wanted her . . . always?

And he could have her and her inheritance without delay and with as little effort as it took to procure a special license and say a few meaningless vows.

Wasn't that precisely what he'd intended all along?

Blast it all, he didn't seem to know anything when it came to Gillian—with the exception of her response to Toussaint. He was all too aware of his feelings about that. Every time he thought about her minimal resistance to his attention, his irritation increased. Why, the woman had nearly succumbed to his advances without so much as a respectable struggle. Certainly that was his original plan, yet it wasn't nearly as satisfying as he had envisioned.

It may well be time to end the sittings altogether. There was no need for Toussaint's attempts at seduction when Richard had already succeeded. Even so, she had found a confidant of sorts in the artist, and it certainly wouldn't hurt to know what was going on in the vixen's mind.

Not that he had so much as a vague inkling of what was going on in his *own* mind. He hadn't the least idea anymore of what he really wanted. And how he wanted to get it.

He needed to sort through his confusing thoughts, his odd feelings and everything else. Needed a place where bewitching blue eyes didn't follow his every move. Painting had always freed his thoughts to deal with other matters, but apparently not when the work was the subject of his quandary.

There were other forms of labor that would serve the same purpose, and more than enough of them awaited him at Shelbrooke Manor. He'd neglected the estate shamefully in recent weeks, far too caught up in furthering Toussaint's career. And then came this business with Gillian.

Society would no more tolerate an earl performing manual labor than it would a titled gentleman painting for a living. Nor would it understand why a man in his position would hesitate for a moment to marry a woman whose fortune would ensure he never had to do either again.

He heaved a frustrated sigh. Damnation. He only wished he understood it himself.

"Richard's gone." Emma glanced up from the note in her hand.

"What do you mean Richard's gone?" Gillian drew her brows together in disbelief.

"That scruffy lad brought yet another note, my lady," Wilkins said with an air of disdain.

Gillian shot him an impatient glance. Wilkins shrugged as if to say it was none of his business if communication in London had fallen to so lowly a level, and left the room. "What does it say, Emma? Where has he gone?"

"Home."

"Why?" Surely Emma was mistaken. A hard knot formed in the pit of her stomach.

Emma scanned the page. "He doesn't say exactly, only that he has matters to attend to and should return by the end of the week."

"The end of the week." A good three days from now. Her heart sank with disappointment and, perhaps, a touch of pain. How could he leave without telling her? How could he leave her now? How could he leave her at all? She struggled to keep her voice level. "He didn't say a word last night."

"Perhaps something unexpected has happened," Emma said hopefully.

"Perhaps." Something unexpected had indeed happened, but right here in this very room. Something exciting and important to them both. At least Gillian thought so. She still wasn't certain of her true feelings or his, but how on earth was she expected to determine anything with him away? The one thing she had no doubt about was her desire to be with him.

Aside from everything else between them, her grandmother's annual house party was at the end of the week, and she'd planned on inviting Richard to accompany her.

Regardless of what they had or hadn't said last night, they'd been seen together publicly at Lady Forester's ball. Nothing the slightest bit out of the ordinary ever went unnoticed there. The attentions of the standoffish Earl of Shelbrooke to the unapproachable Lady Gillian were definitely the stuff gossip was made of.

By now, her parents, aunts, uncles, assorted cousins, and anyone else associated with the Effington family had already heard enough to have them all wondering about her relationship with Richard.

If she didn't appear at the yearly gathering, it was entirely possible someone, even a full delegation, would be appointed to find out exactly what was going on. And that could well lead to the discovery of her great-uncle's legacy and its accompanying conditions.

Not that it mattered in the long run. Oh, certainly her parents would insist she give up the idea of marrying merely to gain her fortune. They were an odd family, all in all, with very definite ideas about such things.

No, the duke and duchess would not approve one bit and would pressure her to accept more financial support from them than she already did. She clenched her jaw in determination. They were a persistent lot, but she was just as stubborn, and she would not allow them to dissuade her.

However, her life would be a great deal easier if they knew as little as possible for the moment. Besides, she was no longer certain what, if anything, the legacy had to do with her plans to marry Richard.

And she certainly couldn't find out if Richard was nowhere to be found.

"Your brother is something of a coward, isn't he?" Gillian said thoughtfully.

"Richard? Of course not." Emma bristled. "He's really quite courageous."

"Is he?"

"I think so. I think it takes a great deal of courage to change your life the way he has." Emma's eyes flashed. "He didn't have to, you know. He could have abandoned all of us out in the country and left us to fend for ourselves.

"Father had already arranged for some beastly man to marry me, and Richard put an end to that. He has refused to allow any of us to turn governess, although we could certainly use the money.

Furthermore, he's doing something, I have no idea what, but he assures us it is not against the law, and it's apparently proving quite successful. I'm assuming it's some kind of business endeavor, but Richard won't say, probably because society would never accept an earl actually earning a living wage. But he's managed to pay off all of his debts and many of Father's—"

"Whatever could he be doing?" Gillian said more to herself than to Emma. She hadn't really thought about it before, but Emma was right. If indeed Richard was making inroads into the debts left by his father, quite extensive from what she understood, he had to be earning money in some way.

"—and he's certainly not squandering money on himself. Why, he won't even show me where he stays when he's here in London. He says his rooms are not an appropriate place for a proper lady."

"Indeed." How very odd to realize she too had no idea where Richard lived. Or for that matter, how he spent his days. In point of fact, while she thought she knew rather a lot about the man, there was apparently a great deal she didn't know.

"He has no carriage, merely a single horse. And his clothes—"

"His coats are always shabby," Gillian murmured, wondering why she found his frayed cuffs rather endearing.

"Exactly," Emma nodded. "Beyond that, when he is home, he helps the tenants with planting or harvesting. He mends fences and works in the stables and does all manner of things no other man of his position would lower himself to do."

"Does he?" So that explained the slight roughness of his hands.

Emma raised her chin and met Gillian's gaze defiantly. "I think that's all quite courageous."

"My apologies, Emma. You're right, of course. I had no idea." Gillian shook her head, touched by Emma's fervent defense of her brother and touched as well by this glimpse of a side of Richard she had no idea existed. "It could be his courage simply fails him when it comes to . . ." To what?

"Matters of the heart?" A smile spread across Emma's face. "What a delightful idea."

"It is, isn't it?" Gillian said thoughtfully. Was it at all possible hers were not the only fears that lay between them? "Perhaps it's time to find out."

"I daresay it won't be easy. Richard keeps a great deal to himself."

"We shall have to break him of that habit. It is indeed time to find out the extent of your brother's courage." She returned the younger woman's grin. "And I think it's past time I paid a visit to Shelbrooke Manor."

Perhaps this wasn't a good idea after all.

Gillian's carriage turned onto the drive that led up the gentle rise to Shelbrooke Manor, and she released a long breath. Uninvited guests were not always welcome, particularly when the host was not merely in residence but possibly in retreat.

Gillian had wanted to follow Richard the moment Emma had told her he had gone, but it had taken a full day just to arrange to borrow one of Thomas's carriages and a driver. She'd had Wilkins bring him a note saying she needed the transportation. He'd agreed, but had responded with a note of his own, saying that he'd heard some rather intriguing rumors and should like to discuss them with her at the first opportunity. She wasn't at all pleased that Thomas was suddenly adopting a newfound role of protective older brother. Still, she was grateful he hadn't come in person, and he had sent the carriage.

The vehicle bounced up the rutted drive, bordered by shaggy grasses that crept here and there onto the road itself. A scattering of flowers—too obstinate to know they couldn't possibly grow without care—nodded over long-abandoned gardens. At the top of the drive, Shelbrooke Manor gazed out over the countryside like a matron who'd seen better days but was nonetheless content with her lot in life.

Gillian wasn't certain what she'd expected. Given the family's history, something ancient and forbidding, perhaps. decrepit with age and neglect. Instead, while it was obvious that prosperity had not visited for some time, it struck her as a rather pleasant place, one that could easily be called home. A place *she* could call home.

For a moment, she could see the manor as it once had been. And could be again. Noble and proud. With manicured lawns and well-tended gardens overflowing with spring blossoms. And with her laughing children racing across the grass. Richard's children. Their children.

A large, shaggy dog appeared from nowhere and bounded along beside the carriage. Oh, and yes, a dog. There would definitely be a dog.

The carriage pulled to a stop before the front entry, and Gillian pushed open the door and stepped down with equal amounts of eagerness and dread. What would Richard say when he saw her?

The creature leaping about her feet was obviously thrilled by her presence. And quite overwhelming.

"Henry," a female voice snapped.

Henry sat at once, his long tail thumping a frantic rhythm on the ground. Gillian bent forward and scratched him under the chin.

"You shall have his undying love forever now, you know."

"So I see." Henry gazed up at her adoringly. Gillian laughed and straightened. "There are far worse things than undying love."

"I would think so." Intelligent brown eyes gazed at her from behind gold-rimmed spectacles. A mass of pale blonde curls caught the sun and danced around her head like a halo. From Emma's description, this must be Marianne, the sister rarely seen without a book in her hand.

"You're Lady Gillian, aren't you?" The girl stood in front of the now open door and studied her with frank curiosity.

Gillian stared in surprise. "How did you know?" The young woman shrugged. "I daresay there isn't anyone else you could be. We've heard all about you."

"Have you?" From Richard?

"Well, not all about you, I suppose. Richard never tends to tell us more than he thinks is best. It's really quite annoying. But he has mentioned your name, and I know Emma is staying with you." She craned her neck to see around Gillian to the carriage behind her. "Isn't she with you?"

"Actually, she preferred to stay in town." To work is what she'd said, and she was of age and well chaperoned by Wilkins and his wife, but Gillian wondered if there wasn't more to her desire to remain behind.

"Alone?" Marianne considered her for a moment. "You're letting her paint, aren't you?"

"Paint?" Gillian said cautiously. She had no idea if the other members of the household shared Richard's views on Emma's secret passion. "Why do you say that?"

"It simply makes sense. I've always thought the moment Emma was out from under Richard's nose she'd do exactly as she wished. And that's very likely the only reason Emma wouldn't accompany you."

"So you know about her painting?"

"Of course. Emma and I are very close. Becky knows, too. I'm not entirely certain about Jocelyn, but then, one never knows if she is ever aware of anything that has nothing to do with her. Even Aunt Louella knows. She doesn't particularly like it, but she tolerates it because she knows Richard would disapprove." Marianne paused. "I'm Marianne."

"I guessed as much." Gillian smiled and stepped up the broad stairs.

"It's the spectacles, isn't it?" Marianne heaved a resigned sigh and pushed them back up a nose a shade too pert to support them properly. "I couldn't possibly be Jocelyn because she would rather perish than wear spectacles. I would rather see. And Becky is much too young to be me."

She hooked her arm through Gillian's and started toward the door. "I can't wait to see their faces when they meet you. Richard never mentioned a word about your visit."

"It was rather an impulse on my part." The weight in Gillian's stomach returned. "Richard doesn't know."

Marianne halted, her eyes wide. "He doesn't?"

Gillian shook her head. "Do you think he'll mind?"

"I have no idea. I long ago gave up trying to guess anything whatsoever about what my brother might or might not do. He's never really been one for surprises, though." Marianne's brow furrowed. "He's been unusually reticent since his arrival, as if he has something rather pressing on his mind. Indeed, he's thrown himself into all sorts of jobs around here, not that there isn't plenty to be done." She started back toward the door. "At this very moment he's trying to fix one of any number of holes in the roof."

Gillian stopped and stared. "Good Lord, he's not on the roof, is he?"

"How else would one fix it?"

Gillian glanced up, half expecting to see Richard peering over the edge of the eaves three, no, four stories tall. The knot in her stomach twisted. "It's rather high, isn't it?"

"Oh my yes." Marianne grinned. "We can get him down if you'd like or you can go up—"

"How lovely," Gillian said under her breath.

"—there's a ladder in the back, but I think Richard used the trapdoor from the attic. Odd to have one, I know, but I suspect it was originally to serve the needs of spies or pirates—"

"Pirates?" What was this woman talking about?

"—years ago, but that could just be my own imagination. I do read a great deal. Do you read?"

"I do on occass—"

"Wonderful. Now then, you must meet the rest of the family. Aunt Louella and Jocelyn will want to know all about London and the season. And Becky will no sooner say good day than she'll be out here to meet your horses—"

"Well, they're not really—"

"—and of course we shall all want to hear how Emma is getting on. Do you think there's a chance she could really make a good match?" Marianne paused for breath and looked at her curiously. "Are you going to marry Richard?"

Gillian choked. "Am I—"

"I am sorry, that was extremely rude of me. You see, we've discussed this quite a lot and it simply makes sense that anyone willing to take in his sister would only go to such trouble if she cared a great deal about him." Marianne beamed. "And now you're here to surprise him and, well, it's altogether delightful."

"Delightful," Gillian said with a weak smile. Apparently Henry wasn't the only member of the household who had a tendency to be over-whelming.

"Come along then." Marianne pulled her toward the door. Henry trotted into the house in front of them. "Did I tell you how very much I like your hat? It's quite lovely and what a wonderful—"

"I thought you were the quiet one?" Gillian blurted.

"Oh, Emma is much more reserved than any of us, but in truth," the girl's eyes danced with laughter, "at Shelbrooke Manor, there are no quiet ones."

Chapter 12

Gillian drew a deep breath, gathered her skirt tight around her, and climbed up the wide slats of the slanted ladder leading to the roof. Richard's sisters had assured her it opened onto a flat surface running the length of the roof. She stepped out cautiously and stood with care. There was indeed a flat area and of a good size, but it was far too small for the comfort of anyone with a sensible aversion to heights.

She took a tenuous step away from the opening. It wasn't as if she was terrified of heights, she simply preferred to be closer to solid ground, where words like *plummet* and *plunge* did not linger in her mind. Still, greeting Richard here, where she was no doubt risking her life, was far more desirable than with an audience of four curious females. Not one of which could be considered *quiet*.

She glanced around, taking care to avoid looking

past the edges of the manor. It would take a bit more courage than she had at the moment to admire what she was certain would be a stunning vista of rolling green meadows and woods and fields. She was not quite ready to appreciate scenic beauty.

The level surface occupied about a third of the area. From here the roof sloped downward to the eaves. Several evenly spaced chimneys dotted the flat portion. Others, taller and wider and more decorative in design, sprouted from the slope.

Hammering rang from the back of the house, obviously coming from the slanted section of the roof. She inched toward the noise. The pounding continued, then abruptly stopped, halted by a long string of creative curses. She grinned.

"Richard?"

The obscenities stopped.

She bit back a laugh and tried again. "Is that you?"

"Gillian?" Astonishment rang in the word.

She pulled a steadying breath and stepped quickly toward the sound of his voice. She drew close enough to spot him over the edge. "Richard, how lovely to see you again."

He sat on the side of the roof, one foot braced on a chimney. He stood and shifted to stare up at her. Her insides fluttered at the precarious nature of his position. "What in the hell are you doing here?"

"Here on the roof or here in the country?"

"Both."

What was she doing here? She really had no idea

what she'd expected to gain by following him. "Why, Richard, London was simply unbearable without you."

"Was it?" A smile tugged at the corners of his mouth.

"Unbearable and quite, quite boring." She sat down, perching on the flat surface and gingerly resting her feet on the roof's downward slope. At once she felt a bit more secure. "I couldn't tolerate it one moment longer. Why, I had nothing to do but contemplate the threadbare nature of my carpet."

"I had no idea it was that bad." He pressed his lips together as if trying not to grin.

"Oh, my yes. Extremely worn. Rather a hazard, in fact."

"A hazard?"

"Indeed, someone could trip or . . ." Heat flushed up her face.

"Or?" He raised a brow.

She shifted uncomfortably on the hard surface, a painful reminder of skin scraped raw by the blasted rug.

"Or?" he said again. Amusement shone in his eyes, and she ignored the warmth in her cheeks and elsewhere.

"Or," she met his gaze directly, the level of his eyes slightly below hers, "suffer some other kind of painful injury. I should be happy to show you exactly how such a thing could happen."

He stared for a stunned moment, then burst into laughter.

She grinned back and savored the look of him. Richard's stance on the roof was as relaxed as a goat on the side of a mountain. A gentle breeze teased strands of his dark, just a bit too long, hair. Faded breeches molded to his form so closely that she wondered they didn't tear at the slightest movement. A leather pouch filled with nails hung from a strap at his waist. His shirt, too, was well worn and open at his throat, with sleeves rolled up to his elbows, revealing forearms strong and already a bit browned by the sun, evidence of a man who did indeed work out of doors. Why hadn't she noticed before?

He raised a curious brow. "Are you staring at me?"

Whether at a ball or on a rooftop, he was a handsome devil. "Yes, actually, I am." She nodded at his clothes. "I've never seen you attired like this before. It suits you."

"Does it?" He chuckled wryly. "Well then, perhaps I should abandon this earl nonsense altogether and hire myself out as a jack-of-all-trades."

"And would you prefer that to being an earl?"

"I must confess I've never considered such a thing. However, there is much to be said for honest labor. For working with one's hands. Particularly when one works out of doors. I quite enjoy it." He hefted the hammer in his hands thoughtfully, then grinned at her. "On occasion. I rather doubt I would relish it as much if I had no other choice."

She pulled her feet closer and wrapped her arms

around her knees. "Then you like your position in life?"

"Again an intriguing question, and again one I have given little thought to. Why do you ask?"

"Curiosity." She shrugged. "It strikes me that I don't know nearly as much about you as I thought I did. We have never really discussed matters like this."

"No, I suppose we haven't. Very well then." He paused for a moment to consider the question. "I do not, in general, dislike my position in life. I am rather proud of my title, and, for the most part, proud of my lineage. I am the fourteenth Earl of Shelbrooke, you know."

"And today the fourteenth Earl of Shelbrooke is patching holes in a roof," she said mildly.

He chuckled. "It does seem somewhat absurd. I'm certain my ancestors are turning over in their graves at the very thought. No doubt they were far better at wielding a sword than a hammer. What a pity I have no invaders to fight off, only rot and neglect to do battle with." His expression sobered. "It is not my lot in life that I dislike, merely the circumstances surrounding it."

"You must resent it a great deal."

"Resent it? How could I not? Still . . ." His brow furrowed in thought. "I have come to realize that the loss of my family's fortune and good name has perhaps been the best thing to happen in my life."

"Really?" She rested her chin on her knees and studied him. "What do you mean? It sounds quite awful to me."

"It has not been altogether pleasant." He shifted the hammer from hand to hand absently. "Do you recall years ago when we first met?"

"Vaguely."

"Then perhaps you don't remember the type of man I was then?"

"Not directly. But I remember your reputation. You were quite a scoundrel, according to gossip."

"Oh, I was a magnificent scoundrel. A rake and a rogue of the first order. There was no game I did not play, no wager I would not make. I left no bottle undrunk, no woman untouched." He heaved a dramatic sigh. "I had a great deal of fun."

"I can imagine," she murmured.

"There are moments when I quite miss those days." He flashed her a grin. "However, they are gone and I am here, on the roof of the home of my ancestors trying to keep the rain from the heads of my sisters because, Gillian, there is no one else to do it." He gazed out over the countryside. "This small patch of England has been in my family for generations. I never truly appreciated it until I was faced with the very real possibility of losing it all. I am the only one left who can ensure it remains for those generations yet to come."

He fell silent, and she studied his handsome profile, the determined set of his chin, the resolute gleam in his eye. She had chosen well.

"Look at it from up here, Gillian, how could I possibly let it go?"

"It's very . . . nice." Even to her own ears she did not sound entirely convinced.

His gaze shot to hers and his eyes widened with realization. "You haven't looked around at all have you?"

"Well, I did see much of it on the drive here," she said weakly.

"But from this vantage point one can see forever."

"No doubt." She grimaced as she spoke. "However, I've avoided looking at anything other than my feet and where to place them since I stepped onto this roof in an effort to avoid any horrible accidents. Plunging to my death and the like."

"You are not fond of high places?"

"Apparently not."

He laughed and held out the hammer. "Here, take this." She steeled her nerves and bent forward cautiously to grab it, trying not to look down. He scrambled up the slope of the roof to stand beside her and reached out his hand.

She hesitated.

He smiled down at her. "I won't let anything happen to you."

Her gaze caught his. Her heart leapt, and she knew she had nothing to fear. She placed her hand in his, and he pulled her to her feet and into his arms. For an instant she could do nothing but stare up into his dark eyes. Did a thousand unsaid words pass between them at that moment? Or did she only wish they had?

"You never truly kissed me, you know."

"No?" Amusement lifted the corners of his mouth. "I thought I kissed you quite thoroughly."

"Well, you did. But not . . . what I mean is . . ."
Annoying man, he knew full well what she meant.

"Are you quite certain? I couldn't possibly have
forgotten something like that. Perhaps you simply
overlooked it?"

"I doubt that." She raised her chin, her mouth a
scant few inches from his.

"So you are trying to make me believe I never
lowered my lips to yours," he said as he moved his
mouth closer. "And did anything like this?" His
lips lightly brushed hers.

"Blast it all, Richard, you did that." Obviously
she would have to take matters into her own hands.
She tossed the hammer aside, ignoring the thud
when it hit the roof.

"Careful, I have no need of yet another hole to—"

"This is what you didn't do." She threw her arms
around him and planted her lips firmly on his.

He hesitated for no more than the space of a
heartbeat, then pulled her tighter against him,
crushing her breasts to his chest. His lips greeted
hers with a hunger that matched her own. Fire shot
through her, and she clutched the warm back of his
neck. Her mouth opened, and his tongue met hers
in an exploration of greed and desire. A plundering
born of his need and her own. Her heart raced and
her knees weakened and still she couldn't get
enough. He invaded her senses, swept away her
substance until she was falling into an abyss from
which there was no escape. And no escape needed.

He pulled away and stared down at her, a bemused expression on his face, as though he too had

lost his wits for the span of a few brief moments or the length of a lifetime. His voice carried an odd, unsettled note that belied the teasing nature of his words. "Was that what you had in mind?"

She struggled to catch her breath and nodded. "Yes, well, something like that."

He laughed and kissed her again quickly, then turned her around to face the countryside before she could protest. His arms held her protectively, safely, against the strong length of his body, and she relaxed into the security of his embrace. "Now then, Gillian, look at it all."

Rolling hills and meadows stretched into the distance. Copses of trees dotted the landscape. A stream danced in the sunlight.

"I can see why you love it," she said softly, moved as much by this man's affection for the land of his forebears as by the beauty of the setting.

Endless moments stretched silently between them. A sense of serenity and contentment flowed through her. She could easily stay like this for the rest of her days, here on the top of his world, content in the warmth of his arms.

"When I stand here, overlooking this place," he said at last, "I see the past and the present and the future, all bound together by the land and the people who have come and gone and will come and go. And I feel a great responsibility to them all."

"Do you?" she murmured.

"I do. I suspect this tie to this spot of England runs in my blood. My sisters love it as well, yet they don't see it as I do." His voice was pensive.

"Emma sees the beauty: colors and patterns and textures, lines and spaces, contrasting and complementing. In Becky's eyes, it's a countryside rife with possibilities for adventure, although the hoyden has scoured every inch of it and knows it far better than even I.

"Marianne is convinced it's not merely our home but the home of fairy folk and all manner of magical creatures, unseen but there nonetheless. And Jocelyn," he chuckled wryly, "in many ways Jocelyn sees it precisely as it is: sadly in need of a great deal of work. She's too young to remember when it wasn't, but I suspect she imagines what it was like and will be again."

"And all you need is money," Gillian said softly.

She felt his body tense against hers. "Is it?"

"Well, you do get a wife in the bargain." She paused, ignoring the unease washing through her. "You haven't changed your mind, have you?"

"I would be something of a fool to do that, wouldn't I?" His arms tightened around her, and he leaned forward to rest his cheek close to hers. "What do you want from me, Gillian?"

"I . . ." What did she want? Passion? Excitement? Love? "I don't really know." She held her breath. "And what of you, Richard? What do you want from me?"

"It seems we are well matched, then." He straightened and laughed softly in the manner of a man who suspects he is the subject of the joke. "I don't know either."

"I suppose you could say, either of us could say,

we want nothing more from one another than to share my inheritance," she said lightly, hoping he'd deny it.

"Indeed you could say that." The casual tone of his voice matched her own.

Disappointment stabbed her, followed at once by irritation with herself. What did she expect from him, anyway? A declaration of undying devotion? An assertion of eternal love? If she was unwilling to so much as suggest such things aloud, how could she expect him to?

"But perhaps it's time for a question that actually has an answer," he said in a matter-of-fact way, as if they'd been discussing nothing more substantial than the prospect of rain.

"A question with an answer?" She forced a teasing note to her voice. "However will we manage?"

"However, indeed." He laughed, and she couldn't hold back a smile. "So, tell me, Gillian, have you given any more thought to your far-fetched, impossible, and more than a little foolish idea?"

"My what?"

"Didn't you say that in addition to the obvious attraction of financial independence you wanted this inheritance because of a far-fetched, impossible, and—"

"More than a little foolish idea." She nodded slowly. "I may have said something like that."

"Well, what is it?"

Her mind raced and came up with nothing but the truth. And hadn't she decided from the start she would be honest with him? Of course, she hadn't been entirely honest about Toussaint, although Richard had never asked about him, knew nothing, in fact, about the sittings, so she'd never truly lied to him.

"Gillian?"

"Well, what I've thought . . . that is, what I've decided to do . . ." According to Emma, Richard wasn't going to like this one bit. He would have to be told sooner or later, although she much preferred later. Perhaps it would be best not to tell him everything at once. To ease him into the idea gently. She gathered her courage and braced herself for his reaction. "I want to provide a place, room and board, for promising artists so they can concentrate on their work instead of merely surviving from day to day."

She cringed and waited. He was quiet for a long moment. She longed to turn and see his face, but she forced herself to keep still.

"Room and board," he said slowly. "A kind of orphanage for adults. How intriguing."

She whirled in his arms and stared up at him. "Do you really think so?"

"I do." He nodded, his brow furrowed with thought. "It would be the answer to a prayer for many with a great deal of talent who have no choice but to abandon their muse to turn their attention to keeping body and soul together."

"My thoughts exactly," she said eagerly. "I propose to buy a building, a large house or mansion, perhaps a hall or an old abbey in the country—"

"No, no, the country won't work at all." He shook his head. "The market is in London. The academy, the galleries, the dealers, even the critics."

"Very well, the city it is, then. It shouldn't be difficult to find the kind of house I have in mind." Relief coursed through her. "I can't tell you how pleased I am that you approve of the idea."

He chuckled. "I doubt Lady Forester will approve. This proposal of yours will mean far fewer artists to choose from when it comes to the kind of patronage she's always been fond of."

"Oh, Lady Forester won't mind at all. To my knowledge, she's never been particularly interested in sponsoring women anyway." The words were out of her mouth before she could catch herself.

"Women?" He frowned down at her. "What do you mean, *women?*"

"Didn't I mention that?" Gillian said brightly.

"Not that I recall."

"Oh. Well . . ." So much for easing him into the idea. "I intend for this facility to be strictly for the support of female artists."

"What kind of female artists?" His words were measured, and he released her.

She stepped away from him and the edge of the roof. If they were going to discuss this now, and apparently they were, she was not about to do battle tottering on the brink of a physical precipice as well as a verbal one. "Serious female artists."

"There are no serious female artists."

"I have encountered a few in recent years. Not many, I admit, but—"

"And have you ever stopped to consider why there are not many?"

"Why yes, I have. I have given it a great deal of thought." Annoyance surged through her. "Women, no matter how talented, are simply not taken seriously."

"Gillian, my dear, there is a reason for that." His voice carried a tolerant note, as if he were trying to explain something very basic to a very small child. Or to someone incredibly stupid.

"Is there?" She struggled to keep her voice level. "Oh please, Richard, do tell me more." He didn't seem to note the sarcasm in her voice. Surely if he had, he would have tempered his smug attitude.

"Women are suited for dabbling in watercolors or perhaps charcoal sketches. I will go so far as to say I have heard of one or two who have a fair hand at miniatures, but that's the extent of it."

She stared at him in stunned disbelief. Emma had warned her about his attitude, but she'd never expected him to be quite so, well, pompous.

"Even Emma realizes as much. I'm not sure if you're aware of it, but she paints. Watercolors, of course. Oh, certainly she was interested in more serious work once, but she has accepted the wisdom of my advice on this subject."

Gillian clenched her fists. "Has she?"

"Indeed." He smiled condescendingly. "Women simply don't have the temperament for oils, for legitimate art."

"Why, Richard, I had no idea," she smiled pleasantly. "I never so much as suspected you were quite so narrow-minded, sanctimonious, and, well, silly."

Richard's eyes widened. "Silly?"

"Don't forget sanctimonious and narrow-minded."

"I doubt I shall ever forget sanctimonious and narrow-minded." He drew himself up and stared down at her. "I have been called many things in my life, indeed I have called myself many things, but never sanctimonious and narrow-minded."

"Then I expect I should offer my congratulations on achieving new levels of smug male superiority."

"Well, men are super—" He stopped abruptly. Apparently his superior male intellect was at last understanding precisely what he was facing.

She crossed her arms over her chest. "Men are what?"

"Men are . . ." Indecision crossed his face. Finally he rolled his eyes and heaved a resigned sigh. "Sanctimonious and narrow-minded."

She bit back a smile. "And?"

"Deeply repentant." He swept an exaggerated bow. "A thousand apologies, madame."

"And?"

"And"—he studied her cautiously—"what?"

"And wrong."

"Wrong?"

"About women and *legitimate* art."

"I am sorry, Gillian, as to my high-handed manner, but," he said shaking his head, "on the subject of the suitability of women for serious work,"—he bent over and picked up the hammer—"I'm not wrong." He started toward the door.

She hurried after him. "You won't even consider the possibility?"

"No."

"Whyever not?"

He stopped, blew a long resigned breath, then turned to face her. He settled his back against a chimney and absently tapped the handle of the hammer in one palm, looking for all the world as if he was about to begin a debate in which he had no doubts as to the merits of his argument and no intention of listening to an opposing point of view.

"Marianne is convinced fairies live on the estate. Becky thinks that's complete nonsense. However, she harbors a secret belief that not only can she talk to Henry but, given enough attention, Henry will one day speak back."

"What does that have to do—"

"I am trying to make a point. To continue: Jocelyn has no doubts whatsoever that she is destined to marry at the very least a duke and possibly a king."

"And what does Emma believe?" Gillian said, intrigued in spite of herself.

"Emma is far too practical to believe in anything she can't see or hear. As am I." He shook his head. "I will admit, given Jocelyn's determined nature, she could well marry a king. But I have neither encountered fairies nor heard Henry say a single word. And I have never seen the art of a woman that is equal to that of a man. I seriously doubt I ever will."

"Perhaps you simply haven't looked."

"Perhaps. However, I consider myself rather well acquainted with the work of modern painters."

"I thought you told me you didn't know a great deal about art?"

He shrugged. "False modesty."

"It must be quite difficult, concealing your superior male qualities behind a mask of feigned humility."

"Why, Gillian, it's that very ability that makes us so superior," he said loftily, then softened his words with a teasing grin.

She should have realized from their first meeting that he was not merely an astute observer when it came to art. His comments were far too perceptive and knowledgeable for someone with nothing more than a passing interest. Now that she knew he had once painted himself, his opinions were at least based in substance. Inaccurate though they may be.

"So you don't accept what you haven't seen with your own eyes." She chose her words with care. "What if I could prove you wrong?"

"Admittedly, Gillian, it's conceivable that you could dredge up a female or two, even half a dozen, whose work is passable—possibly even acceptable. And I would gladly concede that in those instances I am wrong. But that changes nothing. In the scheme of the world as a whole the place of a woman is not before an easel. The life of an artist, especially one who has not achieved any measure of success, is extremely difficult."

"Which is precisely why I wish to help—"

"And precisely why that help should not be wasted on those who cannot possibly gain from it."

"Wait just a moment, Richard." She fisted her hands on her hips. "First you tell me women are not suited for serious work, then you tell me even for those who are, there is no place for them."

He nodded. "Exactly."

"Exactly what?"

"Exactly my point." He smiled in an all too patronizing manner. "Even if I am wrong about the abilities of women, and I daresay I'm not, but if I were there is still simply no place for them in the world of art.

"Regardless of any potential talent, you know as well as I do—you even admitted it yourself a moment ago—they are not taken seriously and never will be simply because they are women."

She drew her brows together and glared. "Well, that reeks."

He shrugged. "It's the way of the world."

"Disregarding ability and skill and intelligence just because someone had the misfortune to be born female makes no sense whatsoever." She paced back and forth in front of him.

"Possibly, but—"

"It's totally and completely unfair. Talent should be nurtured, recognized, and rewarded regardless of where it's found."

"Ideally, but—"

"And to discard the potential of fully half the population without so much as minimal consideration is stupid."

"It is?" A smile tugged at the corners of his mouth.

"This is not funny, Richard, not one bit." She halted and leveled him an irritated look.

"Of course not," he said solemnly, but laughter danced in his eyes.

"You are so infuriating." She stepped toward him and shook her finger. "You wouldn't find this even remotely amusing if the situation were reversed. If we were discussing . . . I don't know." What was it his sister had said about their father putting an end to Richard's painting? *No way for a future earl to spend his time?* "What if the issue wasn't the abilities of women or their positions in life but that of titled noblemen?"

His eyes narrowed slightly.

"What if we were talking about the talent of earls not being valued simply because they're earls?" She poked her finger at his chest. "What if we were talking about you?"

Chapter 13

❦❦❧

"About me?" Richard's words were measured, his voice cool and slightly amused. "That's rather far-fetched, isn't it?"

"Of course it is." Apparently Emma was right about Richard's reluctance to speak of his own painting no matter how long ago it was. What else could put such an odd look in his eye? "It's just an example to point out that you'd hardly find it so very humorous then."

"Actually, I would and I do." He caught her hand. "My compliments, Gillian, you understand completely. Society has certain expectations of us all, regardless of whether we are women or merely earls. In this instance, there's little difference. Whether by a female or an earl or a prince for that matter, such work would be seen as inconsequential and given no serious consideration." He pulled her finger to his lips and kissed it. "As I said, it's how the world is."

"Well, I don't like it one bit."

"I can certainly understand that." He kissed a second finger, then turned her hand and kissed her palm.

Shivers washed through her. "What are you doing?"

"Arguing with you. Or rather, disarming your argument." His gaze met hers, but his lips found the sensitive skin of her inner wrist. She was at once rather grateful she'd discarded her long-sleeved pelisse before joining him on the roof. "Is it working?"

"Not at all," she lied. His mouth trailed to the crook of her elbow. She drew a long, shuddering breath. "Are you quite certain you've reformed? You seem somewhat well practiced to me."

"It is all coming back," he murmured. "Rather like riding a horse after a long absence."

"I suspect you were excellent in the saddle." She snaked her free arm around his neck, reached up, and kissed the spot right below his ear.

"Indeed I was."

"I will not give up on this proposal of mine, Richard."

He wrapped his arm around her waist and gathered her to him, his lips nuzzling the side of her neck. "You won't?"

"No indeed." She gasped and nibbled the line of his jaw. "It's as important to me as paying off your debts is to you."

"It's a ridiculous idea." The hammer slipped from his hand and clattered at their feet with a dim distant sound, as though it were very far away. "I shall never approve."

"Will you continue to attempt to dissuade me then?" she whispered and tasted the flesh at the base of his throat.

"Whenever possible." His lips met hers, and passion flared once more between them.

Reason vanished, dashed aside by need and desire. She wanted him here. Now. And knew he wanted her. She wondered if they would sink down on this very spot on the top of the roof, entwined in each other's arms, to lay together high above the ancestral lands of the Earls of Shelbrooke with only soaring hawks and blue skies as witness. How wanton. How wonderful.

Sheer delight swept through her. Laughter echoed in her head. Delicate and high in pitch, like bells of silver or the clinking sound of fragile, costly crystal.

Richard stilled. His lips spoke against hers. "Someone is laughing at us."

"Don't be absurd." She sighed the words. How could he hear what was only in her head? "It was nothing at all." She laughed softly, the sound distinctly different than a moment ago.

Muffled giggles sounded from the direction of the attic door. A resigned grin lifted the corners of Richard's mouth.

"We are no longer alone, Gillian."

"Could it be Marianne's fairy folk?" She smiled up at him.

"Worse."

"Worse than fairies?"

"Much worse. Sisters. I would wager on at least two of them, possibly all three."

"What? No Aunt Louella among them?" Her teasing tone belied any disappointment at the knowledge that the sky and hawks would have to wait a time to bear witness to whatever might have passed between them.

"No need. She will certainly receive a full report." He drew away from her and directed a firm voice toward the opening. "You may come out now."

Silence greeted him.

"It's no use pretending. We know you're there. You might as well come up."

"You're not angry, are you?" A hesitant voice drifted from the door.

"Probably not." His voice was unyielding in spite of the smile on his face.

Becky scrambled onto the roof. "Are you showing her all of Shelbrooke Park?"

Jocelyn's head popped up in the door opening, but she made no move to join them. "Or are you doing something else altogether?" Richard narrowed his eyes, and Jocelyn stared back innocently. "Fixing the roof, perhaps?"

Richard slanted a quick glance at Gillian, then nodded. "Perhaps."

"You can see everything up here." Becky moved

to the rooftop's edge with an unconcerned manner. "It's quite wonderful. Don't you think so?"

"It is lovely." Gillian smiled and turned her attention to Jocelyn. "Aren't you joining us?"

Jocelyn heaved a theatrical sigh. "I am not permitted on the roof."

"In point of fact," Richard said, "no one is allowed up here unless I am with them."

"But Jocelyn doesn't get to come up even then." Becky's voice was smug. "The view is rather wasted on her, she can't see past the nose on her face."

"I most certainly can," Jocelyn snapped.

Becky snorted. "Hardly. Besides, she's more than likely to walk right off the edge."

"Thank you for your concern," Jocelyn said in a haughty manner. "It's always nice to know one's sisters have only one's best interests at heart."

"Indeed I do. Always." Becky's eyes widened with feigned concern. "I should hate for you to unknowingly stroll off the roof and plunge to the ground. Why, it would most certainly make a nasty mess for the rest of us to have to clean up."

"And I should pray all the way down to make the biggest mess possible," Jocelyn said in an overly sweet manner.

"That's quite enough," Richard said sharply.

Gillian stifled a laugh. Richard certainly did have his hands full with these two.

"You're right, of course, Richard." Jocelyn traded a quick glance with her sister. Despite their bickering, it was apparent to Gillian they were allies of a sort. Richard's youngest siblings might squabble endlessly, but they were no doubt cohorts when it came to serious matters. She wondered if he realized as much. "Lady Gillian, we do apologize for our behavior, don't we, Becky?"

"Oh, yes, of course," Becky said. "And we weren't trying to spy on you or anything of that nature."

"Oh, we would never suspect anything of the kind," Richard said solemnly.

"No, never." Gillian nodded.

"Still, I am curious as to what drew you up here." Richard's gaze shifted from one sister to the next and back.

"We were just wondering"—Becky seemed to choose her words with care—"that is, we were curious—"

"Just say it, Becky," Jocelyn huffed impatiently. "Lady Gillian, why exactly are you here?"

Gillian started with surprise. "I thought I'd mentioned earlier—"

"Oh, you said something vague about an invitation." Jocelyn waved dismissively.

"But we think it must be rather important for you to come all this way," Becky said. "Even though it's barely half a day's ride from London."

"Still," Jocelyn said pointedly, "it's not as if we were right around the corner."

"So we were wondering what kind of invitation." Curiosity colored Becky's words.

"Well, not what kind exactly," Jocelyn corrected. "But to what. Exactly."

Becky nodded. "And precisely whom you were inviting."

"Precisely." Jocelyn leaned forward eagerly.

In spite of the differences in their coloring and manners, at this moment they shared the exact same expectant expression, and there was no doubt they were sisters.

"Actually," Gillian said with a touch of regret, "the invitation is for Lord Shelbrooke."

"Richard?" Becky said.

"Just Richard?" Disappointment broke on Jocelyn's face.

"To what?" Richard said mildly.

Gillian hesitated, then plunged ahead. "My grandmother has a party every year at Effington Hall. It's a rather involved occasion with a ball and, of course, the Roxborough Ride."

"Ah, yes, the Ride. I have heard of it." Richard nodded.

"What is the Roxborough Ride?" Becky asked.

"It's a somewhat unusual equestrian event put on by Lady Gillian's family. Best described, from what I've heard, as a fox hunt without the fox."

"Just horses and riders then?" Becky's eyes widened. Gillian nodded. "How delightful."

Gillian smiled at the girl. "Perhaps we can arrange for you to come next year." She turned back to Richard. "It's expected that everyone in the family will attend. I should very much like for you to accompany me."

"You wish for me to escort you to this family

gathering?" He raised a brow. "Are you certain you're quite ready for that?"

She swallowed hard. "Not at all, but I really have little choice. My birthday is fast approaching, and if indeed we are to . . ."

"To what?" Jocelyn's gaze flicked from Gillian to Richard and back.

"None of your concern," Richard said coolly. Gillian's gaze met his, and once again unanswered questions hung heavy between them.

"No one ever tells us anything," Jocelyn said under her breath.

"Well, I should be on my way," Gillian said. "I had planned to travel back to London."

"Oh, but you must stay the night," Jocelyn cried. "We haven't had even a moment to talk."

"Please stay." Becky hooked her arm through Gillian's. "I can't remember the last time we had a guest, and we have any number of things to ask you."

"Well, I hadn't planned—"

"Do stay, Gillian," Richard said. "Even if you leave now, it will be dark before you arrive home, and I prefer not to consider the hazards of an unprotected woman on these roads at night. Granted our accommodations are not as grand as they once were—"

"But we have any number of unused bedchambers," Jocelyn said.

Becky nodded. "And it will take no time at all to prepare one for you."

"Besides, if you leave I will have to deal with

their disappointment." Richard chuckled. "You cannot abandon me to such a dire fate."

She laughed. "Very well, then. I'll stay."

"Wonderful." Becky led her toward the roof door. "You can tell us everything about the city."

"And everything about the season," Jocelyn added, then disappeared into the attic, her voice trailing after her. "The balls and the routs and what grand gowns the women are wearing."

"And London itself." Becky released Gillian's arm and started down the ladder. "I want to hear all about riding in the park and Astley's Amphitheatre and Vauxhall . . ." Becky vanished after her sister.

Gillian turned to start down the ladder.

"Thank you for staying." Richard smiled. "I don't wish to think of the weeping and wailing I should have had to endure if I'd let you go."

Gillian laughed. "I quite like your sisters, Richard, all of them. And since I don't think it's wise, given everything else, to invite them to grandmother's party, staying the night is the least I can do to ease their disappointment."

"Their disappointment?" His tone was lighthearted, but his eyes gleamed. "Why, Gillian, I was talking about me."

Where was the blasted man?

Gillian paced across the chamber allocated to her, with only the moonlight from the tall windows illuminating her path. She'd extinguished the lone candle long ago, suspecting it was something of a luxury in this house to burn candles indiscriminately. Besides, she had no need of candlelight. There was not much of anything to get in her way here.

Furnishings at Shelbrooke Manor were adequate but sparse, no doubt sold through the years by Richard's father. A pang shot through her at the thought. Regardless of Richard's assertion that he was a better man for his family's trials, she still regretted the difficult path he'd had to take.

Of course, all his problems would be solved if they wed. *When* they wed. And she would marry him. How could she live without him?

But was this need to be with him every moment of every day love? It certainly wasn't at all what she remembered with Charles. That had been a gentle longing, a bonding of two souls meant to be as one from the moment they first played together as mere children. They were, from the start, halves of the same whole with the same desires and needs. Their lives had fit together as perfectly as if intended by nature herself. There had never been so much as a moment of doubt, a glimmer of hesitation, a single tremor of fear.

There was scarcely a moment with Richard when there weren't questions or unease or fear. Or excitement or adventure or passion. If this was indeed love, it wasn't what she'd known before and not at all what she'd ever anticipated. So how on earth was she expected to recognize it?

She glanced at the door. She'd left it open a crack to avoid undue noise when Richard arrived. If he arrived. Oh, certainly she hadn't invited him to her room aloud, but surely he'd understood the meaning in her manner. And she couldn't possibly have mistaken the smoldering promise in his eyes.

She blew a long, frustrated breath. It was entirely possible it wasn't love at all. It might be nothing more than lust. Incredible, uncontrollable, mind-numbing lust. Desire that made her senses reel and overwhelmed all notion of propriety and restraint. Why, just look at her now. Waiting in the dark for him to appear and make her his. Over and over and over again.

She gasped. How could she think such things? This wasn't at all like her. Perhaps she was wanton after all. Could it be she just hadn't realized it before now?

Certainly men had made advances, but she had not had as much at stake with other men as she did with Richard. Perhaps their arrangement, coupled with those long years of celibacy, had left her as ready for his touch as a ripened fruit was for picking.

But hadn't Toussaint's touch done much the same to her? Hadn't he too sent chills down her spine and weakened her knees and left her gasping for breath? And didn't she live only when he was near and count the minutes and hours until she saw him again?

Of course not. What an absurd thought.

Gillian stopped short.

That was the difference, wasn't it? She didn't want to be merely in Richard's arms but in his presence, too. She didn't want to share just his bed but his life as well. She wanted to study his face when he spoke of his home, watch the way he tried not to smile when he chastised his sisters, hear his laughter ring in her ears. She wanted to debate with him and fight with him and graciously accept his apology. She grinned at the very idea.

A quiet knock sounded at the door, and it creaked open. Richard's dark silhouette appeared in the entry. "Gillian?"

She grabbed him and pulled him into the room. He resisted only long enough to close the door firmly behind him, and then she was in his arms.

"You're late," she whispered between frantic kisses.

"Am I?" he murmured against her neck. "My apologies."

"Accepted," she said breathlessly and ran her hands over his chest and the thin fabric of his shirt.

"Is there some reason why we are in the dark?" He pushed her nightrail over her shoulders and followed its progress with his lips.

"No." Her head dropped back, and it was hard to form a lucid sentence. "Although . . . there is something rather . . . thrilling about all this . . . in the dark."

"What is more mysterious and exciting than a man whose face is hidden?" He gathered the fabric of her nightclothes in one hand until his fingers met the bare flesh of her leg. "Or a man with secrets?"

"Why does everyone keep saying that to me?" she said more to herself than to him.

"I don't know." His voice was ragged. "Why?"

His question made as little sense as the comment preceding it, and she ignored it. Ignored everything but the sensations of his lips against her skin.

"Richard?" Her fingers slipped across his stomach and lower, to trail over the hard bulge of his breeches.

He sucked in a sharp breath, his answer scarcely more than a gasp. "Yes?"

"Am I wanton?" She bit the lobe of his ear in emphasis.

"If there is a just and merciful God," he mumbled, pulling her nightrail up and over her head to toss it aside in one quick motion. He scooped her into his arms and strode across the room.

"I'm serious, Richard."

He dropped her on the bed. "As am I."

"Richard."

"No." His voice sounded impatiently amid the rustle of clothes being removed. "You are not wanton."

She propped herself up on her elbows and stared at his dark form. "Are you certain?"

"I suspect I can still recognize wanton when I see it."

"Of course." Still . . . "Not even a bit?"

"Perhaps a bit." He climbed onto the bed and pulled her hard against him. His naked skin pressed to hers, warm and irresistible. "However, any skill can be improved with hard work and practice."

"Even wantonness?"

"Especially wantonness."

His lips crushed hers in a frantic greeting of hunger and greed and she met him in kind. Then, without words, each acknowledged the need for more than mere release and his kiss became a slow, measured promise of the passion to come. His mouth caressed hers with a deliberate ease that belied his arousal and the hard length of him pressing against her.

His hands trailed over her breasts, her stomach, her hips in a leisurely, teasing manner until her existence centered only on the sensations he aroused with touch and tongue. A delicious torture of sensual awareness and anticipation.

She explored him in return, running her palm over the hard planes of his chest and savoring the feel of the muscles that tensed beneath her touch. She trailed her fingers down the valley along the length of his spine and traced circles on the firm mounds of his buttocks. She kissed his lips, his neck, his shoulders and reveled in the taste of him until she knew his body with an intimacy she'd never dreamed of.

And with each passing moment, every caress, every touch her excitement grew until she could bear no more. Restraint vanished amidst an onslaught of searing heat and spiraling desire. Nothing existed, nothing mattered beyond the sheer pleasure of his touch. She lost herself in the delicious pleasure of hard work and practice. He was an unrelenting taskmaster, and she, a more than willing apprentice. Or was she the master craftsman and he a humble disciple? His heart thudded against hers and her blood throbbed in unison with his, and the differences between them blurred and melted with their union until the world itself exploded around them.

Much later, secure in his arms, she wondered if she would ever truly know all this man's secrets and realized she now had at least one of her own.

And with a smile to herself, she realized as well that there was a great deal to be said for hard work and practice.

Chapter 14

$\curvearrowright\!\!\curvearrowleft$

A few days later, the grounds of Effington Hall teemed with horses and riders, many still in the heated competition that was part and parcel of the Roxborough Ride. Others were content to watch from the sidelines. Richard had eyes for only one.

Gillian maneuvered herself and her horse through the increasingly difficult course with its obstacles, jumps, and hazards with ease. Her bearing more than anything else, proclaimed her heritage. The daughter of the Duke of Roxborough possessed a natural grace in the saddle, just as she did everywhere else.

Richard was only grateful he could acquit himself as well on the challenging Ride. Admittedly, his skills on horseback were a bit rusty, but he'd managed every section of the course with little difficulty.

There were a hundred or so participants divided into teams of about twenty riders each. The teams progressed through the Ride in a staggered manner, clearing one course before the next team began, for both ease and safety. Gillian was in the second team behind his, and he now had more than enough opportunity to study her performance. And entirely too much time to think.

They'd arrived late last night, separately as per his suggestion, although she'd agreed a certain amount of discretion was wise. Not that it would make any difference. No doubt each and every Effington here was aware that Gillian had invited a newcomer. And aware as well that she would not have done so if he was nothing but a mere acquaintance.

It was unnerving to realize the formidable Effington family would be assessing his every action. The next two days would be a trial of sorts. Gillian knew it as well as he.

"I must say, Richard," Thomas said as he trotted up beside him, "you have offended me deeply."

"Have I?" Richard pulled his brows together. "How?"

"I have invited you to take part in the Ride for years, yet you've never accepted my hospitality." Thomas nodded toward Gillian's figure on the course. "Apparently, I simply didn't know how to ask."

Richard's gaze followed his. "She is much prettier than you are, Thomas."

"Thank God." Thomas laughed, then sobered. "She is also my sister."

"I am well aware of that," Richard said mildly.

"And you are probably my closest friend."

"I am aware of that as well."

Thomas leaned toward him, his voice lowered. "Then why in the name of all that's holy have you been avoiding me?"

"I haven't been—"

Thomas snorted. "Of course you have. When I last came to pick up a painting, you weren't even there although I'd sent you a note and you should have been expecting me. I simply walked right in. You must learn to lock your doors."

Richard shrugged. "There is nothing in my rooms worth stealing."

"Well, you could certainly be a better host." Thomas huffed. "I was forced to drink two full glasses of that disgusting stuff you call brandy while waiting for you—and you never did arrive."

"My heartfelt apologies," Richard chuckled.

"If I were a more suspicious man I would think your obvious aversion to my presence in recent days has something to do with the rumors spreading through the *ton*."

"Rumors? What kind of rumors?"

"Oh, you know, the typical kind of speculation that usually occurs when a lady who has never been seen in the company of any men save her oldest friends is suddenly noticed to be the object of attention of a gentleman who is widely known for his reserved and indifferent manner. A gentleman who, while once enjoying something of a notorious reputation, has not publicly directed his regard to any woman in years. And has, in fact, reformed to the point of reclusiveness and utter boredom."

"Boredom?" Richard said indignantly. "Do you think I'm boring? Now I'm offended."

"It's not what I think but what the rest of the world thinks. After all, I know how you spend your days. I and I alone know the true identity of Etienne-Louis Toussaint." Thomas studied him carefully. "Or am I mistaken? Does Gillian know as well?"

"No," Richard said, his tone a bit sharper than he'd intended.

Thomas chose his words with care. "What precisely is your relationship with my sister?"

"Are you asking me my intentions?"

"Father was unable to be here so apparently, that leaves me as the head of the family, although I wouldn't wish to mention the fact to my grandmother." Thomas nodded slowly. "I am indeed asking about your intentions toward Gillian."

Richard drew a deep breath. He knew this discussion was inevitable. Knew as well that it would occur during his stay at Effington Hall. Still . . . "Very well, Thomas. You're right. I have been avoiding you, and we do have a number of things to discuss. But this is neither the time nor the place."

"Absolutely right. However," Thomas grinned, "if I recall you once played a wicked game of billiards."

"Rather a long time ago. It's awkward to play when one cannot afford to wager on the outcome of the game."

"Even so, such skills once learned tend to return when called upon. And I'm certain we can come up with appropriate stakes. Effington Hall has an outstanding billiards room. I cannot think of a more perfect place to hold such a discussion. Perhaps tomorrow evening, before the ball?"

Richard nodded.

"Excellent. I shall thoroughly enjoy trouncing you."

Richard raised a brow. "Even at my worst, I was always better than you."

"We shall see." Thomas laughed.

They exchanged a few more bantering comments, with Richard carefully avoiding the subject of Gillian, then Thomas was hailed by a woman on horseback and rode off to join her.

Richard's gaze drifted back to Gillian. What were his intentions? And why weren't they clearer in his own mind?

He could indeed now marry her and share her inheritance. She had certainly proved she could fully be his wife. He grinned at the thought of just how well she had proved it. His only condition to her proposal had been that she share his bed. Now that she had, why did he hesitate? Why didn't he marry her at once?

He'd wanted a wife who wanted him, and that was precisely what he could now have. Was it no longer enough? Did he want not just her body but her soul? Not just her hand but her heart? Her affection? Her love?

Did he want her to love him? And if he did, why? No doubt it was nothing more than a point of pride with him. Damnable pride.

The very notion of love was absurd. He'd never given any consideration to the emotion. Never particularly looked for it or longed for it. He had no idea if he'd even recognize it if he saw it. Besides, love was not part of their agreement. Should it be? And why did he care?

Gillian sailed over a particularly difficult jump, and Richard's heart caught in his throat. She had no concept of the dangerous nature of the obstacles on the course. She was indeed an excellent rider, but even the most experienced equestrian could take a serious fall. If anything were to happen to her—

The thought pulled him up short.

Surely he wasn't falling in love with her? She filled his mind from dawn to dusk and lingered in his dreams when he slept. And yes, even his work could not erase her fully from his thoughts. And indeed, he seemed to truly live only when she was with him. And had he ever before lain with a woman whose touch inflamed not merely his flesh but reached into his very soul?

He pulled a shaky breath. Was this, then, love?

Gillian's laughter drifted through the air and shivered in his blood.

Was that why he was reluctant to forge ahead with their agreement? If indeed he loved her, could he marry a woman who did not love him in return?

Gillian was right when she'd told him, or rather told Toussaint, it had all become complicated and quite confusing. He knew exactly what he'd wanted when they'd begun. But now . . .

A rider called to him, and he headed back to join his team and continue the competition. The next section of the course was the most difficult so far, and he looked forward to it eagerly. It would take all his concentration to make it through without mishap.

And for the next few minutes at least he could banish any disturbing questions regarding his chaotic emotions and all thoughts of, perhaps, the woman he loved.

Gillian had scarcely spoken two words to Richard all day, as she was far too caught up in the exhilaration of the Ride and reacquainting herself with friends and relatives she rarely saw more than once a year. Whenever she caught his eye, he'd smile wryly, although he did seem to be having an enjoyable day.

Now she and her cousin Pandora stood near the lake that marked the end of the course. Here, long tables overflowed with a veritable feast of meats and breads and all manner of sweets to suit the voracious appetites of riders and onlookers alike.

Pandora's gaze was locked on the sight of a sodden, but triumphant, Earl of Trent, who had just emerged from a rather amusing display in the water, part of the odd wager Pandora had with the man. The stakes were nothing less than marriage.

"Do you love him?" Gillian said.

Pandora shrugged. "Is it a completely unpleasant emotion?"

Gillian laughed. "It gets better. And what of the earl?"

Her cousin's voice was wistful. "I wish I knew."

"You don't think this is an indication? After all, the man has put on a rather ridiculous, although vastly entertaining, public display. For you."

"He's very competitive. He wants to win."

"What he wants is you." *Not your legacy, not your presence in his bed, just you.* Gillian pushed the annoying thought aside.

"That much I know," Pandora said sharply. "What I don't know is why. Am I a reward for winning? Or does he truly care for me?"

"You could always ask him." Gillian kept her voice light. Why was it so much easier to give advice than heed it?

"I've tried."

"Have you?"

"Well, I've never actually said 'Do you love me?' But I have given him more than ample opportunity to tell me of his feelings. Whatever they may be."

"Pandora, men are truly charming creatures, relatively intelligent on occasion and more than competent to chose a good horse or a fine brandy, but when it comes to things like love, they rarely seem to know what's in their own hearts." What was in Richard's heart? She only wished she knew.

She laid a hand on Pandora's arm. "Ask him.

Trent will give you an honest answer, and honesty between a man and a woman is as important as trust. And love." *Trust?* Could she trust a man with secrets? The more she learned about Richard, the more she discovered she didn't know at all.

"I can't." Pandora shook her head.

"Because you're afraid of the answer?"

"Perhaps. Besides, I don't want to force him into some kind of halfhearted admission. I want him to tell me how he feels."

"Poor Trent. Effington stubbornness is always a force to be reckoned with."

Pandora raised a brow. "You are scarcely one to point fingers."

Gillian laughed. "I'll grant you that."

"So what do I do? How am I to know how he feels?"

Gillian pulled her thoughts together. How indeed? How did you determine how any man truly felt? Odd, reticent creatures that they were. Her words were measured. "It's always seemed to me, the relationship between men and women is very much like that of hounds and foxes."

Pandora groaned. "So I've been told."

"A very good hound will chase a fox until he drops from exhaustion. A lazy hound, a hound whose heart isn't in the hunt, will lose interest. But a hound who truly wants the fox will let nothing stop him. He'll follow the fox anywhere and follow him forever." Gillian studied Trent. "That seems to be a rather determined hound."

"As of today, the possibility of his winning our

game is excellent, and I will not marry him unless he loves me," Pandora said firmly.

Gillian's gaze snapped to hers. "How will you avoid it?"

"I have no idea. But it does appear I have now become the fox, and the hound is gaining fast. I have to find a way to both elude the beast and determine if his heart is truly in the hunt."

"If his heart is in the hunt . . ." Gillian murmured. Where was Richard's heart in the odd game they were playing?

"So, Gillian, tell me." Pandora glanced around and nodded. Gillian followed her gaze. Richard stood talking with two of her aunts. "Are you the fox or the hound?"

"Neither. Or perhaps both." Gillian heaved a frustrated sigh. "Actually, Pandora, I'm not involved in, well, a hunt at all."

"No?" Pandora raised a brow. "Then do tell me precisely what you are involved in?"

"Well, I . . ." What was she involved in? Her mother joined the group around Richard, and Gillian groaned to herself. "I really don't know."

"You'd best sort it out, and quickly. It's not at all fair to subject a gentleman, any gentleman, to the scrutiny of the Effington females unless it is well worth his while. As I suspect it is."

"Pandora!"

"Come now, Gillian." Her cousin's eyes twinkled. "After all, as far as I can recall you have never brought a guest to Grandmother's party before."

"I have too," Gillian said indignantly.

Pandora waved dismissively. "Oh, Weston and Cummings perhaps, but they are your oldest friends and scarcely count. You've never brought anyone like him before." She studied Richard curiously. "Is he as interesting as he looks?"

Gillian sighed in surrender. "More."

"I see." Pandora considered her for a moment. "Gillian, what are your plans for this man?"

Gillian drew a deep breath. Her gaze lingered on Richard. "I suspect I shall marry him."

"Then let me ask you what you asked me: do you love him?"

Do I? "Perhaps."

"Perhaps? Then does he love you?"

Does he? Could he? "I don't know."

"Then it seems to me you should follow your own advice."

"Oh?" Gillian glanced at Pandora. "And which of my sage words of wisdom would you suggest?"

"The simplest and possibly the most difficult as well." Pandora favored her with a smug smile. "Ask him."

"There it is." Gillian's horse delicately stepped around one tree, then another, and into the clearing.

"And what, exactly, is it?" Richard's wry voice sounded behind her.

"It's a temple, of course, a Greek temple." She slipped off her horse and wrapped the reins around a low-hanging branch. The small white structure glowed in the dappled, late afternoon sunlight.

Round in shape, with a domed roof supported by equally spaced columns, it sat on a base two steps high, like a fancy cake with white sugar frosting on a fine china plate.

"Of course." Richard trailed after her. "Silly of me not to have realized it. One often finds Greek temples lurking in the woods of English estates. Sneaky things, temples."

"You do have to watch them every minute." She studied the building affectionately. "This one is quite special."

"Is it?"

"Indeed it is." Absently she took off her gloves and removed her hat. "I spent a great deal of my childhood playing games right here with Kit and Robin and . . ."

"Charles?"

She nodded, her mind drifting back through the years.

"I am sorry, I didn't mean to—"

Her gaze met his. Sympathy shone in his eyes.

"It's quite all right," she said with a smile. "I have nothing but the fondest memories of those days." She climbed the shallow stairs and stepped into the temple.

He followed her. "It's a bit odd though, isn't it? For a girl to have male playmates?"

"Probably. But then my family has always been a bit unusual." She dropped her hat and gloves onto one of the curved benches that occupied alternate spaces between the columns. "Charles's and Kit's and Robin's family estates all border this one.

I can't recall how the four of us grew so close and why Thomas was never one of our party although I suspect it was because he was a bit older and the heir."

She walked slowly around the perimeter of the circular floor, trailing her fingers over the cool marble. "We, all four of us, really grew up here." She looked at him over her shoulder. "Did I tell you it was called the Duchess' Folly?"

"No." He shook his head. "Why?"

She crossed to the far side of the structure and nodded at the landscape. "You can see the lake from here but you can't see the temple from the lake, and it does seem rather foolish to locate something like this where it can't be seen. My grandfather built it for my grandmother shortly after they were married. Whenever anyone has the audacity to ask why he placed it here, she simply smiles a rather private smile."

"But she doesn't explain?"

"Never." Gillian crossed her arms and settled against a column. "It is a beautiful spot, though. Peaceful and serene and secluded."

"And special," he said softly.

She slanted him a quick glance. He leaned against the column closest to hers and stared at her intently. "Very special." Her gaze returned to fix on the lake, but her mind's eye saw the years gone by. "This folly has been witness to two generations of Effingtons. It's seen any number of declarations of love and proposals of marriage. It's been the site as well of heartbreak and deception.

"For imaginative children, it's served as everything from a ship sailing off to unknown adventures to a fort in the wilds of America besieged by savages to a castle high amid the clouds guarded by fire-breathing dragons—"

"With a princess or simply the daughter of a duke?"

She smiled. "Without question a princess. Ever so much better than the daughter of a duke."

"And was the princess waiting for rescue by a handsome knight?"

She adopted a dramatically haughty manner. "Why, nothing less would serve. That is, after all, what princesses trapped in castles by fire-breathing dragons do."

"And was Charles the knight riding to the rescue?" His manner was offhand.

"It was as likely to be Kit or Robin then," she said quickly and turned her gaze back to the lake and the past. Richard was right of course: Charles was, more often than not in their silly games, her knight. And eventually, her love. "I loved them all dearly."

"But it was Charles who captured the heart of the fair Princess Gillian."

"Yes, it was Charles." A touch of sadness lingered in her heart whenever she thought of Charles and probably always would, but she could talk about her husband now without pain or grief. Odd how the years had at last healed the anguish of his loss.

"It must have been very hard," he hesitated, "when he . . ."

"Was killed." She paused, wondering that she could say the words so easily now. "I was devastated. I thought I'd never be able to go on without him. And I didn't, not really, not for a very long time." She met his gaze directly. "But the time came when I did."

"I'm glad," he said simply, the look in his eyes dark and intense, and her breath caught.

"As am I."

For a long moment they stared. The air around them sparked with the tension of unsaid words. Silent declarations. Unspoken promises. She could follow her own advice, should follow her own advice, and simply ask him. What was he thinking? What was he feeling? Did he love her? Could he love her? But the fear she'd thought she'd conquered swept through her, and she couldn't form the words. Couldn't face his answer.

"So," he said, in a strange, strangled voice, as if he, too, was fighting to keep his wits about him. "Were there other games played here besides princess and knight?"

"All kinds of games." Relief coursed through her at the abrupt change to a far safer subject. "Let me think." She ticked them off on her fingers. "Horse and rider and hot cockles and hide-and-seek and . . ." She grinned. "I'll show you one that was a great favorite for years." She picked up her hat and gloves and stepped out of the temple, backing away until she could see the top of the dome.

Richard walked after her with a curious half smile. "What kind of game is this?"

"Do you see the finial on the roof?" An ornate brass rod crowned the top of the dome. He nodded. "We used to take a hat, actually *they* used to take a hat—usually one of mine—and try to toss it onto the spindle."

"Did any of you ever succeed?" His tone was skeptical.

She laughed. "A couple of times."

He narrowed his eyes and studied the brass rod glittering in the sun. "How did you get it down?"

Gillian nodded at a nearby oak. "One of us would climb up there, inch out on that thick branch that hangs over the temple, and flip the hat off with a long stick."

"It looks rather tricky to me."

"I think the tree is a lot taller than it used to be." She shook her head. "Silly game, I know, but we'd spend hours trying. It was quite a challenge."

"Did you ever make it?" he said thoughtfully.

"Kit's the only one who ever managed it. Twice, if I remember right."

"Charles never did?"

"No." She drew out the word slowly and shook her head. "What are you—"

"Give me your hat." He held out his hand.

"I will not!" She snatched the bonnet out of his reach and hid it behind her back. "Richard, this is the only hat I own that matches my riding dress, and I refuse to let you throw it anywhere, let alone on top of the temple."

He shrugged and moved toward her. "I doubt if I can manage it at any rate. I haven't tossed hats for years. It never was a great skill of mine."

She moved back. "It may well be years before you have an opportunity. You shall not toss this one."

"Oh, come now, Gillian." He grinned. "If you didn't want me to attempt this, you would have left it on the bench where it was safe. You can't fool me. You want me to try."

"That's ridiculous. I want nothing of the sort." She took another step backward and tried not to laugh. "Was this the kind of nasty little boy you were? I can see you now, trying to steal bonnets from unsuspecting little girls."

"I was a wicked child, but I never once stole a hat from a girl." An equally wicked light shone in his eyes, and again he stepped toward her. "A kiss, perhaps, from little girls. Unsuspecting or otherwise."

"A kiss? Not merely wicked but quite advanced for a mere boy, don't you think?"

"Some of us grow up faster than others. Now." He drew closer. "Give me your hat."

"Absolutely not." She laughed and pulled it from behind her to clutch it to her chest, its long plume bobbing at him like a floppy sword. "Never."

"You're going to back into that tree behind you, and then I'll have you precisely where I want you."

"Tree? Hah! I'm not falling for that. I know every—" She smacked into something rough and solid and knew without a doubt exactly what it was. "I did that deliberately, you know," she said in her loftiest manner.

"Did you?" He rested his forearm on the bark directly over her head and gazed down at her. "To what purpose?"

"Purpose?" Barely the span of a hand separated his body from hers, and at once the familiar, sweet ache of desire throbbed deep within her. "To force a trade perhaps."

"What do you propose?" His voice was lazy, enticing. His gaze flicked to her mouth, and without thinking she moistened her lips. His gaze drifted back to mesh with hers.

"Well . . ." She raised her chin in an unspoken challenge. "What did you say you stole as a wicked boy?"

He laughed and bent his mouth to hers. She closed her eyes and wondered if it was at all possible that the exquisite delight that surged through her whenever their lips touched would do so every time they kissed.

Without warning, he straightened and snatched the hat from her unresisting hands. She snapped her eyes open. "Richard, that wasn't at all fair."

"Once again, it's the way of the world." He grinned and headed toward the temple.

"You really are wicked, you know." She hurried after him.

"It is my nature, Gillian. It's why women find me charming and irresistible."

"I don't find you irresistible at all."

He stopped and turned so suddenly that she nearly stumbled into him. "You don't?"

"No!"

"Not even a bit?" His tone was hopeful.

"Perhaps a bit."

"Only a bit?" He flashed a grin.

She laughed in surrender. "Very well, more than a bit. Now give me back my hat." She gazed at it longingly. It was a pretty little thing, claret colored to match her habit, with a long, full feather dyed a becoming shade of green.

He hefted it in his hand. "It's not going to be easy. It has no weight to it whatsoever."

"Then let me have it!" She grabbed for it, but he pulled it out of her reach, turned, and strode toward the temple. She sighed and followed.

He paused, his gaze assessing, then nodded. "I'll try it from here."

"Richard, this is ridiculous."

"No doubt of that," he said absently.

"You can't possibly succeed."

"You're probably right."

"If you're trying to prove a point, I told you Charles never managed to—"

"Charles has nothing to do with this," he said mildly.

"Then why—"

At once he turned, pulled her close with his free arm, and kissed her hard and long. Then he drew back and smiled down at her. "I never had the pleasure of rescuing the fair Princess Gillian from a fire-breathing dragon."

"Oh." It was more a sigh than a word. How could the blasted man affect her like this?

His smile widened. "The least you can do is allow me the opportunity to toss your hat." He kissed her quickly. "Just once."

"Very well." She huffed, and he released her. "But you get only one try."

"One is all I'll need."

She snorted. "I do hope your ability lives up to your confidence."

He ignored her, took careful aim, and tossed the hat. It sailed heavenward in a graceful arc, and for a moment she thought he'd actually succeed. Then a gust of wind caught the bonnet and carried it higher, until it snagged in the branches of the tree directly above the temple.

She slanted him a pointed glance.

He stared up at the oak. "Damned close I'd say. Pity." He brushed off his hands. "Well, that's that then. Let's go."

"Go? What about my hat?"

He looked at her cautiously. "It's in the tree."

"I know it's in the tree." She crossed her arms over her chest. "How do you plan on getting it down?"

"I don't." He nodded and started toward his horse.

"Then I suppose I shall have to."

He turned and considered her carefully. "You're going to climb the tree?"

"Granted, it's been a long time."

"But you have climbed it before?"

"Perhaps not that particular tree . . ."

He raised a brow.

"Very well," she snapped. "Not that tree at all."

He rolled his eyes toward the heavens and took off his jacket. "Find me a rock."

"What are you going to do?"

"I'm going to try to knock it out of the tree." He tossed the jacket onto a nearby bush.

"I do hope your aim is better with rocks than bonnets," she muttered and searched the ground. It wasn't an especially rocky area, but within a minute or so she'd found three good-sized stones and held them out.

He selected one, took aim, and let it fly. The rock sailed past the hat. She bit back a laugh.

He glanced at her. "I suppose you can do better?"

"Perhaps." She shrugged, handed him one stone, and kept the second.

"After you, my lady." He swept a sarcastic bow.

She took careful aim and threw as hard as she could. The rock bounced off the top of the temple. Richard smirked. "Good try."

She smirked back. "You will probably need a few more stones."

He laughed and threw the last rock. It hit the hat squarely. The bonnet tumbled out of the tree, missed the finial by a hairsbreadth, and slid down the dome to fall to the grass at the base of the temple. Richard stepped to it and plucked it from the ground. He turned and presented it to her with a flourish. "Your crown, Princess Gillian."

She accepted the hat and bobbed a curtsey. "I am in your eternal debt, noble knight."

"Eternal?" His tone was light, belying the serious look in his eyes. "That's a very long time."

Her heart caught in her throat, and she nodded. "It is, isn't it?"

For a long moment neither spoke. Gillian wasn't sure what to say. She wanted to tell him she thought—she was fairly certain—she loved him. Wanted to hear him say it in return. But the words wouldn't come. He smiled slowly and picked up his jacket. She exhaled a breath she didn't know she'd held.

"We should probably get back." He offered his hand, and she didn't hesitate to take it. Warmth flowed through her. Perhaps the time wasn't right. Not yet.

They walked in companionable silence to the horses, and he helped her mount, then swung up into his own saddle. He turned and stared back at the temple for a long moment.

"It really is special, isn't it?" she said softly.

"Indeed it is." A pensive note colored his voice as if he was thinking of something else altogether. "It lacks only one thing."

"What would that be?"

He grinned. "A hat."

Chapter 15

～◯◯～

Richard took careful aim, drew back the cue, and tapped the red ball firmly. It rolled across the table, deflected off the right side, and gently smacked a white ball, propelling it into a side pocket.

"I see you haven't lost your touch," Thomas said wryly.

"It's all in the wrist, old man." Richard straightened and grinned. "Another game?"

"Why not?" Thomas gathered the balls, arranged them on the green cloth surface, then took his position at the end of the table. "Grandmother's party doesn't begin for another hour yet." He positioned a ball, struck it firmly with the cue, and watched it rebound from the end cushion.

There were far worse ways to pass the time, and the billiards room at Effington Hall was as opulent as the rest of the grand house. Richard hadn't fully appreciated the difference between Gillian's family background and his own until he'd come face to face with it. While Shelbrooke Manor and Effington Hall were comparable in design, the similarities ended there. Effington Hall was twice the size of the manor, beautifully furnished, and well maintained with a staff of servants to see to its occupants' every need. Shelbrooke Manor was very much a poor relation in comparison.

It chafed a bit, knowing he could not provide this kind of luxury for Gillian without the inheritance that was by rights hers alone. He could take some comfort in knowing she could not acquire it without him—still, the knowledge nagged at him.

"Now then, Richard." Thomas cleared his throat. Regardless of his comments yesterday, Richard had the distinct impression his friend had no idea where to begin this query into Richard's intentions toward his sister.

"Spit it out, Thomas."

"Very well. What precisely is going on between you and Gillian?"

Richard strolled around the table to Thomas's side, studying the position of his opponent's ball. He chose a shot. "Precisely?"

"Yes," Thomas huffed. "Precisely."

"Well." Richard leaned over the table and positioned his cue. "I rather expect I'll marry her." He hit the ball. It rebounded from the far end and rolled back to beat Thomas's attempt by a good two inches. "Is that precisely enough for you?"

"Nice shot." Thomas stared at the table.

Richard raised a brow.

"Oh, about Gillian, you mean." Thomas shrugged. "Yes, I suppose that answers my question, but I must say I'm rather confused. As far as I knew, other than that salon she invited you to, I was under the impression you were scarcely so much as acquainted."

"At that point we were. Now, however, we know each other much better." Much, much better. He stifled a smile. "You don't seem terribly surprised, or concerned by my announcement."

"I'm not. For Gillian to invite you here in the first place says a great deal about the serious nature of your relationship, though most of us expect that she'll never remarry at all."

"And never someone like me."

"Frankly, when it comes to Gillian's preferences in gentlemen, we had no expectations whatsoever. As far as the family knows, Charles is the only man she's ever been involved with. Her name hasn't been linked with anyone since his death. You know as well as I, it's impossible to keep any kind of affair secret from the *ton*. But there's never been a hint of gossip or rumor about her and any man until recently."

"Until me." Richard considered his next shot.

"As for any concern on my part," Thomas grinned, "I can't think of anyone I'd rather have as a brother." He studied Richard thoughtfully. "However, I am still a bit perplexed about one aspect of all this."

"Yes?" Richard said absently, positioning his cue.

"I can understand why Gillian might wish to marry you, but, well, I don't understand why you would wish to marry her."

Richard's cue slipped and his ball veered away from its intended target. "Oh?"

Thomas grinned, leaned his cue against the table, and stepped to a nearby sideboard bearing a decanter of brandy and several glasses. He poured two snifters and offered one to Richard. "Here. You'll find this much more palatable than the swill you're used to drinking."

Richard accepted the fine crystal glass and pulled a long, bracing swallow. "Nectar of the gods."

"There's nothing better than good brandy." Thomas took an appreciative sip. "When you married, in spite of your reluctance to do so, I'd always assumed it would be to alleviate your financial troubles. I know how frustrated you've been by the speed at which you've been able to pay off your father's debts."

"Or rather the lack of speed," Richard muttered.

"With your title and your now respectable reputation, you've had no end of opportunities to select a bride with excellent prospects or a substantial dowry. So," he paused, "why have you settled on Gillian?"

Richard laughed. "Have you so little faith in your sister's charms?"

"Of course not." Thomas had the good grace to look abashed. "It's simply that this liaison was not anything I would have foreseen." He swirled the brandy in his glass. "Now, answer the question: why Gillian?"

"It's really quite simple, Thomas." Richard kept his tone casual. "She asked me."

"What?" Thomas's brow furrowed with confusion. "She asked you? Why on earth would she do that?"

"I see you have no faith in my charms either."

"Faith has nothing to do with it." Suspicion sounded in Thomas's voice. "What is going on here, Richard?"

"Precisely?" he said with a smile.

"Precisely." Thomas's eyes narrowed.

Richard stared at the brandy in his glass and considered his options. Eventually, Gillian's entire family would learn of the inheritance. His own financial standing was known well enough that no one would imagine that their newfound wealth after their marriage was his doing, and the truth would come out. Thomas already knew all his secrets and had kept them well. Gillian's brother was perhaps the only person in the world Richard truly trusted.

"Will you give me your word you will not repeat this?"

Thomas's brows pulled together, and his tone was cautious. "Certainly."

Richard drew a deep breath. "Are you familiar with your relations in America?"

"My grandfather's brothers?"

Richard nodded.

"I'm aware of their existence, but I really know very little about them."

"Well, Thomas, I hate to be the bearer of bad news, but one has recently died. He did, however, leave a considerable fortune. And he bequeathed it to your sister." Quickly, Richard told Thomas the details of Gillian's legacy and the conditions it carried.

Thomas blew a long, low whistle. "Six hundred thousand pounds, eight ships—"

"More or less."

"And a great deal of land." Thomas's eyes glazed with shock.

"In America," Richard added and watched Thomas carefully. Under other circumstances, the stunned look on his friend's face would have been amusing.

"Bloody hell." Thomas downed the rest of his drink. "And you say Gillian has agreed to a real marriage between the two of you?"

Richard nodded. He hadn't told Thomas all the specific details of his agreement with Gillian and how she had fully proved she could live up to them. Thomas was, after all, her brother.

"Then I have but one question." A slow grin spread across Thomas's face. "When is the wedding?"

"The wedding?" Richard wasn't sure what kind of reaction he'd expected, but this wasn't it. "Then you approve?"

"Approve?" Thomas slapped him on the back. "Of course, I approve. I can't blame Gillian for

wanting such a fortune. I'm only grateful she selected you. She had a list, you say?"

Richard nodded.

"A list. And you at the top of it." Thomas chuckled. "Well, she's always been rather too independent for a woman. This solves her problems and
yours as well. It's perfect for both of you." He
shook his head in disbelief. "Six hundred thousand
pounds."

Richard smiled wryly. "Not to mention the ships
and the land."

Thomas turned to the sideboard and refilled his
glass, then offered the decanter to Richard. Richard
held out his snifter and Thomas obligingly
splashed in the liquor, then replaced the decanter.

"I must say, I'm relieved by your reaction," Richard said. "How do you think the rest of your family
will take this?"

"You've already made a good impression on my
mother and my aunts."

"Have I?"

Thomas laughed. "Don't think for a moment you
haven't been the subject of a great deal of discussion since your arrival. From what my mother
said"—Richard raised a brow—"oh yes, I have
been thoroughly quizzed about you. At any rate
she said you were quite charming without being
overbearing. They like that."

"What about my past?" He hesitated. "My father?"

Thomas shrugged. "Your father's actions are of
no concern to my family. We Effingtons tend to

judge a man more by who he is rather than his parentage. Odd, I know, but there you have it. After all, there are any number in our lineage who were scoundrels in their own day.

"As for your past," Thomas lifted his glass to him, "you are a reformed rake, and the Effington women, one and all, are of the opinion a reformed rake makes the best husband."

"So there should be no objections," Richard said under his breath.

"Then why are you hesitating?" Thomas's voice was sharp.

"I'm not—"

"Oh, but you are." Thomas's gaze pinned his. "Don't forget, Richard, I know you nearly as well as you know yourself. In this case, perhaps even better. Besides, you said you rather expected to marry her. Not entirely definitive to my mind." His voice softened. "This is the answer to your prayers and you may be the best thing to happen to my sister in years, so why, old friend, are you reluctant to see it through?"

"I'm not . . ." Richard shook his head. "I don't know."

Thomas stared for a long, considering moment. Then his eyes widened and he laughed.

"There is nothing funny about this," Richard said indignantly. "This is about my future and your sister's future as well. What do you find in this situation that's even remotely amusing?"

"You." Thomas aimed his glass at him. "You're in love with her."

"I am not." Even to his own ears, his denial lacked a ring of truth.

"Oh, you may not want to admit it—"

"Because it's not true." Why was there no conviction in his voice?

"No?" Thomas snorted. "I've known you for too many years, Richard, to accept that. If you didn't love her you would have procured a special license and be married by now."

"I have a special license," he muttered. "I got it when this whole thing began."

"But you haven't used it. Why not?"

Why not indeed? Hadn't he been asking himself the same question? "The opportunity hasn't—"

"Come now. What utter nonsense. I don't believe it for a moment. What I do believe is, because you love her—"

"I don't know that."

"—you are now finding it difficult to go ahead with this arrangement because . . ." Thomas eyed him with the same concentration he'd use to study a billiards shot. "In spite of the promise of great fortune that alone isn't enough."

"No?" Richard downed his brandy, set the glass on the sideboard, then turned back to the billiards table. He picked up the red ball and shifted it from hand to hand. "Well then, Thomas, since you seem to have a better grasp on all this than I do, you tell me. If six hundred thousand pounds, eight ships—"

"More or less."

"—and land in America isn't enough, what is?"

"Love." Thomas smirked.

"Love?" Richard scoffed. "I told you, I don't—"

"Oh, but you do. Only a man in love would sport a smile as stupid as the one on your face. You look like a smitten schoolboy. And what you're waiting for," Thomas paused dramatically, "is for her to love you as well."

"I rather doubt that." Richard's voice was firm, but his stomach twisted at the abrupt realization that Thomas was more than likely right.

"You really needn't worry, old man, I suspect Gillian does indeed love you."

"Why would you say that?" Richard said slowly.

"She brought you, for one thing. She could have simply married you without subjecting you to the scrutiny of the whole family. Besides, regardless of the circumstances, I rather doubt my sister would truly marry anyone she didn't love."

"Do you think so?" Richard kept his manner offhand, but he couldn't hold back a smile.

"I do," Thomas grinned.

An odd sense of joy washed through Richard. Was Thomas right? Did Gillian indeed love him?

"Richard loves Gillian," Thomas said in a singsong manner.

"Now who's acting like a schoolboy?"

"I can't help it. I find it quite entertaining, and I can scarcely wait to see what happens next. You get my sister, you both get an impressive fortune," Thomas's grin widened, "and Gillian gets Etienne-Louis Toussaint in the bargain."

"Ah yes." Richard's smile faded. "Etienne-Louis. How could I have forgotten?"

Thomas frowned. "Whatever is the matter now, Richard? No doubt Gillian will be delighted by the revelation of your secret life."

"Delighted might not be the appropriate word," Richard said under his breath.

"Why on earth not? I daresay she's—"

The door to the billiards room swung open, and a small, elderly lady with a regal bearing stepped into the room. "Good evening, Thomas."

"Grandmother." Thomas set his glass on the table and hurried to her side. She tilted her face toward him, and he placed an affectionate kiss on her cheek.

So this was the dowager duchess, the matriarch of the Effington family. By reputation she was quite formidable, but Gillian had assured him she was not as daunting as she might appear. Still, Richard had no experience with dowagers of any sort, let alone those who headed large, noble, and wealthy families.

"Grandmother," Thomas turned to Richard, "I don't think you've met the Earl of Shelbrooke yet."

"No, but I have heard a great deal about him." She held out her hand.

Richard dropped the ball onto the table, stepped to her, and took her hand in his. He bowed and brushed his lips across it. "Your Grace."

He straightened, and her gaze met his. Her eyes were blue and bright and nearly the same shade as Gillian's. An amused light twinkled there.

"Thomas," she said without looking at her grandson, "are you finished with your game?"

"Not quite."

"Even so you may take your leave," she said, her manner pleasant but firm.

"Grandmother, do you really think—"

"Yes, Thomas, I do."

A distinct look of unease crossed Thomas's face. He glanced at Richard apologetically. "Very well, then. Richard." He nodded and left the room, closing the door behind him.

The dowager smiled. "He's quite concerned for you, my lord, but I can assure you I am not the dragon you may think."

"I thought nothing of the sort, madam."

She laughed. "Liar."

He grinned. "You do have a daunting reputation."

"One I have done all in my power to earn." She stepped to the billiards table and ran her hand along the edge. "Entertaining game, billiards."

"Do you play?"

"On occasion. I quite like it." She slanted him a sharp glance. "You needn't look so startled. I have been on this earth for nearly eighty years, but I am not yet dead."

"Would you care for a game?"

"Not at the moment. You would, no doubt, consider it only polite to allow me to win." She circled the table slowly. "And while I do enjoy winning, I have always preferred victory on my own terms."

Richard chuckled. "I'm not surprised."

"I didn't think you would be." Her gaze pinned his. "And I am not disappointed."

"Disappointed?"

She ignored him and continued around the table. "I have been a widow now for fully a third of my life. I know what it is to lose a husband, a first love. For some, such as myself, there is one and only one love. I am grateful Gillian is not among those ranks. And I approve of her choice."

"Her choice?" he said cautiously.

"Come now, my lord, you know exactly what I am talking about, although I do admire your reluctance to reveal a confidence that is not yours to divulge."

"You know," he said slowly.

"My dear boy," she said in a patronizing manner, "I know everything. I make it my business to know."

"Does Gillian's father, or rather, does the duke, know?"

"I doubt it. He would never allow her to agree to the conditions of the legacy."

He chose his words with care. "But you will?"

"Not at all. And if her involvement with you at this point had nothing else to it than her inheritance I would put a stop to the entire endeavor at once. However, I decided from the beginning to see how this game of yours played out. I know my granddaughter well enough to know that no matter how tempting the reward, she would never settle for someone she did not care for deeply. I am quite pleased."

"You are?" He was curious in spite of himself. "Why?"

She laughed. "You are a rather remarkable creature, Lord Shelbrooke. It has taken a great deal of moral courage to turn your life around, to accept the responsibilities thrust upon you." She picked up the cue leaning against the table and studied the tip. "And I quite admire the way you've used your talent to try to recoup your family's fortune."

He widened his eyes in surprise. "My talent?"

Her amused gaze caught his. "I told you I know everything."

"Thomas," he muttered.

"Do not blame him too harshly, he is your true friend and I'm confident he has told no one else your secret." She smiled smugly. "But the boy has never been able to keep secrets from me."

"I can certainly understand that," he said wryly.

"Do you know you come by that talent naturally?"

"What do you mean?"

She studied him for a long moment, then nodded as if making a decision. "In due time. It's of no significance at the moment."

"Am I to understand then that you are allowed to keep your secrets but I am not?" he said in a teasing manner.

"You are an intelligent scoundrel, I'll grant you that. You will make a fine addition to the family. I am quite looking forward to your children." She chuckled. "Now then, my lord, I find I am up to a game after all. Will you allow me to win?"

"Absolutely not." He grinned.

"Excellent." He arranged the balls on the table,

and she leaned forward and positioned her cue, then glanced up at him. "Are you aware that Marie Antoinette and the king of France are said to have played billiards on the eve of their imprisonment?"

He shook his head. "No."

"Pity. Then you don't know the outcome of their game." The dowager cast him a serene smile. "She won."

Perhaps there was something to this business of love after all. Something that made the lights in the ballroom brighter, the colors of the women's gowns more vivid, his senses more acute. Something that made it impossible to keep his gaze off Gillian.

At the moment, she danced with a gentleman he didn't know and, further, didn't like. He sipped the champagne in his glass irritably. Didn't her partner hold her a bit too close? Wasn't her laugh a touch too joyous? Was this, then, jealousy? Irrational, no doubt, but present nonetheless.

He suspected Thomas was right. Richard, who had never considered love at all, was apparently now in the grips of the odd and disquieting emotion. He was a practical man, and his feelings were not at all practical. Or rational. Or even sane.

Rational or not, the man definitely held her too close.

Was Thomas right about his sister as well? Thomas and his grandmother both believed Gillian shared Richard's feelings. Richard wished he could be as certain.

How could he find out? Was she in love with him, or was she simply swept away by the kind of passion she hadn't tasted in years? He had no doubt she enjoyed being in his bed, but even he realized the act of love was not the same as the emotion. He could, of course, simply ask her. But was he ready to hear her answer?

If her partner didn't stop clutching her at once, Richard would be forced to take action.

At first, she'd wanted marriage for her inheritance. He'd wanted a wife for his future.

Now he wanted so much more. But did she? And could he bear it if she didn't? He'd never considered himself a coward, but there it was: he didn't have the courage to face her answer. It was no longer a question of his pride: it was a question of his heart. Damnable heart.

The dance ended, and her gaze met his. Was the look in her eye born of love or merely desire? Love was not part of their agreement. Not expected, not demanded. But now . . .

Thomas was right. Richard couldn't marry her for the legacy alone regardless of his need for her fortune, regardless of his need for her. He had to have her love as well.

She started toward him, and he could see nothing else in the crowded ballroom but her. She filled his gaze and his mind and his soul. He wanted to paint her and nothing but her forever.

What did she want?

For a practical man, he was indeed something of

a fool. But for good or ill, he had to know. Had to determine her true feelings. But how?

She reached him and paused, her smile quizzical. "Whatever are you thinking?" She took the glass from his hand, drained the last of his wine, then returned it. "You look as though you were trying to determine matters a great deal more important than those to be found in the strains of a waltz."

"Do I?" He forced a casual note.

"What is on your mind, Richard?" She gazed up at him. Was it love that shone in her eyes or something less?

"Nothing more important than the next dance." He signaled to a waiter and placed his empty glass on the tray. "Will you do me the honor?"

"Always."

He led her onto the floor and took her in his arms, amazed at how perfectly her body fit to his. They were meant for each other. How odd that he should be the one to think such things.

"Because you pose no threat to my heart!"

The words she'd said in his studio came to mind with the swiftness of a fired shot. She'd admitted more of her feelings to him as Toussaint than she'd ever admitted to him as Richard. Perhaps once again he could break through her reticence, not as an earl but as an artist.

The longer he played this game of deception, the stronger her fury when she learned the truth. And the stakes for all concerned were much higher now. Still, it was worth the risk.

If the Earl of Shelbrooke didn't have the courage to find out if the woman he loved, loved him in return, Etienne-Louis Toussaint was more than up to the task.

Chapter 16

Whatever had possessed her to come here again?

Gillian reclined on the chaise in the dark studio. This was the height of foolishness.

When Toussaint's note had arrived arranging another sitting two days after she'd returned to London, she'd had no intention of keeping the appointment. Still, the more she'd thought about it, the more she'd been convinced she had nothing to fear by coming here.

So far, the Frenchman had kept his distance. She'd been posing for nearly an hour, and they hadn't exchanged more than a few polite comments. He'd been, in fact, both cool and remote. Exactly as she wanted it.

She loved Richard, or at least she was fairly certain she did. Surely, her feelings for him went far beyond the powerful sensations he triggered with nothing more than a smoldering glance or a casual brush of his hand or a simple kiss. And if indeed she were in love with one man, the flirtatious overtures of another wouldn't affect her in the least. It was simply curiosity that brought her to Toussaint's studio. Nothing more than that. Once she knew for certain he had no real effect on her, she could put the tiny seed of doubt in her own mind to rest.

Besides, she did want him to finish the portrait. She'd be well able to pay for it once—when—if—she got her inheritance. Richard seemed in no great hurry to consummate their agreement even though she had met his lone condition to their marriage. She smiled to herself. More than met his condition.

"You have the look of a woman who has been well loved, madame." The artist's heavy accent drifted from the other side of the dark room. The silly man was still playing his absurd game of not allowing her to see his face. He was probably quite ugly.

"Do I," she said coolly.

"I gather you have now been kissed."

"That is none of your concern."

"Oh, but it is. I can only paint what I see." He paused. "And I see a woman whose senses have been awakened after a long sleep. Do I not?"

"You most certainly do not," she snapped.

He chuckled. "Your protest does not carry the ring of truth, madame. Whom do you wish to convince: me or yourself?"

"You." Did she?

"Are you so certain?"

"Yes." Was she? Wasn't that truly at the heart of her confusion? Was she afraid to admit her love to Richard because she feared it wasn't truly love at all but merely desire? Was she afraid that what she felt for him was brought on not by her heart but by his touch? Or were even these arguments in her own mind simply a mask for something else she hadn't considered at all?

"Perhaps you should tell me about this man who has put such a look on your lovely face?"

"I really don't think—"

"Ah, but how soon you have forgotten." He heaved a dramatic sigh. "I am your confidant, am I not?"

"You are not," she said firmly.

"Who else do you have, madame?"

Who else indeed? Not her friends, not her family. Telling this man her secrets was as foolish as coming here in the first place. Yet here she was, and there was a certain amount of ease and freedom in talking to a faceless stranger in the dark. She'd acknowledged it at the last sitting, and nothing had really changed. She heaved a sigh of her own. "I suppose I am rather confused."

"When you were last here, it was your circumstances you found confusing. Now, it is you who are confused?" He clucked his tongue. "That is not a good sign."

"No, it isn't." She shook her head. "My feelings seem to be all jumbled. I think I love him—"

"Do you?" Toussaint's accent eased with the

comment, and for a fleeting instant his voice sounded vaguely familiar.

"Yes, well, that's what is so perplexing. Am I truly in love, or is it exactly what you said a moment ago? He makes my senses reel." She thought for a moment, trying once again to sort it all out within her own mind. "When I am in his arms I can think of nothing but him."

"And when you are not?"

"I can think of nothing but him." She laughed wryly. "Which still doesn't answer the question of whether I truly love him or whether I simply want him."

"And how does he feel?"

"I don't know. One minute I'm certain he must care for me, at least a little, and the next . . ." She shrugged.

"You English are so foolish about matters of the heart." Scorn rang in Toussaint's voice. "Why do you play such games? Why do you not ask him how he feels?"

"Because I'm not entirely certain I wish to hear the answer."

"Perhaps," Toussaint paused, "he is confused as well."

"Perhaps." Was it at all possible that Richard's emotions were as tumultuous as her own? "He does seem to be a man with any number of secrets."

"And what is more exciting than a man with secrets, eh, madame?"

"Or a man whose face is hidden," she murmured. Why did that thought keep recurring in her life these days?

"But now I am confused. What difference does it make if it is love you feel for this man or lust?"

"A great deal, I fear." She searched for the right words. "If what I feel with him is no different than what I would feel with another man, how can I marry him?"

"Again, I do not understand. I thought your marriage was only for the purpose of gaining a great fortune."

"I thought so too." The irony of it all struck her as sharply as a physical blow. She'd intended to marry with no thought for love at all. Now, it was the only thing she could think of. Did he love her? Did she love him? She'd married the first time for love, and how could she marry again without it? Nothing, not the legacy, not the plight of needy artists, not even her own longing for independence, was as important.

Abruptly an overwhelming weariness flooded her. She was tired of trying to sort out her feelings and tired as well of the odd circumstances governing her life. She sat upright, found her shoes, and slipped them on. "I must thank you, though. If nothing else, I do understand a bit more of my own feelings." She rose to her feet. "You have a great deal of talent, monsieur, and I would very much like to have this portrait. Regardless of whether I marry or not, I'm confident I can find the money to pay you for your work." She picked up her cloak and started toward the door.

"Would you care to see it?"

She paused. "The painting?"

"It is not yet finished, but you may wish to see what I see when I look at you."

"But if I came over there I would no doubt see your face and spoil all your fun," she said lightly.

"And that we cannot allow," he laughed. "Put out the candles nearest you, madame, and I will step back into the shadows."

"Very well." She blew out the candles, then crossed the room and stepped to the other side of the easel.

A lone candle burned in a holder affixed to the top of the easel, illuminating the painting. Her face stared from the canvas. It was a lovely likeness, yet was this creature captured in paint truly her? Was her smile that mysterious? Her relaxed pose on the chaise, the line of her body, that confident? Her eyes that luminous and serene? Had he captured not who she was but who she wished to be?

"You're very good, monsieur," she said softly. "Is this once again how you see my soul?"

She caught the movement of a shadow out of the corner of her eye, and the candle snuffed out. The room plunged into darkness.

Toussaint's voice sounded behind her, his tone intense. "It is indeed how I see you."

"What are you doing?" she said with a sigh.

He rested his hands lightly on her shoulders. "Nothing more than what you wish."

"What I wish?" She shook her head. "I doubt that."

"You want to know if it is lust you feel for this man or love." He drew her against him, and she didn't have the strength to protest. "What do you feel for me?"

"Nothing."

"Nothing?" He laughed softly. "That too is a lie. When I kiss your neck"—he brushed his lips along the side of her neck, and a shiver rushed through her—"you feel a great deal."

Did she? "No, I don't."

"Another lie."

"No." Was it?

"It is, how do you say, a test, perhaps? Test yourself, ma chérie. If I were to kiss you as you should be kissed, as no man has kissed you before," his voice dropped to a whisper, "you would know."

Without warning, anger filled her. She whirled to face him and glared at his dark figure. "Very well then, monsieur, test me! Kiss me!"

Without hesitation he pulled her into his arms and crushed his mouth to hers. Fire shot through her from his touch, and for a moment she was swept away by desire, stark and unrelenting and undeniable. Realization flooded her and caught at her breath and stilled her heart.

The emotion gripping her now in Touissaint's arms was exactly like that she felt with Richard. The heat of his embrace, the press of his body, the feel of his lips on hers, was the same. How could two such different men create the same response within her?

She wrenched herself out of his grasp. "Good

God!" Unreasonable anger surged within her, and without thinking she drew back her hand and cracked it across his face. "So much for your test!"

"Madame, I—"

She turned on her heel and groped her way across the room. "And, apparently, Toussaint, I failed!"

And failed miserably. She found the door, flung it open, and stalked down the stairs toward a waiting Wilkins. She barely glanced at him, nodding sharply for him to follow. She climbed into the hired carriage without a word, and it started off at once.

She was furious. With Toussaint certainly, but more with herself. If this stranger could do this to her, what did that say of her relationship with Richard? What did it say about her? She was indeed wanton. No better than a common trollop.

Richard was a good man, an honorable man, and he deserved far more in a wife than a woman who would melt at the foot of any man who so much as kissed her. Although it was an impressive kiss.

What on earth was she going to do now? She buried her face in her hands and tried to think. A flurry of thoughts crowded her brain, and she couldn't separate one from the other.

Still . . .

She lifted her head and narrowed her eyes in concentration. She only felt this desire for the artist when she was in his arms. She didn't long for his touch, didn't yearn to be with him. Then . . . wasn't this nothing more than lust? Didn't her feelings for Richard go far beyond that?

She straightened in her seat. Toussaint was as accomplished at seduction as he was at the easel. Everyone knew that. And Richard had been rather versed in that arena as well at one point. Why would anyone in their right mind think the kisses of such men wouldn't have a devastating effect on her senses? She was, in a very real sense, not terribly experienced, in spite of a bit of hard work and practice.

Had she passed the test after all? Perhaps it wasn't only what she felt when she was with Richard that mattered. Perhaps what she felt when she wasn't with him was equally—no, more—important. She wanted him when she wasn't in his arms and wanted him for so much more than his touch alone. Hadn't she already realized that? And if that wasn't love, well, what in truth was? Now, she simply had to tell him.

She could ignore Toussaint's kiss, it was of no real significance. It wasn't as easy to ignore the persistent question lingering in the back of her mind.

How could the kisses of two different men be so very much alike?

Was there ever a man who approached his level when it came to total idiocy and sheer number of mistakes?

Richard lay on the chaise in the dark studio, his hands laced behind his neck, and stared up at the night sky. And at the moment there was surely not a man as miserable. How could he have done that to her? Any of it? He was the worst sort of cad. He'd placed her in an awkward situation for his own purposes. He'd lied to her, deceived her. Once for pride, once for money, and finally for love, although he doubted Gillian would either note the difference or care. Worse, none of it had really gotten him anywhere.

The stars above winked in accusation.

He was no closer to knowing her feelings now than he had been at Effington Hall. Of course, he had managed to find out that she was as hesitant to confront him as he was to talk to her. That, no doubt, was in his favor. A small point, but far better than nothing.

He stared upward at the stars hoping for inspiration, some new strategy. Preferably brilliant.

It had been such a delightfully clever plan in the beginning, and he still wasn't sure when it had all gone awry. He probably should have put an end to it and told her the truth the moment there had no longer been a need for a twofold assault. But by then, too many confusing emotions were muddling his mind. What little mind he seemed to have left.

There really weren't many options remaining at this point. He blew a long, resigned breath. He would have to confess and throw himself on her mercy. Tell her everything, from the moment he'd seen his own painting in her house to his impromptu deception at Lady Forester's masquerade to this ridiculous business tonight.

He would explain it all, and eventually she

would understand. She was as practical in her own way as he was in his. Oh, certainly, at first she would be a bit overset, perhaps even furious, but that would pass. Didn't it stand to reason that if they shared the same sort of fear over each other's feelings then surely they shared additional emotions as well? Surely she loved him just as he loved her?

Her grandmother had said it had taken courage to change his life. Telling Gillian he loved her as well as the rest of it would forge the greatest change of all. And take far more courage than he'd ever dreamed possible.

Still, she wasn't entirely innocent. She hadn't mentioned a word to him about her sittings with Toussaint or about the artist's advances, although she hadn't exactly lied.

He snorted in self-disdain. She'd never donned a disguise to accost him in a garden, never adopted an accent to seduce him. No, perhaps it would be wise not to mention Gillian's actions. No doubt she wouldn't equate her relatively minor lies of omission with his very real duplicity.

He did have to admit, at least to himself, he'd rather enjoyed playing the role of the rakish Frenchman. Toussaint's manner was very much like his own had once been. It was surprisingly easy to fall into the portrayal. To be, once again, a rogue absorbed by nothing more than his own interests and desires.

Well, he would pay dearly. Now, he'd do whatever he needed to do to make it right between them. Beg. Plead. Even grovel.

In truth, how long could it take? Sooner or later she'd probably see the humor in it all. One of the things he loved about her was how easily she laughed. They'd have quite a good laugh together over it. She'd forgive him because she loved him. He just hoped she loved him enough.

He smiled up at the stars. Of course she loved him. Given her comments, and her confusion, it made sense. How could she not?

Gillian glanced at the clock on the overmantel once again. Its hands had scarcely moved since the last time she'd checked. Or the time before or the time before that. She suppressed the impulse to snatch it off its perch and see if the damnable thing was still functioning. Besides, it had indeed been working when she'd examined it only a few minutes ago.

Where was he? She paced the room. Was she doomed to spend the rest of her days waiting for him to make an appearance? According to his note he should have already arrived. Where was he, anyway, and more to the point, exactly what was he up to?

She could add that to the ever-growing list of items they needed to clear up between them. Not that she thought he was spending his time doing anything less than honorable. She agreed with Emma on that score. Still, it would be nice to know.

She'd been about to send a missive of her own

when his note had arrived, brought once again by the same grubby boy Wilkins was convinced marked the decline of English civilization as they knew it.

She'd decided on her way home last night that it was past time to resolve all the questions between them. She was fairly confident she understood her own feelings. Now she needed to determine his. It would take rather a lot of courage, though.

Courage? The thought stopped her in her tracks. She'd never really considered the attribute before. It had, of course, taken a certain amount of courage to approach Richard with her marriage proposal in the first place. And hadn't it taken courage to continue with her life after Charles's death? Certainly it had.

Or was it courage? She drew her brows together in concentration. Didn't courage imply some risk? Had she ever really chanced anything in her life?

Marrying Charles had involved no uncertainty. They'd known each other since childhood, and she'd assumed they'd be together forever. After his death she'd gone on, although, when she looked back with the perception born of distance, what choice had she had?

But had she truly carried on with life?

Hadn't she protected herself, protected her heart, at every turn through the years? Hadn't she used Robin and Kit as convenient escorts and companions who demanded nothing in return? Even her salons had been held with an eye toward introducing patrons to those who could use their help, but she had been nothing more than an intermediary. As much an observer as Richard had always appeared to be.

She shook her head at the revelation. Gillian had never really reflected on her life before. And she wasn't at all sure she liked what she saw. Had she lived all these years or simply existed? Perhaps it was time to take a risk. Perhaps, she straightened her shoulders, nothing in life that was worth having was possible without it.

Voices sounded in the foyer, and she braced herself.

"Gillian." Richard appeared in the doorway.

"Richard." Her voice was calm, but her heart tripped.

He strode into the room. She hadn't seen him since they'd returned to London, yet he didn't seem at all pleased to see her. It was almost as if he was as nervous about their meeting as she was.

She didn't know what to say, where to begin. She stepped to the sideboard and poured him a glass of brandy. "I've been expecting you."

"Yes, well." He ran his fingers through his hair, and at once she realized he was indeed as uneasy as she. Why? "I've been thinking . . ."

"As have I." She groaned to herself and took a quick sip of the liquor. They sounded like two complete strangers having a polite conversation about nothing whatsoever.

"About?"

"Us?" she prompted.

"Among other things," he murmured.

Was he, too, reluctant to begin? This was getting them nowhere. "It seems to me, we haven't been entirely honest with each other."

"We haven't?" he said cautiously.

"No." She drew a steadying breath.

"About anything in particular?"

"In particular, well . . . feelings, I suppose." This was far more difficult than she'd ever imagined. "How we feel about one another."

"Does it matter?" His gaze searched hers.

"Of course it matters. We are going to be married."

His words were measured. "It didn't matter in the beginning."

"No, but it matters now."

"Why?"

Because I love you. Because I want you to love me. "Because everything has changed since the beginning."

"Has it?" he said casually. Too casually.

"Why, yes, I believe it has."

"How?"

She took another quick sip. "Are you going to answer every question with a question?"

"Are you going to offer me something to drink?"

She looked at the glass in her hand with surprise. She'd obviously forgotten to give it to him. "This is yours."

Amusement curved his lips. "You have the oddest habit of drinking my drinks for me."

"Do I? Well, I don't really drink much," she murmured.

He raised a skeptical brow, stepped to her, and plucked the half empty snifter from her hands. "Now then, was I doing that?"

"Doing what?" She shook her head in confusion.

"Answering a question with a question."

"You know perfectly well you were."

"Oh, well, if I was," he shrugged, "I do apologize. Go ahead then." He sipped at the brandy. "Ask me a question, and I shall endeavor to answer it without hesitation."

"Very well." She drew a deep breath. "How do you . . . feel about me?"

"Feel about you?"

She frowned.

"Oh. I've done it again, haven't I?" A wry smile quirked his lips. "Sorry. Well, let me think." He stepped around her, circling her as if considering a purchase, his gaze assessing and quite annoying. "You're intelligent. I do like that in a woman."

"Do you," she said, wondering why that should surprise her.

"Indeed I do. I find women lacking in intelligence to be quite boring." He narrowed his eyes. "You, my dear, are never boring.

"In addition, you are lovely to look at, you have a ready wit, and," he flashed her a wicked grin, "you are not adverse to hard work and practice."

A blush warmed her cheeks, and she ignored it. "That's all very well and good, but it really doesn't answer my question."

"I thought I answered it quite nicely."

"Well, you were wrong." She heaved a frustrated

sigh. "I'm not asking for a list of my charms—"

"I quite like your charms."

"And I like your charms as well, Richard," she snapped, "but what I want to know is if you . . . if you . . ."

"Care for you?"

"Exactly," she said with relief and looked at him expectantly. A second passed, and another, and another. "Well?"

"Well . . ." He chose his words with care. "Of course I care for you."

"Is that all?" The words were out of her mouth before she had a chance to think. " 'Of course I care for you'? That's it? Nothing more than that?"

"What do you want me to say?" he said slowly.

I want you to tell me that you love me! "I don't know exactly," she lied. "Something, well, *more*, perhaps?"

"Shall I get down on one knee and pledge my eternal devotion? Shall I clasp my hands to my heart and vow my undying love? Shall I throw open the windows and proclaim my everlasting ardor to the world?"

"Yes, I should quite like that!" This was not going at all the way she had envisioned it.

"Is that what Charles would have done?" His words were cool, but there was an intense gleam in his eye.

She drew her brows together in confusion. "Charles has nothing to do with this."

"Doesn't he?" He drained his glass and set it on a table. "Hasn't Charles had a great deal to do with everything from the moment you first approached me?"

"No, not at all." She shook her head. "Oh, in the beginning, there was a certain amount of guilt, but I've gotten over that."

He snorted. "Indeed you have."

She glared. "That's what comes of hard work and practice."

"I am not at all like Charles."

"No, you're not!"

"Then why did you choose me?"

"I had a list!"

"*A list.*" He fairly spat the words. "With me at the top. A position I occupy only because you see in me the very same noble qualities your beloved husband possessed."

"Yes, I suppose if you wish to—"

"Then is it me you want or a copy of what you once had?"

"That isn't at all—"

"But you didn't want a husband in the beginning, did you, Gillian? Not a real husband. You wanted nothing more than a means to an end." He stared at her. "What do you want now?

You. "I don't . . . know."

"Don't you?" He was silent for a long moment. The air between them simmered thick with tension. With fear. With questions unasked and unanswered.

"Your husband was a fool."

"Why?" Anger rose within her. "Because he thought it was important to serve his king, his country? Because he gave his life for what he believed in?"

"No." Richard's dark gaze bored into hers. "Because he left you."

Chapter 17

Richard turned on his heel and stalked out of the room, slamming the door behind him.

His words struck her like a blow. She stared after him, her mind reeling with the import of his charge.

Because he left you.

She sank down on the settee.

Because he left you.

His voice thundered in her mind. An unrelenting echo. And at once she understood everything. About Richard and more about herself.

It wasn't love she feared. It was loss and the devastating anguish it carried. She'd given her heart to Charles fully and without reservation, and regardless of the nobility of his reasons, he'd left her. Forever.

How could she be certain Richard wouldn't?

"Honesty between a man and a woman is as important as trust."

Honesty? And trust? To this point they hadn't had a great deal of either. Certainly he had his secrets, but whatever they were, he was an honorable man and she could trust him. Implicitly. And she could trust him with her heart as well. She could see it in his eyes. She might never completely eliminate her fear of loving him and losing him, there was nothing she could do about death after all, but she had to trust him enough to know he would never leave her of his own accord.

She had to love him enough. It was a risk that would take far more courage than she'd ever thought she had. Or ever thought she needed.

She had to tell him how she felt with no more hesitation, no more delay. There was no need to wait for his declaration of love. No need for him to actually say the words. Doubtless he'd never said them before, and possibly he even couldn't. But he did love her. She could see it in his eyes, feel it in his touch. And if he possibly didn't, she shrugged, she would cross that road if she came to it. It was a risk. Probably the first of many with this man. But the rewards would be glorious.

She jumped to her feet and headed toward the door. She'd have to go to his rooms at once. The thought pulled her up short. She had no idea where he lived. She was completely at his mercy as to where and when they would meet. She could send a note through his solicitor as she had done when she'd invited him to their first meeting. But that may well take a day or more, and she didn't want to waste so much as an hour.

If she could find that boy who'd brought his note. . . . Hadn't Wilkins remarked that it was the same youth who had delivered Toussaint's messages? Obviously, Richard's rooms and the artist's studio were in the same area of the city. Toussaint would know how to reach the boy, and she could have him deliver a note to Richard. Better yet, she would insist on being taken there in person. She'd surprise Richard and pour out her feelings. And hopefully, allow him to reveal all his secrets in return.

This would give her the chance to end these silly games with Toussaint. She'd tell him in no uncertain terms there would be no more of that nonsense about love or lust. And there would be no more night sittings. She strongly suspected that the attraction he'd held for her had had very much to do with the slightly exotic atmosphere of his studio— with its chaos and odd scents of oil and turpentine—and, of course, the mysterious magic of the dark.

There would be no magic in the daylight. Not with Toussaint. But there would be revelation: she'd finally get to see his face. Not that she really cared. It was a matter of nothing more than idle curiosity.

She started toward the door. She needed to go at once before she lost her nerve. She'd have Wilkins hire a carriage and—

The door swung open, and Robin stepped into the room. "Gillian, we need to talk."

"Not now, Robin," she waved him away. "I'm in something of a hurry." She sidestepped him and continued toward the door.

He grabbed her arm. His gaze pinned hers. "Now, Gillian."

"Goodness, Robin, I have neither the time nor the inclination for whatever it is you want." She tried to pull away, but he gripped her firmly. "Now, do let me go."

"No." He studied her with an air of resignation, then pulled her into his arms and kissed her, long and quite thoroughly.

Shock coursed through her, and she was too stunned to so much as breathe.

He drew back and looked down at her cautiously. "Well?"

"Well . . . what on earth was that?" She stared up at him.

"It was a . . . a testament. To my undying devotion." He released her and stepped back. His chin raised slightly. He looked like a man facing a firing squad. "I love you, Gillian, I have always loved you. I cannot allow you to marry a man you do not love. Marry me."

"You're not serious." It was all she could do to keep from laughing aloud.

"I have never been more serious."

"But you don't especially want to marry me," she said slowly. "Or do you?"

"Of course I do." He squared his shoulders.

"I can always tell when you're lying." She studied him carefully. "Now, what are you up to?"

"I want to marry you," he said staunchly.

She raised a brow.

"Well, I would rather like to marry. And it might as well be you."

"Do be careful. You'll turn my head with your compliments," she said dryly.

He ignored her, clasped his hands behind his back, and paced the room. "You need to marry in order to get your inheritance. I want to marry because I'm bloody tired of my entire family throwing young women in my direction, not one of whom has your wit or looks, for that matter—"

"Now, I truly am flattered. And rather touched. I had no idea you thought so well of me."

He stopped and stared in surprise. "You didn't? My apologies then, Gillian, I have always regarded you highly." He considered her for a moment. "I will confess, I was a bit disappointed all those years ago when you decided to marry Charles."

"Robin." She widened her eyes in disbelief. "I had no idea."

He waved a hand dismissively. "I got over it."

"No doubt."

He cast her an amused look. "I didn't say I was heartbroken, merely disappointed."

"Thank you for making that clear."

"At any rate, Gillian"—he stepped closer and took her hand—"I have always loved you in my own way and I feel certain you have always loved me."

"Well, yes, but—"

"And even if it's not precisely the same kind of love you had for Charles, I know we would get on rather well together."

"Very likely, but—"

"Therefore if you were to marry me, it would be for love, of a sort, and you won't have to marry Shelbrooke."

At once she understood. "So that's what this is all about."

Robin nodded. "If nothing else, Gillian, we have been friends for far too long for me to allow you to marry a man, any man, simply to get your inheritance."

"Robin," she said gently, pulling her hand from his, "I'm not marrying Richard simply to get my inheritance—"

"You're not?" A grin broke on his face. "Excellent. I knew you wouldn't go through with it. I can't tell you how—"

"—but I am marrying him."

"You are?" He stared at her in confusion. "Why?"

"I love him." She smiled apologetically and wondered why it was so much easier to tell this old friend of her feelings and so hard to tell the object of her affection.

"You love him?" Robin's eyes widened. "How can you possibly love him? I don't even like him."

"Then it's a good thing you're not marrying him," she said with a laugh.

"Are you certain of this, Gillian?"

"I am."

"Does he return your feelings?"

"I don't know. But that's exactly what I hope to find out." She whirled and started toward the door, then stopped and turned back. "Could you lend me your carriage?"

"Of course." He stepped to the window. "My driver should still—"

The doors flew open, and Kit burst into the room. "Gillian." He started toward her, and instinctively she backed up. "I love you, Gillian, I have always loved you. I cannot allow you to marry a man you do not love. Marry me."

"What?"

Kit moved closer. "I love you, Gillian, I have always loved you." His words had the ring of a well-rehearsed recitation. He grabbed her shoulders and pulled her to him. "I cannot allow you to marry a man you do not love. Marry me."

She stared up at him. "You're not going to kiss me, are you?"

"I hadn't planned on it . . ." Indecision sounded in his voice. "But I suppose . . . if you think I should."

"Oh, I don't think you should." She raised her voice. "What do you think, Robin? Do you think he should?"

"I suspect it would be somewhat pointless," Robin said wryly.

"Robin?" Kit peered around her. "I thought we'd agreed to do this separately?"

Robin crossed his arms and leaned against the

window frame. "That was the original plan."

"Yours is not the first offer of marriage I have received today." She bit back a grin. "You may release me now."

"Oh. Of course." Kit's hands dropped as if she were on fire. "Sorry."

"Perhaps one of you would explain exactly what the original plan entailed?" She glanced from Kit to Robin.

"It's really quite simple, my dear," Robin said with a sigh. "We've decided—"

"Last night, actually," Kit said helpfully.

"—that this farce of yours with Shelbrooke had gone on long enough."

"Did you?"

"And it was up to us, one of us anyway, to save you." Kit's gaze slid from her to Robin. "So . . . you beat me to it, old man. Thank God." He collapsed onto the sofa and blew a long, relieved breath. "I don't mind telling you I was willing to go through with it—"

"Yet another compliment. How will I keep my head?"

"—but I'd really rather not."

"I won't be able to stand much more."

"It's not you, Gillian," he said quickly. "Well, not entirely. I just think you and I get on much better as friends, dear friends, of course—"

"Of course," she murmured.

"Than we ever would as something more. Besides," he said, leaping to his feet as if he couldn't bear to stay still, "there really is someone else I'd rather marry."

Gillian and Robin traded glances.

"You see, Gillian, she's the real reason why I stayed in London. With you and of course her brother gone, I thought—" He paused, and his eyes widened. "Blast it all. When you tell Shelbrooke you're marrying Robin instead of him, you don't think he'll hold it against me, do you? I really don't think he likes me."

"Oh, he doesn't." She smiled sweetly. "Not in the slightest."

"And we're not getting married," Robin added.

"You're not?" Kit frowned. "Well, I suppose it doesn't really surprise me. I never thought she'd accept either of us." He directed his words toward Robin. "Emma thinks Gillian's in love with Shelbrooke. I told her she was daft. Gillian was far too practical—"

"She is in love with him," Robin said glumly.

"Really? That does change everything then, doesn't it?" Kit thought for a moment, then his expression brightened. "I daresay, this will work out in everyone's favor. If you could put in a few good words for me."

"I shall see what I can do." She laughed. "After I put in a few good words for myself."

"Oh, that won't be necessary," Kit said confidently. "Emma's fairly certain he loves you as well."

Gillian stilled. "What makes her think so?"

"Because he hasn't married you yet." Kit cast her

a smug smile. "Emma thinks if all he wanted was your inheritance, he would have married you by now."

"Emma knows about the legacy?" Gillian said.

Kit winced. "I'm afraid so. I am sorry, Gillian, I couldn't help myself. Besides," he looked down his nose in a lofty manner, "we don't think two people who love each other should keep secrets between them."

"No, they shouldn't," she murmured. "So do you know all her secrets?"

"I know about her painting." He turned toward Robin. "She's quite wonderful, if I do say so myself."

"High praise coming from someone whose idea of great art is a well-rendered painting of a horse and hound," Robin said.

Kit ignored him. "However, Gillian, you do need to do something about Shelbrooke's attitude about that as well."

"Oh, I intend to." Was Emma right? Did Richard love her? His sister's reasoning made sense. Gillian could only hope her assessment was accurate.

"I never thought it would when this all began, Gillian, but it seems to be working out quite well," Kit grinned. "I love Emma and she loves me. You love Shelbrooke and he loves you. Of course, he hates me—"

Robin snorted.

"—but with luck and your influence, he'll get over that in time." Kit smirked at Robin. "Although this does leave you rather out of it."

"I shall do my best to bravely carry on." Robin's voice was grim.

"Poor Robin." Gillian shook her head. "And of all of us, you have always been the one most inclined towards love and marriage."

Robin shrugged. "The irony is overwhelming."

"Do not despair too much, dear friend," Gillian grinned. "There may be hope for you yet. You see, Richard has more than one marriageable sister."

"Monsieur Toussaint?" Gillian rapped on the door once again.

"Perhaps he isn't there, my lady?" Robin's driver called from the bottom of the stairs.

"Then I shall wait right here. All day if necessary." She was determined to find the boy who could take her to Richard. The time had come to resolve everything between them, and she would not be put off.

Toussaint could well be here, too absorbed in his work to notice a knock on the door. She fisted her hand and pounded impatiently, the sound echoing in the stairwell. "Monsieur, are you here?"

The door cracked open.

She paused. Was he inside, or did the silly man actually leave his studio without locking his door? If he was foolish enough to allow the possibility of any stranger entering, he deserved unexpected visitors.

She pushed the door open and poked her head inside. "Monsieur?"

No one was there. She opened the door wider

and cautiously stepped inside. In the daylight, the single room looked much as she'd imagined it. Disheveled and disorganized, it was obviously the domain of a man without a maid to occasionally shovel out debris.

Canvases were stacked against the walls. Battered tables held paints and artist's tools. In a far corner, Toussaint's bed was heaped with unmade bedclothes. There were few other furnishings aside from the chaise where she'd posed, the stool next to it that held the candelabra, his easel, and the screen set up beside it to hide his face. A large blue splatter of paint stained one wall.

She stepped across the room to the other side of the easel. A cloth covered her painting, and she gently pulled it off. Her face gazed back at her, and again the sensation of his capturing more than her mere appearance swept through her. The portrait was nearly finished, just a bit of the background remained to be filled in. She stared at the likeness with a sense of awe.

Toussaint's skill was impressive. No wonder his work was starting to be appreciated. His talent deserved to be recognized, and she would do what she could to assist him. She probably owed him that much.

At the very least, she did owe him an apology. She wandered around the edges of the room, stopping to study a sketch here, a preliminary drawing there. She had asked him to kiss her, after all, and it had been only her anger with herself that had made her strike him. He had simply been doing what obviously came naturally to a man of his nature.

She smiled, anticipating his reaction when he found her here. Throughout their acquaintance that ridiculous nonsense of his not allowing her to see his face had given him the upper hand. Now, the tables were turned.

She really didn't think Toussaint was ugly, but she doubted he was overly handsome, either. He was probably quite ordinary. One would no more stare at him on the street than one would notice him. Still, whatever his appearance, the expression on his face when he saw her here would be quite enjoyable.

And he had to return eventually. She would wait as long as was necessary. Toussaint was her only link to the boy, and he her only link to Richard. After today, however, with any luck at all, there would be no more secrets between them. Not where he lived or what he did or how he felt.

A half-finished landscape caught her eye. It was a lovely scene, a wooded setting with a small Greek temple off to one side. It looked a great deal like the Duchess's Folly. Gillian bent to study it closer.

Of course, one folly looked a great deal like any other, but the resemblance was remarkable. The proportions were right, as was the number of columns, and . . . she narrowed her eyes and leaned closer.

Perched on the top of the finial was a claret-colored bonnet with a jaunty green plume.

Her hat? Toussaint had painted her hat on top of

what looked suspiciously like her temple. How in the world. . . . She sank down on the floor and studied the painting closely.

It wasn't just the temple but the clearing, the arrangement of the trees, and wasn't there the hint of a lake in the distance? This was definitely the Duchess' Folly. Since she'd never seen Toussaint's face, it was unlikely, but not inconceivable, that he'd been a visitor to the Effington estate. Possibly even at this year's house party or the Ride. But only she and Richard knew about the hat.

Richard? Could he have commissioned Toussaint to produce the work? Of course not. He had no money for such frivolities. He used every cent he made doing whatever it was he did . . .

"I'm assuming it's some kind of business endeavor but Richard won't say, probably because society would never accept an earl actually earning a living wage."

Emma's words rang in her ear.

What had Richard said?

"Whether by a female or an earl or a king for that matter, such work would be seen as inconsequential and given no serious consideration."

Her breath caught. Was it possible? Surely not.

Her blood pounded in her ears. It was ridiculous. A quite mad idea.

The landscape seemed to pulse before her eyes.

Were Richard and Toussaint one and the same?

At once, a myriad of tiny details and minuscule moments that had had no significance at the time joined together in her head like pieces of a puzzle. Fitting perfectly into one astounding picture.

Good Lord! Of course. It all made sense. Toussaint's refusal to let her see his face. His insistence on nighttime sittings. His thick, overdone accent, not to mention the way it seemed to lessen on occasion. He probably didn't even speak French.

And there was so much more. The same boy delivering notes from both men. Richard's comments about the hard life of an artist. His far too astute knowledge of art. Emma's observance as to the similarities between Toussaint's painting and the work Richard used to do. Used to do? Hah!

And the vague scent of turpentine after their first night together!

Why hadn't she seen it before? Was she that foolish? That enamored with the man? No, she shook her head impatiently. Never in a hundred lifetimes would she have ever even toyed with the idea of the Earl of Shelbrooke being Etienne-Louis Toussaint.

But why didn't he tell her? She of all people would not condemn his painting.

"What is more mysterious and exciting than a man whose face is hidden? Or a man with secrets."

Was that what this was all about? Was he using Toussaint to gain her affections so she could live up to his condition for their marriage? If so, it hadn't worked. Not really. It was not Toussaint's arms she had ended up in. Not Toussaint's arms she truly wanted to be in.

Realization struck her, and she gasped. Why, she wasn't a trollop after all! She felt the same way when Toussaint kissed her as when Richard kissed her because it was the same man. The same man she loved. It wasn't lust. Well, it wasn't lust alone. After all, other men had kissed her, Robin most recently—and quite thoroughly at that—and she'd felt nothing whatsoever.

So why hadn't he told her the truth?

"Perhaps he is confused as well."

Was he? And was he confused because he too was in love? An absurd sense of joy bubbled up inside her, and she wanted to laugh out loud. Of course. That was the only answer. And what did she expect? Was there anything else in the world as confusing as love? And hadn't she told Pandora men had no idea what was in their own hearts when it came to something like love? If indeed he wanted her only for the legacy he could have married her by now. But if his heart was involved . . .

She should be furious with him. Should want to shoot him, or at the very least run him through with a dull sword. Instead all she could do was grin like an idiot.

She got to her feet and dusted off her dress. Poor, dear Richard. In love and confused. One could almost take pity on the man. And she would. Eventually. But not yet. She certainly couldn't let him get away with this little deception unscathed. It would not be a good way to begin the rest of their lives together. Why, the man hadn't begun to understand the true meaning of the word confused.

If there was nothing more mysterious or exciting

than a man with secrets, it was past time Richard found out there was nothing more dangerous than a woman who knew those secrets.

Each and every one.

Chapter 18

W hat exactly had gone wrong?

Richard stared at the canvas and tried to work, but he couldn't get his meeting with Gillian out of his head. He'd gone to her house with the best of intentions. Planning to confess everything. Tell her about Toussaint and tell her he loved her. Instead, an irrational jealousy toward, of all things, her dead husband had reared its annoying head. Until today, Richard hadn't even realized he resented this first love of hers.

But he did. Resented that he hadn't been the first man in her life. The first man in her bed. The first man to rescue the fair princess.

What had she done to him? He should have married her at once, agreed to her terms, claimed her inheritance, and gone on with his life and a wife in name only. At least he'd be out of debt. But his pride wouldn't allow that in the beginning. And his heart wouldn't allow it now.

A knock sounded at his door, followed by a feminine voice. "Monsieur Toussaint?"

Gillian?

"Madame?" He jumped to his feet and strode to the door. "What are you doing here?"

"I should very much like to talk to you." She paused. "May I come in?"

"A thousand pardons, but I am not prepared for a sitting tonight." He couldn't possibly let her in.

"I'll wait." She paused. "Monsieur, I have already let my driver go."

"One moment, s'il vous plaît." Damn. What on earth had brought Gillian here? He raced across the room, lit the candles by the chaise, extinguished the remaining lights, flew to the easel, and lit the candle affixed to the frame. He ran a hand through his hair, drew a deep breath, and settled on the stool in his concealed spot. "Very well, then, madame. You may enter."

He heard the door open and watched her figure move from the dim shadows near the entry to the light by the chaise. "Good evening, monsieur."

"Madame," he said cautiously. She dropped her cloak onto the end of the chaise. "I did not think I would see you again."

"Why would you think that?" She sat on the sofa and slipped off her shoes. "Is the portrait finished?"

"Not entirely, but I do not need you for what is

left to complete. Therefore if you would prefer to leave, I can send for a carriage."

"Not at all." She stretched out on the chaise, her movements languorous and enticing. "I would prefer to stay right here."

"You would?"

"Indeed I would." She laughed softly, a sound deep in her throat, and the muscles of his stomach tightened. "You say you don't need me to finish this portrait?"

"No." However, as long as she was here, he might as well work on it. He picked up a brush. How long did she plan on staying, anyway? As far as he knew, she'd always left Wilkins waiting at the bottom of the stair. Where was the man tonight?

"Then perhaps you would accept my commission for another?"

"Another portrait?" He frowned. "One is not enough?"

"It simply struck me how lovely it would be to have a work that was, oh, a bit different. Something unique."

"All of my paintings are unique," he muttered. It wasn't enough for her to surprise him, now she had to criticize him as well.

"Yes, well, I was thinking of something in a more classical vein."

"Classical?" What was more classical than a woman in a Grecian gown reclining on a chaise?

"You know, in the manner of a sculpture. A Greek sculpture. Yes, that would be perfect. Something that would grace, oh, I don't know, a temple perhaps."

"A temple?" he said, uttering a silent prayer. Hopefully, the landscape he'd started after they'd returned from the country was leaning against a wall where she couldn't possibly see it in the dark.

She swung her legs off the chaise and rose to her feet, her movements at once graceful and provocative. "This gown is perfect for such a painting." She stretched her arms over her head and turned slowly. The candlelight danced off the folds in the sheer fabric and caressed every curve. "Don't you think so, monsieur?"

He swallowed hard. "I do indeed, but I have already painted you in that dress."

"Oh dear." Her lips pursed in a delightful pout, and she crossed her arms over her chest, the action underlining the swell of her breasts above her gown. "Then this will never do."

"Perhaps not," he murmured, his gaze caught by the play of the flickering light on her ivory skin.

"What shall we do instead?" She tapped her finger against her bottom lip.

"I don't know." He knew exactly what he wanted to do, but painting played no role in it.

"I did so desire something in a classic tradition."

"Desire . . . classic." His gaze riveted on the finger against her lips.

"Perhaps even daring."

"Daring." Her luscious, lovely lips.

"Yes, but maybe not Greek exactly, perhaps something more in the manner of the great Italian masters." Her movements seemed as measured as if she moved in a dream. Or perhaps the dream was his. Her hands drifted to the gold cord knotted at her waist. "Botticelli." She untied it. "Or Titian."

It dropped to the floor, and his gaze followed.

"Titian," he echoed, mesmerized by the snake of gold twinkling at her feet.

"No, Botticelli, I should think. Something like his *Birth of Venus.*"

"Madame, Venus was . . ." Her gown fell to cover the cord. His gaze traveled up her legs and higher, over the curve of her derriere and up the valley and planes of her back and shoulders. Her flesh glowed warm and golden. She drew the ribbon from her hair, and her curls tumbled like liquid light to kiss the top of her back.

She looked at him over her shoulder. He knew full well she couldn't see him, yet her gaze seemed to rivet to his. "Venus was . . . ?"

"You have lost your clothing, madame." He could barely croak out the words.

"Not at all, monsieur." She reached down, plucked the gown from the floor, and tossed it to join her cloak on the chair. "I know precisely where they are."

"And do you know what you are doing as well?" He bloody well hoped so, because he had no idea what she was up to.

"Oh, I believe I do. You see, monsieur . . . Etienne—"

Etienne? When had she started calling him Etienne?

"I have been giving my situation a great deal of thought since last night." She moved toward the candelabra, the flickering light skimming her naked body like a luminescent hand. She leaned forward and blew out a candle. "And I have considered what you said."

"What I said?" Why was his mouth so dry?

"Indeed. Everything you said." She puffed out the second candle.

"Everything?" Why was his voice so weak?

"Oh my yes. About how I feel when you kiss me." She extinguished another candle. "And about your test." She glanced at him. "It wasn't fair, you know." She blew out the next candle.

"No?" His heart thudded in his chest.

"No indeed. I wasn't expecting it. I wasn't at all ready." She looked in his direction and slowly licked her thumb, then her forefinger.

"You weren't?" He couldn't breathe. And didn't care.

"No. But now, monsieur." She snuffed out the last candle with her fingers. A slight sizzle sounded in the air. Every muscle in his body tensed. "I am."

"You are?" Was he?

"Test me, Etienne." She practically purred the words, a dark silhouette on the far side of the room.

"What do you want of me, madame?" In spite of his words, he started toward her, his feet moving of their own accord.

"What?" She laughed in a throaty manner he'd never heard from her before. A shiver of desire shot up his spine. "Why, what does any woman want

of Etienne-Louis Toussaint, master painter and
lover extraordinaire?"

"Madame, I . . ." He was a scant step away from
her. He should stop this. Now. Before it was too
late.

"Yes?" She stepped toward him and placed her
hands on his chest, then ran her fingers lightly over
his shirt. He gasped and grabbed her hands firmly.

"Why?" His voice was strangled.

"Why?" She pressed her naked body against
him, her flesh burning his through the fabric of his
clothes. She leaned forward and flicked her tongue
over the hollow of his throat. "I once thought I
could never marry a man I did not love." Her voice
was low and intoxicating. She pulled her hands
from his and wrapped her arms around his neck.
"I also once thought I couldn't be with a man I
didn't love."

"And now?"

"Now?" She tunneled her fingers through his
hair and drew his mouth to hers. "We shall see."

"I . . . we must talk," his mouth murmured
against hers.

"Must we?" She slid her hands over his shoulders, down his back, then slipped them under his
shirt.

He yanked it over his head and threw it aside,
and she was at once back in his arms. "It is imper-
ative . . ." It was hard to form a sentence, a single
thought. ". . . I must tell you . . ."

"Your secrets, Etienne?" Her hands were everywhere at once, touching and exploring and skimming his sides, lower and lower still.

And in that moment he knew it was already too late.

He couldn't resist and didn't want to. She pushed his trousers down his hips, freeing his hard member. Her hands cupped him and caressed him with a shocking confidence, and he moaned with the sheer sensation of her touch.

She drew him onto the chaise, the heat of her body searing his bare skin, numbing his mind to anything beyond the passion in her touch, the need swelling within him.

Here and now, he no longer cared if it was Toussaint she truly wanted or Richard. If she loved the earl or the artist. She was in his blood, in his soul. He wanted her with an ache so fierce it eclipsed all thought of right and wrong. All thought of honor and deception. He loved her and he wanted her and it didn't matter who she wanted, who she loved.

He and Toussaint were one and the same. There was enough of the rakish artist in him to discard the consequences of this moment, enough of the man he had once been to cast aside all thought of repercussions, all concern for tomorrow. There was nothing in this moment but a single man and the one woman he loved.

But even as his body joined with hers and ecstasy swept away caution and control, he knew in some still sane portion of his mind that it would soon matter very much indeed.

It would be all that mattered.

*   *   *

They lay together silently, wrapped in a sense of contentment and serenity he'd never suspected could be the aftermath of the physical act of love. Now might well be the best time to confess all, although any urgency to do so had vanished. She was warm and supple beside him and probably quite receptive to the truth. He had an amazing sense of well-being and the illogical belief that nothing could come between them now.

Gillian sighed, turned to him, and kissed him firmly. "I have never seduced a man before."

"I would not have known," he said lightly, remembering just in time to feign his accent. He chuckled. "You seemed quite good at it."

"Thank you." He could hear the grin in her voice. "I've been practicing."

She sat up and bent over to find her shoes, then rose from the chaise. He watched her shadowy figure grope for the chair. She found it, slipped her dress on and her cloak. At once he realized she'd made certain she knew exactly where to find her clothing in the dark room. He propped himself on his elbows.

"You are leaving? Now?" He'd rather hoped that she'd stay until dawn, when the rising sun would reveal his face to her and alleviate the need for him to bring up the subject of his deception. He'd always been rather more successful at defense than offense.

"Yes, well, my carriage is waiting."

"Did you not say you'd sent it away?"

"Did I?" she murmured. "What was I thinking?"

"Madame?" he said slowly.

"Monsieur, I have had a delightful evening. I do so appreciate your part in it." Her tone was cordial and polite, as if she were thanking him for nothing more than a drive around the park.

She crossed to the door and opened it, silhouetted in the doorway by the dim light. "Oh, and I should hate for you to spend the rest of the night wondering, so I do think I should tell you before I go."

"Tell me what?"

"The answer to your last question, monsieur," she paused, "is no." She closed the door behind her with a firm snap.

"What question?" he muttered and stared after her. He couldn't recall any question of significance. He lay back and stared upward into the night. No stars shone tonight. Clouds obscured the heavens, a blessing earlier for keeping his secret from her, but now they seemed forbidding. An omen perhaps?

What question? He searched his mind. He'd been far too busy dealing with questions of his own to note anything of importance she might—

"I also once thought I couldn't be with a man I didn't love."

"And now?"

He bolted upright.

"The answer to your last question, monsieur, is no."

No? What in the hell did that mean?

He jumped to his feet and promptly bashed his

knee on the chair. Pain shot through him. He muttered a curse, groped for his trousers, and pulled them on, then headed toward the easel, guided by the faint glow of the candle still burning on the wooden frame. He sank onto the stool before the portrait and stared at Gillian's face.

She stared back.

No?

If she couldn't be with a man she didn't love . . .

His stomach clenched.

But she had been with Toussaint. She had in fact seduced Toussaint. And with a great deal of enthusiasm.

Did she then love Toussaint? Had his silly plan worked after all? And had it worked far too well?

The face on the portrait smiled a smug, satisfied smile.

Blast it all, what would he do now? Gillian had fallen in love with the wrong man, even if he was that man. He was his own rival. He ran his hand through his hair and tried to think.

What if he could get rid of Toussaint? His spirits lifted at the thought. Send him back to France, or better yet, kill the scoundrel. Perhaps in a duel? No, no, that would be too romantic. Besides, he'd need witnesses and an opponent.

A duel would create far too much gossip, and the last thing he needed was to draw the attention of the *ton*. What about an accident? He racked his brains for something plausible. A carriage accident perhaps? Or he could drown? That would work. His body would never be found.

Bloody hell, he couldn't kill off Toussaint. Gillian would then be faced with a dead lover as well as a dead husband, and Richard couldn't handle the memory of yet another man in her life. Even if he didn't truly exist.

Of course, he could be wrong about her feelings. No. His heart sank. He should have known right from the beginning, regardless of her intentions, that she was not the kind of woman to share a man's bed without love. And not the kind of woman who married without love.

Damn it all, he loved her. But she loved someone else. And she would hate him when she learned the truth. She'd never believe that this deception of his wasn't strictly to gain her inheritance. And in truth it had been when this whole blasted mess had started.

Now, he didn't care about her legacy. If he had to go the rest of his life painting under another name and trying to make repairs on an ancient roof and struggling to scrape up dowries for his sisters, it was well worth it if she shared that life with him.

He blew a long, resigned breath and met the gaze of the face in the portrait. He loved her. He'd never loved before and probably never would again. But how could he marry a woman who loved someone else?

He couldn't. His pride wouldn't allow it. Neither would his heart. It had all been so simple until love had entered into it. Damnable love.

Once again, irony colored his life. He who had

never thought of love at all now found it was the only thing he could think about. The only thing he truly wanted.

And the one thing he couldn't have.

Chapter 19

❧

It had been three days since her seduction of Toussaint—or rather, Richard—and Gillian hadn't heard a word from either of them. The first day she'd expected Richard to storm into her home raving over her scandalous behavior. She'd rather looked forward to that.

The second day she'd thought he might appear as if nothing had happened at all. That too would have been extremely interesting. Now, she wondered if perhaps he was too overwrought by what had passed between them to do anything at all. She certainly hoped so.

She smiled with satisfaction and finished the note on the desk before her. He'd had his opportunity. Now their future was in her hands. Besides, she had a legitimate reason for requesting his presence. She sealed the note and scribbled an address on a slip of paper.

Feminine laughter rang in the foyer outside the closed doors. A bark sounded in response, followed at once by an indignant voice. Any minute Wilkins would no doubt burst through the doors demanding a return to the calm and serene atmosphere he was accustomed to presiding over. Her house certainly wasn't conducive to this many guests, and since their arrival it had seemed as if the very building would burst from the strain. Still, she was enjoying herself, even if Wilkins wasn't.

Her grandmother was to blame for it all, or, perhaps, to thank. Regardless of her often stated belief that her offspring were well equipped to run their own lives, the dowager duchess was not above a bit of meddling if she deemed it necessary. And apparently, in this case, she had.

As if on cue, the doors flew open, and Wilkins stalked into the room with a vigor he hadn't shown in years. "My lady, I must insist you do something at once or I shall have to take matters into my own hands."

She suppressed a grin. "Whatever it is, Wilkins, it can wait. Right now I need you to bring this note for Lord Shelbrooke to his solicitor and insist it be delivered at once. This morning, if at all possible, but by midday at the latest."

Wilkins's bushy brows drew together. "But what about—"

"I shall take care of it." She stood, picked up the note and the paper, and handed it to the butler. "I've written the address here. Now, tell Lord Shelbrooke's solicitor if this is delivered with due speed he shall be considered favorably by the Dowager Duchess of Roxborough—no—the Duke of Roxborough when it comes to any future endeavor."

"My lady!" Wilkins's eyes widened with shock. "Your father knows nothing about this!"

"No, but he could." She ignored a tiny twinge of guilt. She'd never before used her family's influence, but she'd never before been in a situation where she'd needed it. "And I'm certain he wouldn't mind." She waved toward the door. "Now then, off with you."

He drew himself up in the best manner of a put-upon family retainer and sniffed. "As you wish." Wilkins turned and marched toward the door, muttering all the way. "Blasted business. House full of women." He yanked the door open. "Damnable dog," he muttered and snapped it closed behind him.

She shook her head and grinned. It wouldn't be easy for him, but Wilkins was going to have to accept that if all went as she hoped, nothing in her life would ever be the same. With luck, Richard would be here in a few hours, and she had a great deal to do before then.

Odd how there wasn't a doubt in her mind, or perhaps her heart, that Richard loved her. He hadn't said it aloud, and there was a possibility he never would, but she knew it as surely as she'd ever known anything in her life.

She pulled open the top drawer in the desk and drew out the miniature he'd painted. She should have known it the moment she'd looked at this very personal keepsake, even though she doubted he realized it himself.

It wasn't her soul he had captured in the tiny painting. It was his own.

Richard pulled back the knocker on Gillian's front door and rapped as gently as possible. Even so, the sound reverberated through the house and through his head. He shuddered and clenched his teeth against the pain. He deserved it, had, in fact, well earned it by his concentrated effort to consume every drop of liquor that had come within reach. Still, the knowledge made it no easier to bear.

It had been three long days since the night with Gillian in his studio. He'd wanted to come before now, but he'd had no idea what he'd say to her and wasn't certain he wished to hear what she had to say to him. However, her note today had requested a meeting, had insisted on it actually, and he could no longer delay the inevitable. No doubt she wished to break it off with him in favor of Toussaint.

The door opened with a faint squeal that probably went unnoticed most of the time, but at the moment it sliced through his head like a cold, pitiless blade.

Wilkins stood in the doorway and eyed him with disdain, as if he were to blame for the troubles of the world. "Good day, milord."

"Wilkins." Richard nodded.

With an obvious air of disapproval, the butler stepped aside to allow him to enter.

The light in the foyer wasn't nearly as bright as the afternoon sun, and he was damned grateful for the respite. He blinked and noticed a familiar figure halfway up the stairs, with an open book balanced in one hand and an apple in the other.

He shook his head, winced, then peered at the vision. "Marianne?"

"Oh hello, Richard," she said absently. Marianne cast a last reluctant glance at the book in her hand, then snapped it shut and turned toward him. "We were wondering when you would get here."

"We?" His voice rose. What was going on?

"Um-hum." She smiled pleasantly. "Becky and Jocelyn and Emma are around somewhere. And of course Henry—"

"Henry?" This made no sense whatsoever. Perhaps he was still foxed and this was nothing more than a drink-induced dream.

"Becky refused to come without him. And Aunt Louella couldn't possibly leave Becky—"

"Aunt Louella?" He groaned. Even in his dreams the last thing he needed was his termagant of an aunt in London. Or any of the rest of them. "What is she doing here? What are any of you doing here?"

"I'd like to tell you," she shrugged, "but I can't."

"Why not?"

"Because I really don't know. But I suspect it's quite interesting." She grinned and headed up the stairs.

He stared after her. What was going on here?

The parlor doors opened. Gillian stepped into the

foyer holding a snifter of brandy in one hand. He glanced at it longingly. "Richard, what a lovely surprise." She beamed at him. "I wasn't at all sure when I'd see you again."

He narrowed his eyes in suspicion. "You sent for me."

She laughed lightly. "That's right. How could it have slipped my mind?"

"You insisted I come," he said, his words measured. "Your note said it was a matter of some urgency."

"It did, didn't it?" She studied him carefully. "You look terrible, Richard. Are you ill?"

"Something like that," he muttered.

"I'm sure you'll feel better in no time." She took a sip of the brandy, then handed it to him. "This will help."

"It certainly couldn't hurt," he mumbled.

"Excellent." A wicked gleam flickered in her eye. "Because we do need to talk."

A heavy weight settled in his stomach. No doubt his heart. "Of course."

"But first, you have visitors." She waved him into the parlor. "They came here because they had no idea where to find you. It's the oddest thing. I hadn't realized until now that I had no idea where to find you either. We should probably discuss that as well, although I suppose it scarcely matters now. Besides, there is nothing quite as exciting as a man with secrets." He stepped past her, and she smiled innocently. "Don't you agree?" Too innocently.

"Good day, Richard." His aunt's forbidding tone

grated on his already raw nerves. She sat on the settee and gazed at him in a manner distinctly reminiscent of Gillian's butler.

"Aunt Louella." He nodded a greeting, then dismissed all pretense at polite behavior. He simply didn't have the patience necessary to deal with what was obviously a conspiracy of all the women in his life. "What are you doing in London? And why are my sisters here as well?"

"As always, Richard, it is good to see you." She glared at him, and for a moment he toyed with the idea of trapping her gaze until she was forced to turn her eyes away. But he was in no mood for a test of wills. Given his current state of infirmity, she would probably win and hold it over him for the rest of his life—much as she had everything else he'd ever done.

He downed the brandy in one long swallow and noted the fact that if it hadn't been for Gillian's annoying habit of sharing his drinks, there would have been a great deal more. Although she was right: it did help. He set the glass on a table and forced a smile to his lips.

"Forgive my bluntness. I have not felt quite up to snuff recently, and seeing you and Marianne a moment ago has come as something of a shock." He stepped to her and kissed her lightly on a papery cheek. "However, it is, as always, a pleasure to see you."

She snorted. "Don't bam me, boy. I know you'd just as soon we'd stayed put in the country. Well, it's been years since I've been to London and now that we're here, we're going to stay for a good, long visit. And do sit down. I can't abide you towering over me."

Relief surged through him. He sank down on the opposite end of the sofa and shook his head with a show of regret. "Oh dear, that may prove awkward. I am sorry, but I have the meanest of rooms and you can't possibly—"

"They're most welcome to stay with me as long as they wish," Gillian said from somewhere behind him. He hadn't realized she was still in the room, and he turned to find her leaning against the closed parlor doors. She favored him with that annoyingly brilliant smile of hers.

"Excellent." He cast her the closest thing to a smile he could muster, then turned back to his aunt. "And do forgive me for asking *again*, but exactly why are you here?"

"It wasn't my idea." Louella opened a large fabric satchel wedged on the sofa beside her and rummaged inside. "Where is it?" She pulled out a wrinkled sheet of folded velum and waved it at him. "This is why we came."

"What is it?" What could be so important that it would bring his entire family to town?

"A request of sorts, although it carries more the feel of a command," she muttered.

"A command?"

"Indeed." She craned her neck to see past him to Gillian and leveled her a suspicious glare. "From the Dowager Duchess of Roxborough."

Richard looked at Gillian over his shoulder. "Your grandmother?"

"So it would seem," she said lightly. There was definitely some kind of conspiracy here. Who played which role was still in question, but there was no doubt in his mind there was a plot afoot.

"As I was saying . . ." Louella's voice rang in the room, and he jerked his attention back to her. "I received this letter from the dowager duchess suggesting there were some . . ."—she pursed her lips in obvious reluctance—"aspects of your family's history that you should be made aware of."

He narrowed his eyes thoughtfully. "What aspects in particular?"

"Would you prefer that I leave?" Gillian said quietly.

"No." If Gillian's grandmother thought there was information he should have, Gillian should probably have it as well. Richard studied his aunt. "Go on."

"It appears the dowager was acquainted with your grandmother. She now seems to think you need to know about your father and—"

"I know all I need to know," he said harshly and stood. "If that's what this is all—"

"Sit down, boy," Louella snapped. "You don't know anything."

"Very well." He lowered himself stiffly back onto the settee, tried, and failed to keep the sarcasm from his voice. "What, precisely, does the dowager think I need to know?"

Louella's lips thinned in censure. "Her note suggests you should be told about your father's sister."

"My father's sister?" He drew his brows together. "What sister?"

"I didn't know you hadn't heard of her, although there's no reason why you should, I suppose. She was never really spoken of." Her tone softened slightly. "I had no idea until now you were unaware of it all."

"Unaware of what?" Impatience sounded in his voice.

She paused as if to pull her thoughts together, then drew a deep breath. "It was quite a scandal at the time, although it faded soon enough, as scandals do. She was . . . well, she . . ."

"She what?"

"She painted." Louella heaved a sigh of exasperation. "Not the kind of pleasant, meaningless paintings well-bred young women are supposed to do, but the kinds of works that hang in museums and galleries. I know it sounds ridiculous and I know as well your opinion when Emma has raised the very same issue. Her aunt's blood no doubt."

She sniffed in disdain. "I must admit I agree with you on that score. A woman trying to make her own way, alone, without so much as a husband to help her along, in a world that does not take kindly to such women and doing the work of men to boot, artists no less, will come to no good."

"What happened to her?" An odd, strained note sounded in Gillian's voice.

Richard stared at his aunt. His every muscle

tensed. He wasn't sure why, exactly, but somehow he knew this was important. "Go on."

"Your mother told me all this, mind you, I never knew your father's sister." Louella paused. "I don't really know much more than that. She ran off. Lived with some Frenchman for a time, I believe, and painted as she'd wished. I understand it wasn't long before she became ill and died. By then, of course, she was well, quite forgotten.

"But, as I said, it was something of a scandal in the beginning. Your grandfather disowned her. As for your father," she shrugged, "he wasn't a very strong man."

Richard couldn't hold back a short, humorless laugh. "That I knew."

Louella looked at him for a long time. "But you are."

"Am I?"

"Your father loved his sister yet he did nothing to help her. I believe he even sided with your grandfather. He loved your mother as well, yet he couldn't prevent her death. And he couldn't bear life without her."

"And what of his children?" A bitter note rang in Richard's voice, but he didn't care. "Did he love his children as well?"

"I don't know." For the first time he could remember, there was sympathy in her eyes. For him.

"It's of no significance now, I suppose," he muttered.

"Richard." Louella reached forward and placed her hand on his. "Your father was weak, and I cannot condone his behavior after your mother's death. I may be able to understand it, but I cannot excuse it.

"As for his son," her gaze met his firmly, "I have not been entirely fair to him through the years. Even after you took on the task of setting to right the family's affairs, I did not quite believe you would not end up exactly like your father. I will admit now that I was wrong."

"You? Admit you were wrong?" He raised a brow. "I thought surely it would be the end of the world itself before words of that nature crossed your lips."

"Perhaps, boy," she said as she narrowed her eyes, where a twinkle lingered nonetheless, "it is."

"Pardon me." Gillian joined them, and Richard rose to his feet. "As much as it suits my own purposes, I'm afraid I don't understand why my grandmother wanted Richard to know this? It's a family tragedy, long forgotten. Why bring it up now?"

Louella's brows drew together in irritation. "I don't know, child, ask your grandmother. It doesn't make any sense to me. The dowager is getting on in years, isn't she? Probably dotty in the head."

"She is not," Gillian huffed.

"No?" Louella's eyes narrowed. "Then explain this." She waved the note at her. "Right here it says Richard should know that the true legacy of the Earl of Shelbrooke—his true heritage, in fact—comes not from any man but from a woman. Whatever that means."

Richard glanced at Gillian. "I assume the dowager knows about your preposterous plans.

Gillian smiled smugly. "So it appears."

"Now, I've had quite enough of this." Louella got to her feet. "Unless things have changed, it's getting on to that time of day when everyone who is anyone in London drives through the park. And I would rather enjoy that myself."

"Before you go." Gillian crossed the room. He hadn't noticed until now, but three easels were arranged before the windows, each displaying a painting. All were landscapes, although the settings varied from piece to piece. "I had no idea what your aunt wished to say to you, Richard. I had set these up to make another point altogether."

Gillian gestured at the canvases. "I purchased two of these several years ago. There's another pair upstairs. They were apparently painted by a woman of noble birth who later died." She glanced at Richard. "Poor and alone."

Louella's gaze slid from Gillian to Richard and back.

"There are initials in the corner, bottom right side, but I've never been able to make them out. Lady Louella, do you think . . ."

"I never saw her paintings, probably wouldn't recognize them even if I had. I know nothing about such things, and I don't care to." Louella moved to the nearest painting. "Her first name was Caroline. Lady Caroline Shelton." She leaned closer and peered at the corner. Her brow furrowed in concentration. "Could be a C. Could be an S. I can't say for sure." She straightened. "Is that all?"

Gillian stared at Richard. "They are your aunt's. You know they are."

"Perhaps," he said quietly. There was little doubt in his own mind that these were more than likely the work of Caroline Shelton, a relation he'd never so much as heard of. It was highly improbable there had been more than one woman with her story nearly forty years ago. The disclosure of her existence explained a great deal.

His head filled with his father's long-ago rantings about art and artists, about duty and one's place in the world. And each and every comment now made perfect sense.

He stepped to the first painting, studied it for a long moment, then moved to the second. He barely heard the murmur of voices behind him and scarcely noted doors opening and closing.

Gillian's voice sounded at his side. "They're wonderful."

"Yes, they are."

"A pity such talent was lost to the world simply because she didn't have the funding to properly support herself."

"Yes, I suppose it is." He stepped to the last painting and paused. While the first two were different in subject, the style of the artist was unmistakable. This last work was not by the same hand. "Who painted this?"

"Who?" Gillian called from across the room. Hadn't she been standing beside him a moment ago? He glanced in the direction of her voice. Gillian stood in the half open doorway speaking softly to someone in the hall. Apparently the conspiracy underway here went well beyond Louella's revelations.

He turned back to the final painting with an air of resignation, wondering if he shouldn't admit surrender right now. At least whatever lay in wait for him postponed his discussion with Gillian.

He considered the painting before him thoughtfully. It too was a landscape, well executed, with a nice sense of balance and proportion, light and shadows. Still, whereas the others were somewhat complex, this one struck him as less refined: the artist's strokes not as confident, his skill not as developed. Or more than likely her skill. It was obvious Gillian, and perhaps his family as well, was trying to make a point. As unwilling as he was to acknowledge it aloud, privately Richard had to admit there was considerable talent evident here.

"So, tell me, Gillian, what impoverished female painted this one?"

"I'm afraid I did." Emma's voice sounded behind him.

Richard heaved a resigned sigh, not really surprised. After all, he hadn't abandoned his work entirely in spite of his father's objections. If Richard and this particular sister shared the same talents, no doubt they shared the same stubborn will as well.

"Do you like it?" She stepped up beside him.

He nodded slowly. "Yes, actually, I do."

"Really?" Emma's face lit up, and his heart

twisted. He should have known all along that limiting her opportunities to keep her safe and protected was not merely wrong but futile.

"It needs a bit of work." He pointed to an area where trees and sky met. "Here, if you were to deepen the shadows with a lighter hand and—"

"Richard, your knowledge never fails to amaze me," Gillian said. "One would almost think Emma wasn't the only artist now in the family."

"Oh, but I told you he used to paint," Emma said.

"Did you?" Richard stared at Gillian. She knew he had once painted? Why hadn't she said anything to him?

"I suppose you did." Gillian shrugged. "It must have slipped my mind."

"As has everything else today," he said, as much to himself as to her.

Gillian smiled that knowing smile he was beginning to dislike intensely. "Now that you've seen Emma's work and her obvious talent as well as the work of your aunt—"

"We don't know that." Even as he said the words he knew they were false.

"Aunt Louella paints?" Confusion washed across Emma's face.

"Hardly," he scoffed.

"I'll explain later," Gillian said to Emma, then turned to Richard. "At any rate, now even you can admit the truth."

His breath caught. "What truth?"

"That you were wrong about the ability of women to create serious art—"

"I should take my leave," Emma murmured.

He released a relieved breath. "I'll admit nothing of the sort. I will concede that you have managed to present me with two exceptional women of unusual talent. It goes no farther than that and it changes nothing."

"What do you mean it changes nothing?" She frowned with annoyance. "It changes everything."

"You can best discuss this without me," Emma said and edged toward the door.

"Not at all." He glared at Gillian. "Women, regardless of their talent, do not belong behind an easel. The life of an artist is not an easy one. It's no life for a woman, and no life for my sister, and I will not condone or permit it!"

"Just as your father would not condone or permit it for his sister!" Gillian snapped.

Emma gasped.

Gillian sucked in a hard breath, and her eyes widened with shock as if she couldn't believe she had said such a thing.

The words hung in the air between them. Her accusation struck him with the force of a physical blow, catching at his throat and stilling his heart.

"Richard," she said as she stepped toward him. "I didn't mean—"

"No," he held out a hand to stop her and drew a shaky breath. "You're right, of course. That was no doubt exactly what my father would have said. Perhaps there is a great deal of him in me after all."

"Perhaps that's not entirely bad," Gillian said softly and put her hand on his arm. "Someone once told me a man who is too good can be, well, tedious and even boring." Amusement glimmered in her eye. "Don't you agree?"

"What are you up to, Gillian?" His gaze searched hers.

"I say, I realize this might not be the best moment . . ."

Richard rolled his eyes toward the ceiling, then glanced once again in the direction of the door. Cummings had joined them. Who on earth would be coming through that blasted door next? Cummings stepped to Emma's side, and the two of them exchanged glances in a far too intimate manner.

Richard grit his teeth. "How perceptive of you."

"It may well be the perfect moment, Kit," Gillian said, ignoring the glare Richard cast her.

Emma whispered something in Cummings's ear. He squared his shoulders and met Richard's gaze without flinching. "I wish to marry your sister, my lord."

"And I wish to marry him," Emma said firmly.

"And if I forbid it?" Richard crossed his arms over his chest and glared at Cummings. Perhaps he couldn't win a battle of wills with his aunt, but this man was another thing altogether.

"Well, you did forbid her to paint," Gillian said casually.

Emma cast him an innocent smile, and Richard couldn't help wondering if she had taught that particular smile to Gillian or if it was the other way around.

Gillian leaned toward him in a confidential manner. "Kit knows it's not really necessary to ask for Emma's hand because, after all, she is of age, but he thinks it's a nice gesture."

"I don't like him," Richard growled.

"He doesn't like you much either—"

"Not at all," Cummings said pleasantly.

"—but Emma apparently loves you both—"

Emma nodded. "Of course I do."

"—and you did wish for her to make a good match—"

"I shall do everything in my power to make her happy, my lord." Cummings's voice rang with sincerity.

"Enough!" Richard threw up his hands. "Do as you wish! Marry! Paint! Run naked through the streets for all I care!"

"Richard." Gillian frowned and shook her head as if she were chastising a small boy. "Is that necessary?"

He resisted the urge to act completely like a child, wanting nothing more than to stick out his tongue, but he settled for slanting her a look any small boy would be proud of.

Emma grinned. "Thank you, Richard. We shall."

"Which?" Cummings said curiously.

"All of them." Emma gazed up at Cummings with an adoring smile and a look in her eye that told Richard his responsibilities toward his oldest sister were at an end. An odd sense of relief and regret swept through him.

"Emma of course will no longer need the services that I propose to provide for women such as herself, but she has agreed to work with me. I have no idea precisely what kind of facility will be best, what artists really need."

"It scarcely matters at this point." Richard drew a deep breath. Gillian's comments were the perfect opportunity to say what had to be said. It had been put off long enough. Whether he liked it or not, it had to be done. "You will not have the funds for such a project." He couldn't marry a woman who loved another man regardless of who that other man truly was. "You will not acquire your inheritance through marriage to me. I have made my decision."

He met Gillian's gaze squarely and hoped his breaking heart would not show in his eyes.

"I will not marry you."

Chapter 20

His words rang in the room.

"No?" Gillian looked at him for a long moment. "Are you certain?"

He clenched his fists by his sides. "Yes."

"Quite certain?"

"Yes," he said grimly.

"Is there nothing I can do to change your mind?" she said with little more than idle curiosity. Why wasn't she more upset?

"No." Why wasn't she upset at all? He certainly was.

"Oh dear." Gillian tilted her head and frowned.

"Now we should definitely leave." Emma started toward the door, pulling Cummings behind her.

"Why?" Cummings grinned. "This should be quite interesting."

"That's exactly why." Emma jerked open the

door, pushed a protesting Cummings out, and pulled the door closed behind them.

Gillian shook her head. "Well, that's that, then." She shrugged. "At least there is still sufficient time remaining until my birthday to find a suitable husband."

"That's it?" He stared in stunned disbelief. "That's all you have to say to me?"

"I shall have to make up another list," she said absently, then smiled brightly. "Unless you have some suggestions?"

"Me? You're asking me to help you find a suitable husband?" His voice rose.

"I should think you'd be well qualified to do so. You know precisely what I'm looking for. After all, you were once at the top of the list."

He stared in shocked disbelief. Even if she only loved him as Toussaint, he had thought, had hoped, she harbored some feeling for him as Richard. Did she care so little for him that she was able to brush him off without so much as a by-your-leave?

"There is an artist I know who might do quite nicely," she said thoughtfully. "You've seen his work: Etienne-Louis Toussaint?"

"I wouldn't wager any legacies on it," he snapped.

"Nonsense. He'd probably be more than willing to marry me, given the stakes involved."

"You will never marry Toussaint," he said through clenched teeth.

"Of course I will. I see no good reason why not."

"I can give you a very good reason." He squared his shoulders. It was past time for the truth.

"I doubt that." She waved off his comment. "Besides, I rather like the idea of marrying a man of extraordinary talent." She paused thoughtfully. "Of course, he is extremely arrogant, and he has this odd need to keep his face hidden, and oh, yes, his accent is atrocious and quite unbelievable—"

"Atrocious? I scarcely think—"

"Don't forget unbelievable," she added.

"I could hardly forget unbelievable." He snorted. "What is so—"

"Indeed. It was obviously feigned in order to disguise the fact that the man no doubt speaks no French at all. Est-ce que vous ne consentez pas?"

"Huh?"

"That's what I thought. At any rate, I quite like the idea of marrying an artist with a brilliant future ahead of him—nearly as much as I like the idea of marrying a penniless earl."

"You like the idea of marrying a penniless earl," he said slowly.

"Just one penniless earl in particular."

"Just one—"

"Such a pity though," she heaved a heartfelt sigh, "I seem to have found two men who would serve the same purpose—"

"Gillian." He drew the word out slowly.

"—who seem to trigger precisely the same feelings when I'm with them—"

"Gillian." What was she up to?

"—who are in fact so remarkably similar in the

way they do certain things like, oh, say, kiss—"

"What are you saying?"

"—that one might even think they were not two different men at all but one and the same." She smiled sweetly.

"The same?" Was it possible? Did she know?

"It's ridiculous, of course." She stepped closer to him. "Who in their right mind would ever dream the fourteenth Earl of Shelbrooke," she poked him in the chest, "was Etienne-Louis Toussaint?"

"Who indeed?" he said weakly.

"Would you imagine such a thing, Richard?" She poked him once again.

"Me?" He swallowed hard. She knew.

"Or should I say," she poked again, "Monsieur Toussaint?"

"Toussaint?" he said as if he'd never heard the name before.

"Etienne-Louis Toussaint." She emphasized each word with a poke.

"Ouch." He grabbed her hand. "You're hurting me."

"Am I?" She smirked up at him. "And precisely who am I hurting?"

His gaze searched hers, and for the first time in days hope rose within him. "Did Thomas tell you?"

"Thomas? My brother?" Her brows pulled together in annoyance. "He knows of this secret life of yours?"

"Well, yes, in fact." Perhaps he could blame this all on Thomas. "Toussaint was very much his invention."

"Does he know precisely how you've used this invention of his to further your ends?"

"Thomas knows nothing about you and Toussaint," he said with an air of reluctance. "That was completely my idea."

She raised a brow.

"It seemed like a good plan in the beginning," he muttered.

"Before we go any farther, why don't you tell me exactly what that plan was?"

"The plan?" He tried to pull his thoughts together, selecting and discarding one response after another. "It seemed to me, that is I thought—"

"That if I was hesitant to warm the bed of the Earl of Shelbrooke I might be more amenable to share the affection of Etienne-Louis Toussaint?"

"Something like that." It sounded rather absurd when said aloud.

"And did your plan work?"

"Not entirely." His tone was defensive. "But you were simply much more, well, relaxed with Toussaint than you ever were with me."

"But when I did, to use your word, *relax* in your company, why did you continue your deception?"

"I needed to know how you felt. After all, you did confide in Toussaint."

"Somewhat foolish in hindsight." She shook her head. "And did you discover my feelings?"

"Indeed." He scoffed. "You love Toussaint."

"Do I? How did you ascertain that?"

"You said it yourself." A fresh wave of pain

gripped his heart. "You said you couldn't be with a man you didn't love."

"And?" she prompted.

"And you were with Toussaint." He narrowed his eyes. "Quite enthusiastically, I might add."

"Who was, in truth, you."

"Well, yes," he said reluctantly.

"So it all comes down to precisely when I knew the truth, doesn't it?"

"I suppose." As much as he hated to admit it, she was right.

"What if I told you that I went to Toussaint's studio, or rather your studio, to find the boy that brought Toussaint's messages and yours as well—"

"The boy? Blast it all, I used the same boy?" He smacked his palm against his forehead. He'd never for a moment considered that both identities used the same messenger. What a stupid mistake. He probably deserved to be unmasked.

"And while there—do you realize you don't lock your doors?"

He groaned. "So I've been told."

She nodded. "At any rate, while waiting for the elusive artist, I stumbled upon a work in progress. A landscape, very nice, quite scenic, a clearing with a charming temple."

"A temple?"

"With, of all things, a hat on the finial." She paused for emphasis. "My hat."

"Oh." He considered her for a long moment. A tiny glimmer of hope flared within him. "So the night when you—"

"Seduced Toussaint? Seduced you?"

"You knew," he said flatly.

"Um-hum." A smug smile tugged at the corners of her lips.

"But you didn't let me know you knew."

"Where would be the fun in that?"

"You let me believe you were seducing, were in fact, in love with, another man." He glared indignantly. "How could you do that to me?"

"And you let me believe you were another man." She crossed her arms over her chest. "How could you do that to me?"

"I did it because . . . because I wanted—"

"My inheritance? My fortune?"

"In the beginning, perhaps, but I also wanted you to want me. It was as much pride as greed."

"And in the end?" Her gaze trapped his. "What was it in the end?"

"In the end?" He stared into her eyes, as blue and brilliant as any paint he could put to canvas. Simmering with emotions as strong as his own. "Love, Gillian, in the end it was love."

An odd light shone in her eyes. "Do you love me, Richard?"

"Yes. Damn it all. I love you." He glared with all the pent-up passion within him. "And that's exactly why I can't marry you."

She frowned in confusion. "That makes no sense whatsoever."

"Of course it does." He ran his hand through his hair and paced the room. "How can I marry you if you love someone else?"

"Even if that someone else is you?"

"Besides, if I marry you now, before your birthday, how will you ever know that I truly love you? That I'm not marrying you for your inheritance?"

"Then will you marry me after my birthday?" she said slowly.

He stopped and stared. "After your birthday will be too late."

"Answer my question," she said softly.

The moment stretched between them, taut and tense and thick.

"My Lady Gillian." His gaze locked to hers. "I have nothing to offer you save my name, a manor house with a leaky roof, and a talent I can never publicly reveal, yet if you were to do me the great honor of becoming my wife the day after your birthday, I shall spend the rest of my days in an effort to make you happy."

"Very well." A slight catch sounded in her voice. "My Lord Shelbrooke, I shall be honored to become your wife the day after my birthday."

"But what of your financial independence?" He was afraid to say the words. Afraid she'd change her mind. But he had to know. "What of helping artists like Emma?"

"They shall have to make due without me. I—we—will continue with my salons. As for my independence," her eyes glittered with emotion, "it's a paltry price to pay to become the Countess of Shelbrooke."

"Paltry? You are willing to forfeit six hundred thousand pounds, eight ships—"

"More or less."

"And a great deal of land?"

"It's in America." She sniffed. "It's probably little more than swamp. I should never see it anyway."

"You'd give it all up? For me?"

"Yes."

"Why?"

"Why?" Her eyes widened. "I would think a man clever enough to come up with a method of being two men at once would be well able to determine that."

"Say it." He moved toward her.

"Why?" She raised her chin and stepped to meet him.

His heart raced. "Because I need to hear you say it."

"Do you?" She was barely a heartbeat away from him.

"I do."

"Very well, rich or poor, I don't want to live my life without you. Not one more day, one more minute." At once she was in his arms. "Because I love you."

Joy surged through him and his lips met hers, and he didn't care about fortunes found or lost. Secrets kept or revealed. Only this woman for now and forever.

A knock sounded on the door, and it opened at once.

"Pardon me." Jocelyn poked her head in.

Richard groaned, raised his head, and gazed into the wonderful blue eyes of the woman he loved.

"You do know, you get my family as well?"

Gillian laughed up at him. "And you join the Effingtons. Seems like a fair exchange."

Jocelyn cleared her throat. "I couldn't help overhearing."

Richard released Gillian but kept her close at his side. "Not if you had your ear to the door."

"That's neither here nor there." Jocelyn stepped into the room without hesitation. "It seems to me, well to us, really—"

Gillian raised a brow. "Are you all listening at the door?"

"Of course not," Jocelyn said indignantly. "Just Becky and I."

"Hello, Richard." Becky's voice sounded from the doorway, but only her waving arm appeared.

"What do you want?" Richard glared.

Jocelyn glared right back. "As I was saying, it seems to us that if you love her, and you do, don't you? . . ."

Richard rolled his eyes toward the ceiling, then nodded in surrender.

"And she loves you . . ." His sister glanced at Gillian.

"By *you* I gather you're referring to Richard, the Earl of Shelbrooke, and not Richard known by some other name?" Gillian said innocently.

Richard's eyes narrowed.

Jocelyn frowned in confusion. "I mean . . . well, *Richard*."

"I see." Gillian smiled sweetly. "Yes, I do love him."

Jocelyn's expression brightened. "Excellent. Then if you love each other, why on earth would you forfeit her fortune?"

"Why indeed." Gillian grinned.

"Isn't it enough to know that you're both willing to do so?" Jocelyn's voice was eager. "I simply can't see why we—or rather you—should live the rest of our lives—I mean your lives—in poverty—"

"It was never poverty," Richard muttered.

"But it wasn't a great deal of fun either," Gillian said pointedly.

"—when you have a rather exciting fortune yours for the taking."

"In point of fact, Jocelyn, I don't see why either." Gillian tilted her head and studied Richard. "I want you, regardless of whatever you wish to call yourself, for the rest of my life. If I'm forced to choose between you and the legacy, I'll gladly give it all up and spend my days handing you nails on the top of your blasted roof.

"But I think it would be much more enjoyable to spend our lives together with servants to take care of such chores. And funding to assist women with talent like Emma. And decent dowries to help your sisters find men who will hopefully show a bit more intelligence when it comes to such matters as this than their brother has."

Jocelyn giggled. "Nicely done, Gillian."

"You may take your leave now." Richard's words were directed toward his sister, but his gaze remained locked on Gillian.

Jocelyn grinned and stepped toward the door.

She started out, then turned and leaned toward Gillian. "We all think it's terribly romantic, you know. Both of you willing to give up everything for love. We never imagined Richard, he's always been so practical, and—"

"Get out!" he bellowed.

Jocelyn scurried out and closed the door behind her.

"Would you really give it all up?" he said quietly.

"I said it once. I will be the wife of the penniless but honorable Earl of Shelbrooke or the wife of the promising but rather penniless as well Etienne-Louis Toussaint. All I truly want is to be the wife of Richard Shelton. Whether he is wealthy or poor."

"Why?"

"I said it once as well."

"Say it again."

"Because he's the man I love."

"Is he?" He pulled her into his arms, still not quite able to believe it himself.

"Yes." She gazed up at him. "He is."

"You know this changes nothing. I am still not especially fond of your ridiculous idea to assist female artists."

"I also know you promised to make me happy." She grinned with a triumphant gleam in her eye.

"So I did." He chuckled. "You are a wicked woman, my lady."

"And you, my lord, are a very wicked man." She brushed her lips across his. "We sound well matched to me."

"Well, I was at the top of your list." He studied her for a moment.

Once more the ironic twists his life had taken struck him. He'd thought women had no place in art, yet the talent that flowed in his veins came from the blood of a woman. He'd agreed to Gillian's proposal out of a need for wealth, yet money was no longer important at all. His pride had ruled his actions in the beginning, yet love was all that mattered in the end.

"I'm still a bit confused about one thing."

"I do so love it when you're confused," she said with a laugh.

"The other evening at my studio," he said slowly.

"When you believed I thought you were Toussaint?"

"Yes, well, whatever." He chose his words cautiously. "I have never quite been, that is I was somewhat surprised, what I mean to say . . ."

She raised a brow. "You didn't think I was capable of such a seduction?"

"I didn't know anyone was capable of such a seduction," he said with an odd sense of gratitude and awe.

"You enjoyed it then?" She wrapped her arms around his neck.

"Oh," he nodded, "you could say that."

"I think I can do better, though." She pulled his mouth down to hers. "All I need is a little hard work and quite a bit of practice."

"I did promise to make you happy."

His lips met hers and he knew this was just the

beginning of a lifetime of happiness that had little to do with six hundred thousand pounds, eight ships, more or less, and a great deal of land in America. And marveled at the realization that an emotion that was never part of their agreement was in truth a far greater fortune than mere wealth, and he looked forward with hope and joy to the rest of his days with this woman by his side.

And looked forward as well to a little hard work and a great deal of practice.

Epilogue

Four months later . . .

"**R**ather impressive, don't you think?" Lady Forester glanced around the elegant ballroom in the new London home of the newly wed Earl and Countess of Shelbrooke. "And quite a crush as well."

"It's their first ball, you know. Anyone who matters is here, even at this time of year." The lady beside her nodded. "I saw the Duke and Duchess of Roxborough earlier, and any number of Effingtons are in attendance. I heard even the Dowager Duchess is here, and you know she never comes into town."

"It certainly is a far cry from Lady Shelbrooke's salons," Lady Forester murmured. Oh, the lady still gave them, but not as frequently as she had before her marriage. She was apparently far too caught up in arranging for some sort of foundling home for female artists. Lord knows, Lady Forester could well understand the desire to support struggling artists—but women? What was the point of that? And where was the fun in it?

"Did you see her portrait?" the woman said with a note of awe in her voice. "It was painted by that Frenchman. Too-something. It makes her look so . . . so . . ."

"Perfect. No doubt why Toussaint continues to be in great demand." The portrait hung here in the ballroom, the centerpiece of Lady Shelbrooke's extensive collection of art.

"I understand there's another painting he did of her that's really rather scandalous."

"So I've heard," Lady Forester said under her breath.

The lady beside her raised a brow. "Have you made the artist's acquaintance?"

"No," she sighed. "And I doubt I shall have the honor." According to the latest bit of gossip, Etienne-Louis Toussaint was abandoning his rakish ways in favor of fidelity to, of all things, a wife. Pity. She'd never had the opportunity to learn for herself if everything she'd heard about him was true, if he or indeed any man could live up to his reputation.

Lady Forester's gaze drifted across the well-appointed room with its equally well-appointed guests. Musicians played from a balcony overlooking the gathering. A full complement of servants wearing the white mask, tricorn hat, and cloak of Venetian dominos flitted discreetly among the crowd. Lady Forester wasn't sure if she was annoyed by the blatant theft of her idea or flattered.

She spotted the countess, and her gaze lingered thoughtfully. Lady Shelbrooke laughed in response to some comment. It seemed Lady Shelbrooke often laughed these days or smiled a private sort of smile. She carried an air of contentment about her that was altogether too, well, radiant to be proper. An odd twinge of what might have been jealousy stabbed Lady Forester, if indeed she was envious of such things as trite as happiness and true love.

"Lady Shelbrooke looks exceptionally lovely tonight," the other woman said. "Marriage seems to agree with her."

"Doesn't it, though?"

A warm flush colored the new countess's cheeks, and her eyes glowed with a brilliance that could never be feigned. She appeared almost as ethereal as the portrait that hung in a place of honor.

"How does one achieve that, I wonder?" Lady Forester said more to herself than anyone else.

"How? Why, my dear Lady Forester." The Earl of Shelbrooke stepped up beside her, a glass of champagne in one hand. He sipped thoughtfully, directing his words to her, but his gaze fixed on his countess. "No doubt Lady Shelbrooke would be more than willing to share her secret with you. You have always been fond of secrets, have you not?"

"Indeed I have." She laughed and glanced up at him. She could certainly see how he'd captured the heart of the lovely widow. Once more, envy shot through her. "And do you know the secret, my lord?"

He sipped his champagne thoughtfully. "There really isn't all that much to it. First, you have to decide precisely what you want. Then there's nothing more to do but simply, in the case of my wife at least"—a slow smile spread across his face—"make yourself a list."

"A list?"

"Indeed." He smiled the smile of a man well satisfied by life and love. "A husband list."

America Loves Lindsey!

The Timeless Romances

of #1 Bestselling Author

GENTLE ROGUE	0-380-75302-2/$6.99 US/$9.99 Can
DEFY NOT THE HEART	0-380-75299-9/$6.99 US/$9.99 Can
SILVER ANGEL	0-380-75294-8/$6.99 US/$8.99 Can
TENDER REBEL	0-380-75086-4/$6.99 US/$8.99 Can
SECRET FIRE	0-380-75087-2/$6.99 US/$9.99 Can
HEARTS AFLAME	0-380-89982-5/$6.99 US/$9.99 Can
A HEART SO WILD	0-380-75084-8/$6.99 US/$9.99 Can
WHEN LOVE AWAITS	0-380-89739-3/$6.99 US/$8.99 Can
LOVE ONLY ONCE	0-380-89953-1/$6.99 US/$8.99 Can
BRAVE THE WILD WIND	0-380-89284-7/$7.99 US/$10.99 Can
A GENTLE FEUDING	0-380-87155-6/$6.99 US/$8.99 Can
HEART OF THUNDER	0-380-85118-0/$6.99 US/$8.99 Can
SO SPEAKS THE HEART	0-380-81471-4/$6.99 US/$9.99 Can
GLORIOUS ANGEL	0-380-84947-X/$6.99 US/$8.99 Can
PARADISE WILD	0-380-77651-0/$6.99 US/$8.99 Can
FIRES OF WINTER	0-380-75747-8/$6.99 US/$8.99 Can
A PIRATE'S LOVE	0-380-40048-0/$6.99 US/$9.99 Can
CAPTIVE BRIDE	0-380-01697-4/$6.99 US/$8.99 Can
TENDER IS THE STORM	0-380-89693-1/$6.99 US/$9.99 Can
SAVAGE THUNDER	0-380-75300-6/$6.99 US/$8.99 Can